The Otter of Death

The Otter of Death

A Gunn Zoo Mystery

Betty Webb

Poisoned Pen Press

First Edition 2018

10 9 8 7 6 5 4 3 2 1

Library of Congress Control Number:
2017954240

ISBN: 9781464209918   Large Print

Poisoned Pen Press
4014 N. Goldwater Blvd., #201
Scottsdale, AZ 85251
www.poisonedpenpress.com
info@poisonedpenpress.com

Printed in the United States of America

Acknowledgments

The Arizona State Library's Writer-in-Residence program helped considerably in the writing of this book. On the personal front, of particular service were Marge Purcell, Debra McCarthy, Delpha Wright, Judy Par, the ever-faithful Sheridan Street Irregulars, Poisoned Pen Press' brilliant Barbara Peters, and Melanie Gideon of Moss Landing's wonderful Captain's Inn, who told me about the wild otter with the video camera. Any errors in this book are my fault, not theirs.

For today's unsung heroes—our nation's librarians, who tirelessly work to keep the wolf of ignorance from our doors.
And a special shout-out to the dedicated librarians at the Avondale (Arizona) Public Library, where most of this book was written.

Chapter One

Other than a few remaining wisps of fog, the morning was your standard California morning: perfect. The warm Pacific nuzzled at the Gunn Landing breakwater, while overhead snowy gulls swooped through a soft westerly breeze like noisy angels. Even better, it was a Monday, and my day off. Knowing me, though, after I finished my walk around the Gunn Landing Slough, I would probably drive down to the zoo to say hello to my charges. With my new hours, I had too much to do, and too little time to do it in.

My overcrowded schedule meant poor old DJ Bonz had come up on the short end today. After giving my three-legged terrier a short walk through Gunn Landing Park, I'd returned him to my boat, the *Merilee*, and ordered him to keep Miss Priss company. Bonz never behaved well at the Slough and snarl-barked at any otter as if it were a marauding Viking intent upon carrying off every liveaboarder in the harbor. I sighed an "I'm sorry" sigh, not that the little terrier could hear me from here. This end of the Slough—a fifteen-hundred-acre marsh near Gunn Landing Harbor—was a good mile from my boat as the crow flies, not that I'm a crow. My slog around the Slough's many inlets added another mile to my hike, but today I was supposed to turn in my portion of the local otter count to the Otter Conservancy, the marine life rescue organization.

With my count up to fifteen, I rounded the southern edge of the Slough, another reedy area where sea otters sometimes gathered. They didn't disappoint me today. I stopped to watch several females floating on their backs while their pups snoozed on their mama's bellies. Nineteen. Two pupless otters paddled by mere feet away, not bothering to give me a second look. Twenty-one. With their dog-like black eyes and noses, and golden brown coats, they appeared healthy. So far, I'd seen no sign of toxoplasma gondii, the disease that had felled too many of their kind in the past few years.

Approximately fifty yards further, I discovered

that my earlier optimism had been in error. Two otter carcasses lay half-hidden among the reeds. Growing closer, I found no blood, no signs of attack. Possibly toxo. Not having anything to bag and tag the animals with right now, I took several photos and e-mailed them to Darleene Bauer, president of the Otter Conservancy. We would pick them up later and take them into Monterey for autopsy.

Troubled, I headed toward the northern edge of the Slough, where my sector of the grid ended. There I spotted a single otter, perhaps a male. That brought my count to twenty-two live, two dead. This otter had a rock the size of a softball tucked under his arm. Unlike other mammals—primates excepted—otters use tools. Their usual prey was the shellfish that proliferate near the shore; oysters, abalone, and whatnot. Somewhere during their evolution, the animals had learned to use rocks or other hard objects to crack open shells to get at the soft meat inside. Cunningly, they held onto their favorite tools, and it wasn't unusual to see them swimming by clutching metal ship fittings, belt buckles, or pliers. Once I had even seen a large male attempting to open an oyster by using an old glass Coke bottle.

My own territory covered and notations duly made, I was about to return to the *Merilee* when I saw a familiar face lurking in the reeds. Maureen. Number twenty-three. Her thick coat, a prize sought by hunters for generations because of its water-repellent properties, was a brighter gold than most otters, making her easy to spot. Today she was busy opening the hard shell of a clam. As a zookeeper I knew the dangers of treating wild creatures like domesticated pets, but long ago she had stolen my heart with her nightly scratchings and chirpings at the hull of my boat, begging for treats.

Maureen loved herring.

After gulping down whatever it was she'd killed, Maureen spotted me. Perhaps thinking I carried a herring in my pocket, she tucked her tool under her arm and swam toward me, and in her rush, nudged aside a fat male—twenty-four—who had floated into her lane. Upon reaching me she looked up with hopeful eyes.

"No herring today," I whispered, to avoid disturbing the nearby otter mommies.

Maureen can be stubborn. She waggled her head and chirped.

"Maybe tonight."

She chirped again, this time louder. Waved a

webbed paw. When she did that, I could see the tool tucked under her other arm. It was black. Shiny. No rock.

"What's that you've got, Maureen?"

Another chirp. Another paw wave. She did this dance every night at the *Merilee*. It had always worked there, and she didn't understand why it wasn't working now. One more paw wave dislodged the object so that I could see it better.

A cell phone. Wrapped in kelp.

"Oh, Maureen, you didn't!"

Those of us who lived in the harbor were alert to such thievery, and Maureen wouldn't be the first otter to make off with some poor tourist's dropped cell phone. Whenever possible we rescued the phones and traced them back to their owners, careful not to injure the thief in the process.

I reached out my hand. "Give me that."

Maureen sniffed. *Where is my herring?* Her following chirp sounded more like a warning *ack-ack* than a plea.

"You're threatening me now? I'll have you know I've handled bigger bullies than you. Rhinos. Tigers. Even a mean cockatoo."

Chirp?

Another thing about Maureen; she's

entranced by the human voice. That's down to me and my nightly conversations with her, but hey, words sometimes work. Maureen was so intent on translating my words into "otter-ese" that she was unprepared for the quick grab that snatched the cell phone out from under her arm.

"*Aka-aka-aka!!!*" she shrieked, and with teeth bared, made a dive for my hiking boot.

No dummy me, I fled, leaving her behind.

Once on higher, drier ground, I turned my attention to the kelp-wrapped phone, an expensive, water-resistant Zeno-7. To my surprise, it was still on and in camera mode, which meant it had only recently been dropped. Scanning the horizon, I saw no one. I carefully brushed the kelp away to better see the picture on its mud-spattered screen. At first the image made me smile, because the owner—Stuart Booth, whose otter count area included the northern dogleg of the Slough—appeared to have dropped his phone in the act of taking a selfie. It was an odd selfie, though. A dark spot marred his temple, and splatters of reddish-mud half-covered his face. The image was blurry, too, as if he had forgotten to hold the phone still. And there was something…something about the look on Booth's face that made me uneasy. Was it surprise? I pulled my tee-shirt out of my cargo pants and wiped at the screen again. Squinted. Tried to read his expression through green smears of kelp and red mud.

No, that expression wasn't surprise.

It was horror.

And the red drops splattered all over his face? Blood.

I was looking at a murder.

Chapter Two

The San Sebastian County Sheriff and two deputies arrived twenty minutes after my call, and were now wading through the Slough. I stood well back on the dry bank, watching as they poked at the murky water with long sticks. The phone thief was long gone, as were her twenty-three cohorts, but some of the liveaboarders from the harbor had wandered over to join me. We liveaboarders are a nosy lot.

"You sure it's not some dumb kid's idea of a joke, Teddy?" asked Darleene Bauer, just returning from completing her own otter count at the eastern sector of the grid. Darleene lived on the *Fleet Foot*, a Union 36 cutter berthed near my *Merilee*. "That's the kind of thing a teenager would think was funny."

Although the mother of three and the

grandmother of six was superior to me in her knowledge of child goofiness, she had not seen the image. The horror on Booth's face had appeared all too real. "No teen would sacrifice a Zeno-7 just for a joke," I told her. "Too expensive."

"Stolen, maybe, or—"

She was cut off by a shout from one of the deputies. "Over here!"

Joe—that's Sheriff Joseph Rejas, the San Sebastian County Sheriff, who just happens to be my fiancé—slogged his way through the marsh to join the deputy. He studied something in the water, then motioned for the other man to step back along with him. As the two retraced their footsteps, Joe grabbed his radio and barked out orders. Then he took his personal cell out of his back pocket and made a call. He spoke for a few minutes, then shoved the phone back into his pocket and made his way over to me, leaving the deputy standing sentinel over whatever it was they'd found.

After chasing Darleene off, he took out a pen and notepad. "When's the last time you saw Professor Booth?"

"Did…did you find him?"

"Please answer the question, Teddy."

Usually the most patient of men, Joe was all business when it came to his job, so I wasn't offended by his testiness. "Last week sometime."

"How well did you know Professor Booth?"

Did. Past tense. "I've always tried to avoid him."

"You didn't see him earlier this morning? Before finding this?" He held up the bagged and tagged Zeno 7.

"Like I told the 9-1-1 dispatcher, I was the only person around when I got out here, so no, I didn't see him or anyone else. Six a.m. is too early for tourists. It'd be too early for me to be out here, too, but I was doing the otter count when I found the…" I motioned to the phone, "…uh, and I…"

"You've been a member of the Otter Conservancy for how long now?"

"Is that relevant?"

"It might turn out to be important later on."

I had to count on my fingers. "Four years, I think. Maybe five. But this is only my second year helping with the count."

A worry line appeared between his eyebrows. "When and where did you last see him?"

"You found his body, didn't you?"

Joe didn't say anything for a moment, then

sighed. "He'll have to be formally ID'd, but yeah, it looks like him. As soon as the techs get here, I'll drive up to the Betancourt compound and give the bad news to his wife, which I'm not looking forward to. Now help me. When did you see Booth last? And this time, please be specific."

More finger-counting. "Tuesday…No, Wednesday morning, when I visited Betancourt College to give a talk on the effect of pollution on local wildlife. I passed him in the Marine Sciences Building and waved hello. He didn't wave back. It was just before, ah, ten. I don't know if he was headed to his office or to a class. Maybe a class, come to think of it, because he seemed to be in a hurry. That's only a guess. And he had a young woman with him."

Joe frowned. "A student?"

"She was carrying books."

"Would you recognize her if you saw her again?"

"Maybe."

"What did she look like?"

"Young. Pretty, if that's what you're getting at. Blond, blue-eyed. Perfect features. Boob job." Stuart Booth was known for his affinity with female students. Especially pretty blondes with big boobs.

"I meant, did she seem happy or…?"

"Happy, I think. They went by pretty fast."

"How about him?"

"He looked happy, too."

"Hmm."

I wondered if he was thinking the same thing—that Booth's liking for the young and beautiful could have resulted in him lying dead out here in the Slough. He was, after all, a married man. And Booth's wife…I shivered.

"You okay, Teddy?"

I swallowed. "I'm fine."

"Good, because we have to get on with this. Now tell me, did you ever—?"

His question was interrupted by the arrival of two white vans, one filled with crime techs, the other, the van San Sebastian County used to transport the dead. Joe left to talk to one of the drivers, and since he hadn't told me to stay put, I made my way through a growing crowd of curious liveaboarders and headed back toward the harbor. As unpleasant a person as Professor Stuart Booth, PhD, had been, I had no desire to see his body hauled out of the Slough.

Just before reaching the *Merilee*, I was hailed by Lila Conyers, who was trying to shoo away a stubborn pelican from the deck of *Just In*

Time, her decrepit houseboat. Despite the cheerleader-type good looks she had been born with, this morning the thirty-four-year-old Lila appeared almost as run-down as her houseboat. So thin it was worrying, she had dressed herself in a mismatched skirt and blouse she probably bought at the Salvation Army store. It's hard to look like a fashion plate when your only income is a part-time job at Tiny Tots, the local day care center.

"What's going on at the Slough, Teddy?" she called, once the pelican flapped off.

Since she would find out soon anyway, I told her, leaving out the part about the Zeno-7.

"You're sure it was Booth?"

"Pretty sure."

"But you say you didn't see the body yourself."

"The sheriff did."

Her dull eyes livened. "So he's really dead!"

"Yeah."

"Good."

Without another word, she went inside.

Uneasy, I made my way along the dock to Slip No. 34, where the *Merilee*, my refitted 1979 thirty-four-foot CHB trawler, is moored. Now, a thirty-four-foot boat may sound roomy enough, but its actual walking-around room is less than twenty feet. The rest of the boat's interior was taken up by the bulkheads, cabinets, forward and aft bunks, and the galley with its built-in eating area. Living on a boat isn't for claustrophobes.

So why do we liveaboarders do it? In many cases, it's because rents in San Sebastian County have risen so high that the average person—i.e., Lila Conyers—can no longer afford them, whereas the monthly cost of a boat slip is far less onerous. That's if you own a boat in the first place, which Lila did, having inherited the rickety old thing from her grandmother. But other people live on their boats because life in Gunn Landing Harbor is so peaceful. Usually, anyway. For them there is nothing more wonderful than waking in the morning to the gentle rocking of the leeside Pacific, the call of gulls, and the occasional visits of sea otters.

Some of us live at the harbor for more personal reasons, and as I approached the *Merilee*, I spotted my own reason standing on the deck, dressed in something expensive whipped together by the Designer-of-the-Moment. Mother didn't look happy and I suspected why. Ever since she had married criminal defense attorney Albert Grissom, her fifth husband, she'd developed the bad habit of listening to his police scanner. My suspicion proved correct when I stepped aboard and saw three Louis Vuitton suitcases next to her.

"I'll help you pack," she said.

"I'm not going anywhere, Mother."

"Haven't I told you a million times to call me Caro?"

Caroline Piper Bentley Mallory Huffgraf Petersen Grissom hated it when I called her Mother, so I always make certain I use the term at least once a day. Irritating point duly made, I repeated, "I'm not going anywhere."

"Oh, yes, you are. I'm not having my only child live in a place that allows murderers to run around loose."

Here's the thing about Caro.

Ever since my father embezzled millions and fled the country, leaving us destitute, she has been determined to marry her way back up the social ladder. For a former beauty queen who maintained her beauty via countless cosmetic surgeries, marrying up came easy, and each succeeding husband had been wealthier than the last. Now firmly back on the Social Register's A-List, she felt secure enough to pay attention to areas other than financial portfolios, and kept herself busy poking into other people's business. In some cases, her efforts had had beneficial results, such as the mentoring she'd been doing with at-risk girls. In other cases, she was a royal pain in the derrière. Specifically, mine.

"There are no 'murderers,' plural, running around loose in Gunn Landing Harbor," I told her. "Just one."

"That's supposed to make me feel better? That there's only, as you put it, 'just one,' *singular*, murderer out there? Don't be foolish, Theodora. I want you off this boat and safe in Old Town with me, where I have alarms, security cameras, and a good guard dog."

"Are you talking about your Chihuahua?"

"Feroz has excellent hearing. Now let's get you packed." She turned away from me and faced the *Merilee*'s cabin door. "Unlock it."

I crossed my arms in front of my scrawny chest. "No."

"Don't you tell me no." She crossed her own arms across her surgically endowed breasts.

On the other side of the cabin door I could hear DJ Bonz whining. Un-judgmental, as all dogs are, he had always liked my mother and wanted to see her. Our face-off, or bust-off, could have lasted for hours, but was mercifully broken up by a deep male voice.

"Teddy, I need you to make a formal statement. You can either do it here or at my office. Your choice." Joe, with Deputy Emilio Gutierrez in tow. Both knew Caro well, and despite the circumstances, Emilio smiled when he saw her.

"Good morning, Mrs. Grissom," he said. "You're looking particularly lovely today."

Emilio was descended from one of my great-great-great grandfather's *vaqueros* in the halcyon days when we Bentleys owned most of San Sebastian County. A string of bad investments, lawsuits, the Depression, and my father's crimes had changed all that, but the Gutierrezes' loyalties remained steadfast. Last year, when Caro had been arrested on suspicion of murder, Emilio had made certain her cell was comfortable and her food better than the usual jailhouse slop. He had even allowed her manicurist to visit.

Pointedly ignoring Joe, whom she loathed, Caro gave Emilio a friendly nod. "Emilio. How's the baby?"

"Growing by leaps and bounds, Mrs. Grissom."

"Delightful. I remember when you were born and you were so—"

"Which do you prefer for your interview, Teddy?" Joe said, interrupting their lovefest. "Here or there?"

As if he didn't know. "Your office looks pretty good to me right now."

He winked. "Fine. In the meantime, don't tell anyone about the…" he motioned to the pocket where he'd stashed the Zeno-7.

Too late—I'd already told Lila. But I said, "I won't. I promise."

Thirty seconds later I was in my old Nissan pickup, fleeing my irate mother, following Joe's sheriff department cruiser inland to San Sebastian.

Being questioned by the police is never pleasant, even when you're engaged to the questioner. For one thing, there's always a camera in the room, and I knew how scruffy I looked. My own outfit—paint-spattered jeans and faded maroon Blue Seas Marine Laboratory sweatshirt—was no more elegant than Lila's morning wear, and my frizzy red hair had been not-too-neatly pulled back into a Dollar Store barrette. I hadn't had a chance to shower yet, either, and knew I stank.

Joe pretended not to notice. After running through the usual questions and duly writing down the answers, he asked, "I happened to see you talking to someone on the way back to the *Merilee*. Wasn't that Lila Conyers?"

"Um, yes."

"I hear she had some problems with Booth. Could you catch me up on that?"

"Time marches on, Joe. Her trouble happened fourteen or fifteen, whatever, years ago when Lila was a sophomore at UC San Bertram. Ancient history."

"Sexual harassment, wasn't it? She claimed he was always making sexual innuendoes and that several times he tried to get her into his car as she was walking through the student parking lot. I'm thinking that if the harassment was that bad, surely the school would have done something to stop it. Like fire him."

Suddenly the interview didn't feel all that friendly.

I tried to keep the anger out of my voice, but failed. "The university formed a committee— all males, by the way—and after a short investigation, declared there was nothing to her allegations. They even hinted that, if anything, *Lila* was the harasser. Can you say, 'institutional sexism'? The bastards said that, unlike the other girls, Lila refused to take no for an answer, and started showing up places she knew Booth would be. He played off that by telling the committee she even sat under his bedroom window several times, crying. She denied everything, but his version carried more weight than hers, so…"

"She dropped out of school, right? Never g her degree?"

I muttered something about him being co rect.

"My sources tell me Ms. Conyers was majoring in Marine Science, that she hoped to eventually work at that place down the coast."

"Blue Seas Marine Laboratory, yeah."

"Didn't she have a breakdown or something before she dropped out? Had to be hospitalized?"

"It was just for a couple of weeks." *Months, actually*.

"Hmm. She's working part-time at a daycare center now, isn't she?"

"It's a *nice* day-care center!"

Joe narrowed his eyes. "What was Ms.

Conyers' reaction when you told her about Booth?" With his light brown skin courtesy of his Hispanic father, and blue eyes courtesy of his Irish mother, Joe is a startlingly handsome man, but right now he looked downright ugly.

"Who said I told Lila about Booth?"

"Oh, please. What was her reaction?"

I hate it when people keep asking the same question over and over again. "She didn't say much."

"Teddy. What did she say?"

Sighing, I quoted, "'So, he's really dead. Good.'"

Feeling like a Judas, I slunk my way back to the *Merilee*. At least DJ Bonz and Miss Priss, my one-eyed Persian, were glad to see me. Priss even rubbed up against me, purring loudly, but that might have been because I'd stopped off at Phil's Sea Food Market and picked up some herring for Maureen. Pushover that I am, I gave one to Priss. Bonz looked on patiently, knowing that I never fed one without feeding the other. His patience was rewarded with a boneless piece of pork chop from my mini-refrigerator.

I was cooking myself a belated breakfast when I heard someone shout, "Permission to come aboard, Captain!" Darleene Bauer again. Not that permission was necessary, since she had already clambered onto the *Merilee*'s deck. I had always been amazed that a woman in her seventies could be so spry. Then again, sailors tend toward more fitness than landlubbers.

"The body's gone," she informed me, after stepping into the cabin area and plunking herself down at the small galley table.

"Already?" I flipped my two eggs onto a paper plate, grabbed a fork, and began eating while standing up.

Darleene eyed the eggs with distaste. "The cops—detectives, I think—and techs are still there, even put up a tent to shade them while they work. Saw one just like it on *Law & Order.* Weird, though. Makes a crime scene look like a wedding reception. So who do you think murdered Booth?"

Between bites, I said, "What makes you think someone murdered him? Maybe it was an accident." By the time Darleene arrived at the Slough, I had already turned over the cell phone and its horrifying picture to Joe.

"Techs had a problem with the body bag,

and I saw the hole in his head before they got him stuffed all the way in. That was a bullet wound, for sure."

"Since when are you an expert on bullet wounds?"

"I used to hunt."

My mouth fell open and a tendril of yolk dribbled down my chin. Darleene had been a vegan as long as I'd known her.

"Oh, don't look so surprised, Teddy. Nobody's born vegan. Before Lionel had his coronary, we both hunted. Deer. Elk. Grouse. Pheasant. Fish, too. Lionel once caught an eleven-hundred pound blue marlin down in Cabo, that year's record haul, and he hung the gaudy thing above our fireplace. It wasn't half as impressive as my izzly head, but in forty years of marriage you learn to make compromises. You'll be finding that out for yourself pretty soon, won't you?"

She reached down and scratched Bonz behind his ear, making his entire body wriggle with pleasure. Straightening up, she said, "Are you going to be there next Monday?"

It took me a minute to figure out what she was talking about. "Oh, you mean the Otter Conservancy meeting at the church. Of course I'll be there. That reminds me…" I scrabbled in the drawer where I had stashed the partially filled-out otter report. Like the other volunteers, I'd kept track of the otter count on my phone, then transferred the numbers to the official form Darleene had given me. "I haven't had a chance to type it up more neatly, what with me finding Booth and having to talk to the authorities. But I did make it all the way to the northern end of the Slough, where his sector begins. Uh, began."

She took the paper, which still smelled faintly of chlorophyll-rich Slough water. "No problem. I'll type it up for you. Given your love for typos, I always have to redo it anyway."

Stuffing the report into her pocket, she started up the ladder to the deck, then stopped on the top rung. "One more thing, Teddy. Don't bother trying to figure out who killed Booth. Whoever did it has done us all a favor. Besides, I'd hate to see something happen to you."

A friendly warning?

Or a threat.

Chapter Three

I spent the rest of the morning cleaning the *Merilee*. When you live on a boat and work full time, you tend to let the household stuff slide until your bare feet stick to the filthy teak decking and you run out of clean clothes—something Joe kept pointing out.

"Houses are much more sensible," he'd said, more than once.

True, but whoever had set up the facilities at Gunn Landing Harbor recognized the needs of us floating homeowners and had installed a series of public showers and a laundromat. Because the damp ocean air encourages mildew, the washers and dryers were almost always in use, necessitating a long waiting time.

Wherever there's a wait, there's gossip, and laundromats are no different. As I was stuffing two zoo uniforms, underwear, and bedding into an extra-large washer (I'm too unfussy to sort) the gossip train pulled into the station with the arrival of Kenny Norgaard. Somewhere in his late fifties, he lived on the *High Life*, a 1969 Stephens Flybridge motor yacht.

Kenny was one of those people you often find in marinas, having inherited just enough money that he didn't need to work, but not enough to allow him to indulge in the kind of high life his boat was named for. With too much time on his hands, he spent his days lounging on deck sipping margaritas until he ran out of tequila and had to wait until his monthly trust fund check arrived before stocking up on more. Over the years he had learned to spend his dry days dropping in on his neighbors to cadge food and drink. They always complied, because Kenny's gossip was the best.

Today, after plopping down his own laundry basket on the floor, he started right in. "I take it you've all heard about Booth?"

Murmurs of assent from everyone present.

Then my washer started up, and it was so noisy I had to strain to hear what Kenny was saying.

"In case you didn't know," he continued,

"there's a rumor going around that it wasn't an accident, that someone actually shot him. No wonder, considering. But say what you will about Booth, and there's sure plenty to say, he was one slick operator."

"Are you serious? We've heard some damning stories about his behavior with young women." This, from Ruth Donohue, a rawboned soccer player from Florida who now lived on the *Clear Light* with Dee Dee Pascal, a video game designer.

"Never make judgments based on hearsay." For once, Kenny, the master of light repartee, sounded serious.

There was a brief pause before Dee Dee, softer-looking and more easygoing than Ruth, took over. "Where there's smoke there's often a fire. Not always, I grant you, but often enough. Anyway, we heard that after Lila's harassment accusation, Booth had to hurry up and get married. Harper Betancourt was between boyfriends, so…" She shrugged her plump shoulders. "Not that he loved her, or she him, but it kept the scandal-mongers quiet. Besides, Harper had all that Betancourt money, so why not? It made her father happy. Two birds with one stone, if you catch my meaning."

"Which proves absolutely nothing." Kenny gave Dee Dee a crooked smile. Not that it was necessary. No one could ever stay mad at Kenny.

"Lila wasn't the only victim, Kenny. There were more harass-ment allegations hanging fire."

Ruth jumped back into the conversation. "A couple of other female students were saying the same thing, and you know what? Each time, he used the same defense he'd used with Lila, that the girls were the problem, not him. Unfortunately for poor Lila, it worked. As for the other victims, I'm betting Harper's father bought them off."

Kenny frowned. "Victims? You mean *accusers*. Nothing was ever proved."

"You actually believe Booth's side of the story?" Ruth sounded as incredulous as Dee Dee looked.

"Well, not to go that far, but...." He let the sentence hang.

I stepped away from my washer in order to hear better. Ruth was in her early forties, but appeared older, because unlike her partner, she sailed without bothering to apply sunscreen. Right now her sharp, deeply tanned cheeks were flushed. Although she had retired from pro soccer several years earlier, she'd kept herself in good shape. If Kenny was smart, he wouldn't irritate her further.

"So the other girls were lying, too?" she snarled. "All of them?"

"That's not what I said. I just think it's wrong to accuse a person of horrendous things without having any proof."

Ruth clenched her fists.

I had forgotten that Ruth—unlike everyone else in the harbor—had never warmed to Kenny. For that matter, neither had Dee Dee.

When Kenny noticed the discussion was in danger of becoming physical, he raised his pudgy hands in surrender. "Let's just agree to disagree, shall we, dear hearts?

With that, he turned and dumped his clothes in the one remaining washer. Just in time, too, because the door opened again and several more liveaboarders came in lugging armfuls of mildew-endangered laundry.

Three hours later—there'd been a long line of liveaboarders waiting for too-few dryers—I stowed my clothes away in the *Merilee's* too-few cupboards. Concerned that Kenny

Norgaard might drop by to continue his gossip mongering, I decided to have lunch at Phil's Fish Market, a restaurant too expensive for Kenny's end-of-the-month pocketbook. It was also too expensive for mine, but after the morning I'd endured, I felt like splurging. As an added bonus, few, if any, of the other liveaboarders would be there to share their memories of the generally unloved Booth, and I could eat in peace.

So much for my plans. No sooner had I walked through Phil's door than Preston Morrell hailed me from the restaurant's patio.

"Get yourself over here, Teddy! I've got enough food for two."

Dr. Preston Morrell, Chief of Operations at Blue Seas Marine Laboratory, sat hunched over a plate of food big enough to choke a whale. Although somewhere in his sixties, he was still a handsome man. His ruddy complexion and neatly trimmed salt-and-pepper beard and sea-green eyes were set off by his Blue Seas Burgundy sweatshirt. More than one female diner cast c'mere-sexy looks at him.

Preston had chosen one of the restaurant's primo outdoor tables. Sun-drenched, it overlooked both the harbor and the wooded hill that led up to Old Town, and if I squinted, I could see my mother's house. Not that I wanted to. The table also gave me a fine view of the *Merilee* bobbing gently at her berth, so I happily accepted Preston's invitation.

"As it turns out, the Fisherman's Fry-Up is too much for me," he announced, pointing at the heaping plate. "Especially since I was foolish enough to indulge in clam chowder for an appetizer. You know how big the bowls are here."

Without further ado, he slid one of his cod fillets, two jumbo shrimp, a crabcake, and a handful of fries onto an empty bread dish, then scooted it across the table to me.

"That's sweet of you, Preston."

He smiled. "'Sweet' is my middle name. Remember?"

I did, and with some regret. After my father had embezzled millions and vanished into South America with the authorities in hot pursuit, Preston—this was a decade before he became head of Blue Seas—had fallen hard for the broke, bereft Caro, and had attempted to console her as much as was possible for a cash-strapped marine scientist. He hadn't yet matured into the bearded handsomeness he now evinced, and at the time had looked downright geeky, but his open-heartedness made up for his unprepossessing appearance. He gave us rides on the magnificent *Sea Scout*, Blue Sea's research ship whenever they launched *Sea Quest II*, the lab's submersible.

Only around nine years old at the time, I'd been crazy about Preston and the adventures he led us on, so when Caro's divorce came through, I assumed he would be my new stepfather, especially since she seldom used his given name, just called him "Sweet."

"Sweet, could you take Theodora out on that boat again? She wants to see dolphins."

"Sweet, could you get Theodora an all-access pass to the Grateful Dead concert benefiting Sea Quest II?*"*

"Sweet, could you refill my drink?"

Alas, it was not to be. Using her former Miss San Sebastian County beauty as bait, Caro chose a duller man with a bigger bank account.

"How's your mother?" Preston asked, nibbling at a jumbo shrimp. "New marriage working out?"

Poor Preston. Never married, he still carried a torch for her. But even with his ascendancy to the top position at the marine lab, he would never have enough money for my mother.

"She's fine. So's the new marriage."

"Ah."

Then I remembered hearing something else. Before Booth began his career in academia, he had briefly worked for Blue Seas. Directly under Preston, if my memory was correct.

"Say, Preston, you heard about Stuart Booth, didn't you?"

"Yep." He speared another jumbo shrimp, took a bite. "These shrimp are delicious, aren't they?"

"Didn't he once work for you?"

"Mmm."

I couldn't tell if his *Mmm* was an assent or a culinary review. "How long ago was that?"

"Fifteen, twenty years. Time flies. Here, have some Tabasco for that crabcake." He edged the bottle toward me.

"I'm fine. Exactly how long did he work for you?"

"You don't think it's too dry?"

"What?"

He pointed a finger at my plate. "The crabcake."

"I like them dry, keeps them crispy. Why'd Booth leave Blue Seas? It wasn't because he was given a better offer, because I heard he was out of work for several months before he signed on with UC San Bertram."

"Mmm."

"Was there some kind of a problem?"

He opened his mouth to reply, then a seagull flapped down and perched on a patio railing, eyeing our plates. I pulled mine closer to me. Like all seagulls, it had thieves' eyes.

"Ah, yes, I'm glad you brought up Blue Seas. I lost my assistant last week, you know, the one who just got married to that pretty Italian girl who worked in our front office? She was homesick, so he's moving to Italy to be with her. I told him he was making a mistake since she's from Rome and you know what the rents are like there. But, hey, when love walks in, common sense walks out, doesn't it?"

"You didn't answer me, Preston."

He put his fork down. "I can't talk about Booth."

"But he worked for you." The seagull made a dive for my crabcake, and I covered my plate with my hand just in time.

"Awful birds, aren't they? Why last week I was…"

Recognizing another evasion, I interrupted. "How long did Booth work for Blue Seas?"

"Rats with wings," Preston said, shooing the gull away.

"C'mon, Preston. How long?"

"Only a couple of months."

"So there was some kind of problem."

"Like I said, I can't talk about Booth."

"Did you fire him?"

"I can't talk about that."

It sounded to me like Booth had been fired, so I restated my question. "Then he left under a cloud?"

His usually open face closed down. "Teddy, I told you, I can't talk about Booth."

"Something to do with women, maybe? Young ones?"

"I repeat my former statement. *I can't talk about Booth!* Other than to say he left voluntarily."

Stymied, I resumed eating for a few minutes. Then, as I gobbled down the rest of my crab-cake, I remembered a couple of firings at the zoo and the way Human Resources always handled the cases when approached for references.

"Let's see if I've got this right. You're saying that Professor Booth once worked at the lab, then 'voluntarily' left, only to several months later take a less fun, lower-paying job at UC

San Bertram. Frankly, I find that unbelievable, so how about this. Let's pretend that at some point he saw the error of his ways and changed his mind…" I waved my fork for emphasis, "*If* he'd really changed his behavior, would he have been eligible for rehire?"

"No."

"'No,' as in you're refusing to discuss it or 'no' he wasn't eligible for rehire?"

"Mr. Booth—he wasn't *Professor* Booth at the time, that was years away—was not eligible for rehire."

With that, Preston stood up, gave me a friendly peck on the cheek, and scuttled away with the lunch check in his hand.

Chapter Four

When I walked into the Gunn Zoo's staff lounge the next morning, several copies of the of the *San Sebastian Journal* were being passed around. When Frank Owens, the new river otter keeper, handed one to me I saw that Booth's death had made page one. When it bleeds, it leads.

I ignored the pictures and went straight to the copy.

FAMED MARINE EXPERT DEAD!

The deceased man found in Gunn Landing Slough yesterday morning has been identified as Dr. Stuart Booth, 62, a resident of Old Town, the elite hillside community overlooking Gunn Landing Harbor. When questioned, San Sebastian County Sheriff Joseph Rejas stated, "The autopsy will determine cause of death, but in the meantime, I caution everyone to forego idle speculation. Dr. Booth's family is understandably upset over their loss, and rumors don't help."

The sheriff then added, "And as for the press, instead of camping out in front of the Betancourt compound trying to get interviews, you guys should leave them alone to grieve."

Rejas also refused to confirm the rumors that Dr. Booth had died of a bullet wound and that the person who found the body was the sheriff's fiancée, Theodora Bentley, of the well-known Gunn Landing Bentleys. No stranger to death investigations, Ms. Bentley works at the Gunn Zoo and is best known for her regular appearances on Good Morning, San Sebastian, *where she showcases the zoo's animals. When contacted, Bentley would only say that the discovery came as a great shock. She declined further comment.*

Dr. Booth was a longtime resident of San Sebastian County. After receiving his master's degree in Marine Science from the University of California, Sacramento, he briefly worked for the famed Blue Seas Marine Laboratory, then returned to school to get his PhD from UC San Bertram, where he taught for several years. He eventually left to chair the Marine Sciences Department at Betancourt College in San Sebastian.

Dr. Booth is survived by his wife, former debutant Harper Betancourt-Booth. The couple had no children. Both of Booth's parents predeceased him.

"Fame becomes you, Teddy," Frank said. "Even wearing saggy sweats."

I hadn't noticed anyone snapping my picture as I stood talking to Joe. Weren't photographers supposed to get a signed release or something? With my hair wild and my sweatshirt not only saggy but none too clean, I looked terrible, but my bedraggled appearance was beside the point. Why was I even in the paper to begin with, falsely identified as the person who found the body? I was so irritated that I almost missed Frank's next comment.

"They say Booth was working on the sea otter count, too."

"Several people were. Are."

"You don't find that odd?"

I looked up from the newspaper. "Why would I?"

With the river otter keeper's sandy hair, near-perfect features and gym-toned body, Frank was considered a prime catch for just about any unattached female, but the frown on his face reduced his good looks.

"Because of Booth's reaction to the toxoplasma gondii problem," he said. "He once described it as 'that overstated Toxo Terror.'"

Toxoplasma gondii was a parasite that had begun infecting numerous species, from cats to humans. The parasite is sometimes found in the soil and in undercooked or raw meat, but the infection usually goes unnoticed in otherwise healthy individuals. However, its impact on anyone with an impaired immune system—or pregnant women—can be severe. In otters, toxoplasma gondii was lethal, attacking the animals' brains, leading to seizures, paralysis, then death. Recently, the incidence of dead sea otters washing up on shore had increased, making an accurate otter count of prime importance.

Before I could comment, Myra Sebrowski sniped, "Speaking ill of the dead, Frank? Have a little compassion, for heaven's sake."

I shot her a look of amazement. Myra, a flamboyantly beautiful brunette, had never shown compassion for anyone at any time. Myra loved only Myra. Well, and the great apes she took care of.

The other zookeepers stared at her, too.

"*What?*" she said, looking around. "Am I the only one here who cares about poor old Stuart?"

"Poor old *Stuart?*" mimicked Robin Chase, the big cat keeper. "I didn't know you two were acquainted. And since you bring it up, wasn't he a bit old for you? Like thirty years or something? Besides being married, and all."

Myra shot Robin a dirty look. "As if you can talk."

Oh, here we go.

Last year Buster Daltry, the rhino keeper, won an all-expense trip for two on an African photo safari, and having had a crush on Robin for a long time, invited her to go along with him. No fool she, Robin said yes. But two weeks before the departure date, Buster broke his leg escaping a charging rhino. Not wanting to spoil everything for Robin, he gave the other ticket to her and said she could take along whomever she wanted, expecting she would pick a female. Wrong. Robin, for whatever reason, chose Jack

Spence, the bear keeper. While no one believed the two had had any sort of relationship before the Africa trip, by the time they returned, romance was definitely in the air. It broke up Buster's and Jack's long friendship.

Now here's the kicker.

Robin Chase is no beauty. Big-boned, she towers almost six feet and is built like a WWF wrestler. With the exception of her face, her body is covered with realistic, full-color tattoos of every animal she has ever cared for in her years as a zookeeper. Tigers, ostriches, snakes, koalas, foxes, giraffes—well, you get the picture. Robin has taken care of so many different animals, that wherever she goes, her skin walks, crawls, and ripples with wildlife.

Come to think of it, maybe that's the attraction.

Up until the Africa trip, Myra was the zoo's official femme fatale, flirting here, sneaking around there, and she wasn't taking the loss of her crown lightly. Whereas before she had simply ignored the hulking Robin, she now baited her rival every chance she got.

"At least I don't date married men," Robin replied, looking piqued at Myra's verbal slap. "But from what I hear, you…"

"Ahem!" Jack Spence interrupted, sensing a brawl in the offing. "It's time for us to get our butts to the commissary."

The commissary was where we zookeepers picked up our charges' meals, whether it be seeds, hay, or raw meat. It was also where I usually started my actual workday at the zoo. Unfortunately, this was a Tuesday, which meant that I would be taking some animals over to the TV studio to appear on *Anteaters to Zebras*, my live segment on *Good Morning, San Sebastian*. It wasn't a job I particularly liked, but seeing our animals on television helped highlight ecological awareness; it also boosted the zoo's gate proceeds.

I waved good-bye to the other keepers, ignoring Myra's farewell scowl. She had wanted to be the zoo's so-called Television Ambassador, and had never forgiven me for being chosen instead of her. What Myra didn't know was that I had actually campaigned for her to get the job, but my effort bore no fruit. As Zorah Vega, the zoo director, had explained after swearing me to silence, "Myra would make the segment all about herself, not the animal."

Today's star was El Capitan, one of the zoo's ocelots. Raised in captivity, leash-trained, and used to people and cameras, Cappy, as we called him, was certain to be a calm presence. Sharing the spotlight would be Lilliana, the zoo's popular four-foot-long green iguana, also a TV veteran. The only animal I had qualms about was Samuel, the seven-year-old bald eagle we acquired after he'd been hit by a car. Samuel's broken right wing had never properly healed, rendering him unable to return to the wild. He could still fly short distances, but not well enough to hunt. Today would be his first appearance on live TV.

Qualms or not, I would have plenty of help. Although the zoo volunteer who usually accompanied me on my trip to the TV station was out of town attending her daughter's wedding, two trainee keepers would assist. Janet Hewitt, who at the ripe old age of twenty-four still looked like a teenager, normally helped Robin Chase with the big cats. Usually fresh-faced and smiling, her eyes were pink-lined today, which I put down to allergies; they can be hell here in California. The other assistant was Tim Merriam, a jovial fitness buff stationed at the reptile house. Since both trainees enjoyed being around different species, I foresaw no problem.

With the humans, anyway.

The trip from the zoo to KGNN, the television station in San Sebastian, didn't take long, and the animals were quiet during the drive. They remained silent as we carried them into the Green Room, although Cappy hissed at one of the station's security guards. Ocelots have an excellent sense of smell, and he didn't like the scent of the guard's aftershave. Neither did I, for that matter. Cappy settled down when Janet, who had come prepared, fed him a cube of beef heart.

Ten minutes later I was on the air with an iguana in my lap.

Before leaving the zoo, I had changed into fresh zoo khakis, but as usual, *Good Morning, San Sebastian* anchor Ariel Gonzales outshone me. A former Marine helicopter pilot, she now reveled in civilian clothes. Today she wore a particularly stunning lavender Chanel-ish suit and dangly amethyst earrings. She had swept up her dark-brown hair, revealing not only those stunning cheekbones, but also the two-inch scar she'd received in Afghanistan while rescuing several other Marines pinned down by a sniper. There were times I suspected she valued the scar more than the Bronze Star she had received for it, which was why she refused to let the show's cosmetician make it completely disappear.

As I droned on and on about the pros and cons of iguana ownership, Ariel leaned forward to stroke Lilliana's silky skin.

"She feels so smooth!" Ariel exclaimed.

"Yes, iguanas have lovely skin, although people who don't know anything about them think they have scales, which they don't. They are technically reptiles, like snakes, which also have smooth skin. Iguanas can be quite affectionate and love to cuddle. However, they aren't for everyone because they can grow to more than six feet long. That's something many people who've bought a teensy six-monther for a pet don't understand. One day you have a cute little green thing running around the house and snuggling up next to you, and the next day you've got a six-foot-long behemoth scaring the bejesus out of your neighbors."

Lilliana gave Ariel a loving look. Ariel gave her a loving look back.

"She's a sweetie," Ariel said.

"Yes, and so is El Capitan—Cappy, for short—the Gunn Zoo's ocelot." I waved to Tim and Janet, who were waiting in the wings with the ocelot. Tim rushed forward and snatched up Lilliana, while Janet led Cappy in on his leash.

"Oh, my, what a beauty!" the anchorwoman enthused. "Just like a big ol' kitty cat." She was hamming it up, but I didn't mind. It made for good TV, and that's why we were all here.

As expected, Cappy behaved well and sat at my feet as I began my spiel. "Ocelots such as El Capitan here used to be found all through the southern states of the U.S., but because their coats are so beautiful they were hunted to extinction. To find a wild ocelot these days you have to travel to Central and South America, where they still range all the way down to northern Argentina, although deforestation is threatening their habitat in those countries, too. For a big cat, ocelots are relatively small, just about twice the size of a large house cat, but they're ferocious hunters, and eat anything from frogs to iguanas—sorry, Lilliana—or small deer."

At this, Cappy made a noise that sounded like a purr but was actually a subtle growl. It occurred to me then that we hadn't yet had an animal kill and eat another on the show. I guess my concern showed, because Janet said, "Don't worry. I put the iguana where he can't get at her."

Hammed horror from Ariel. The anchor-woman was having a good time.

So were the other people in the television studio. Outside of the brightly lit set, the camera and sound people appeared mostly as shadows, but when Cappy had entered on his leash, those shadows moved forward to get a better look. A couple of them even went "Awww!"

After nodding in agreement, I faced the camera's red light and continued. "You know, I said there were no wild ocelots in the U.S., but I've heard there's a small colony of them living in the swamps of Florida. Escaped pets, or pets that were dumped when they grew too trouble-some for their owners."

Time for my standard public service announcement.

I put on my "stern" face and waggled my finger at the red light. "Which reminds me. If you're thinking about getting an ocelot for a pet, please don't. Most do not tame well, and they simply won't turn into the cuddly lap cat you want. Another problem is that their health can be iffy in captivity, and it's not at all unusual for them to mount up thousands of dollars in vet bills within just a couple of months. Yes, I know they are beautiful animals, but like so many of Mother Nature's creatures, ocelots are best worshipped from afar."

His time in the spotlight over, Cappy favored Ariel with a quick lick on the ankle before Janet led him off.

All good so far.

Unfortunately, one of the reasons *Anteaters to Zebras* had earned such a large viewership was that the animals I brought on didn't always behave as well as Lilliana and Cappy. In the two years the Gunn Zoo segment had aired, I'd been crapped on by a lemur with diarrhea, nipped on the earlobe by a cranky squirrel monkey, and once even had to chase a rampaging honey badger through the studio. Animals don't follow scripts, and they have no respect for those who do.

But Samuel, the bald eagle, appeared calm as he entered perched on Tim's strong arm, which was covered up to the elbow with a leather raptor glove. Leather jesses dangled from Samuel's legs, a necessary precaution to keep him from attempting to reach the studio's rafters.

Ariel let out a gasp. "Oh, my!"

"Being an ex-Marine, I thought you'd appreciate this fine example of our national bird. Magnificent, isn't he?"

And he was.

At approximately seven years old, Samuel was a full-grown male with a wingspan of eighty-two inches. His white neck feathers were ruffled and his pale yellow eyes—the size of a human's—glared at the camera's red light. He behaved so well that I dared hope this might be one of the rare occasions where no one got bit, pecked, or shat on.

Feeling optimistic, I launched into my speech.

"Although bald eagles are threatened these days by lead poisoning and, as in Samuel's case, car accidents, they live longer than you'd think. A captive bald eagle in New York state lived to be forty-eight years old, but in the wild their lifespan averages somewhere between twenty or thirty." I paused to let that sink in, then smiled at the red light. "By the way, a lot of the things people think they know about bald eagles are wrong, such as the rumor that they can carry away children or full-grown sheep. There are a lot of Photoshopped pictures out there showing them doing that, but a bald eagle's lifting power is only around four pounds, so your children are safe. But maybe not your Chihuahua."

Ariel winced, but Tim, who was still holding

Samuel on his arm, looked impressed. Unlike Ariel, he didn't own a Chihuahua.

Enjoying the success of my spiel, I continued. "If Samuel hadn't been permanently injured after being hit by a car, he could fly to an altitude of ten thousand feet at a speed up to thirty-five miles per hour. And speaking of numbers, here's a wowser for you. Did you know that a bald eagle's nest is around five feet in diameter and can weigh up to two tons? That's four thousand pounds, folks! If an eagle's nest ever falls on you, call the undertaker."

Ariel's eyes widened.

"Another thing. Eagles mate for life. There was no female around when Samuel had his accident, but if there had been, after a brief period of widowhood, she would have remarried." Oh, wasn't I the clever one?

For the climax of the segment, I pulled a freeze-dried mouse out of my pocket and tossed it onto the floor. Beaming at everyone out there in Television Land, I said, "Now, you folks watch this!"

Samuel's big yellow eyes zeroed in on the mouse and in less than a second, he had swooped over Ariel's head, grabbed the dead mouse in his talons and gobbled it down. With nary a burp, he lifted off again to return to Tim's leather-sheathed arm.

Unfortunately, as he soared over Ariel, he let loose a foul-smelling stream of eagle poop all over her beautiful lavender suit.

But Ariel wasn't to be out-hammed.

Although dripping, she ignored the mess, stood up, assumed the "attention" position, and snapped Samuel a perfect Marine salute.

"All things considered, that went pretty well," I said afterwards, as we drove toward the zoo.

"Even though they turned to shit at the end," Tim chortled.

"We're just lucky Ariel has a strong stomach and a large wardrobe allowance. *And* likes all sorts of animals. The anchor before her didn't, and it showed."

We drove along in communal silence for a while until we turned off Old Bentley Road onto the lane that led up the hill to the zoo.

That's when Janet, who had been silent so far, said, "I hear you're the person who found Professor Booth's body."

Irked that this misinformation was still being

passed around, I said, "I did not find the body. A sheriff's deputy did."

She didn't say anything else for a while, but as we rolled through the zoo's rear gate, she said in a quaking voice, "I had Professor Booth for two classes—Marine Biology 101 and that new one on the Monterey Trench. What everybody's been saying about him? That he bothers the female students? It's just not true!"

Then she burst into tears.

Chapter Five

Janet quickly got a handle on her emotions and helped return our TV stars to the Animal Care Center where they would be checked over before being returned to their enclosures. Tim gave her a nervous look after he maneuvered the ocelot into a space far away from the iguana. He probably feared she would start crying again and he wouldn't know what to do. Men are funny that way. They can talk down rampaging elephants and subdue charging tigers, but let a woman so much as sniffle, they panic.

As for me, Janet's tears made me curious. Although sorry she had been upset about Booth's death, I wondered why she had taken it so hard. Granted, the man once had a less-than-savory reputation when it came to female undergrads, but word had gone out that he cleaned up his act after marrying Harper Betancourt. And, anyway, Janet would have been a mere child when the harassment rumors began in earnest, too young even for him.

Unless he'd started up again?

No. I was fairly certain Booth hadn't been messing around with his female students. Hardly out of any sense of decency, but because doing so would have jeopardized his access to all that lovely Betancourt money— not to mention his position at the college the Betancourts' gazillions had founded. He might have been a bad man, but never a stupid one. Hoping to find out what the relationship had been between Janet and Booth, I approached her as soon as Tim went back to the Reptile House. I struck out. Not meeting my eyes, Janet told me she'd love to talk, but was due to help out at the big cats' enclosure as soon as the TV animals were stowed away. Then she scurried off.

Oh, well. It wasn't my business, anyway. After my last involvement in a murder case and almost getting killed, I had vowed to keep my curiosity under better control. So after filling out the necessary paperwork for the animals' return, I walked to the Admin Building, picked up one of the radios we zookeepers rely on for communication with each other, and clipped it onto my belt. Then I went down to the garage, climbed into a zebra-striped electric cart, and headed out on my rounds.

The Gunn Zoo is part of the twenty-five-hundred-acre Gunn Estate, which also includes a one-thousand-acre vineyard and a five-hundred-acre elephant sanctuary. The entire estate is ringed by full-growth eucalyptus trees which give it a sealed-off, Eden-esque quality. Although I have lived in Gunn Landing most of my life—with the exception of my short marriage to Michael when we lived in San Francisco—the joy I feel walking the zoo grounds never diminishes. Laid out in animal "neighborhoods," the zoo offers California Habitat with coyotes, condors and river otters; Tropics Trail with the giant anteater, Andean bears, and parrots; Africa Trail with rhinos and big cats; Verdant Veldt with giraffes, ostriches, and elands; Colder Climes with the polar bear cub, puffins, and Icelandic foxes; Down Under with koalas and wallabies; and Friendly Farm, where less exotic animals like llamas, chickens, and goats reign supreme.

The zoo also has several giant aviaries which

boast more than one thousand species, ranging alphabetically all the way from albatross to Zenaida doves. A great fuss is being made these days by the puffin pair we recently acquired, but my favorite bird (zookeepers aren't supposed to have favorites, but we do) remains Carlos, the Collie's magpie jay. Over the years Carlos has wooed me with numerous gifts, a stick here, a bug there, in an attempt to mate with me. Although I repeatedly turn down the honor— the physical difficulties are insurmountable— he has still won my heart.

Stopping at his aviary, I climbed out of the cart and walked over to receive his latest gift: a dead dung beetle he deposited gently into my hand.

"Oh, Carlos, you shouldn't have!" I cooed, holding the dead beetle close to my unfortunately flat bosom.

Pleased I had accepted his gift, he serenaded me with his mocking-bird repertoire.

"*Whit wheet!*" Curved bill thrasher.

"*Bzzz-zzzz-zzzz!*" Bluebird of paradise.

"*Sweet-sweet-sweet!*" Yellow warbler.

"I love you, too, Carlos, baby." Waving good-bye, I climbed into my cart. I had places to go, other animals to see.

As I drove away, Carlos shrieked in despair—
"*Reedleeee! Reedleeee!*" Boat-tailed grackle.

My next stop was to see Lucy, the giant anteater in Tropics Trail. She had already been fed
and her enclosure cleaned, so my visit with her
wasn't as lengthy as on other days. She made for
great watching, though, being in the middle of
a game of Chase with Little Ricky, her pup. He
was growing rapidly, and had almost stopped
nursing. He was still very much a mama's boy,
though, and five minutes later, he grew tired of
their game, clambered onto Lucy's back, and
promptly fell asleep.

"You're a good mama, Lucy," I told her. "A
very, very good mama."

Lucy didn't reply, not that I'd expected her to,
but I like to think there was a certain amount
of warmth in her eyes when she looked at me.

"That's a weird-looking animal," said a pre-
teen boy who was with a group of similarly
aged kids. Summer camp? Despite his words,
he sounded impressed.

"All the better to suck up ants and termites,"
I told him.

They all liked that.

When I arrived in Down Under, Wanchu the
koala and Nyee, her mate, were sound asleep

in their fake eucalyptus tree, which they usually are since koalas sleep most of the time. Wanchu's as-yet-unnamed joey had grown so large that I could see an ear sticking out of her pouch. It was asleep, too.

I cleaned the koala enclosure quietly, taking care not to wake the sleeping beauties. Shit-shoveling takes up at least half of a zookeeper's day, but it's easy with koalas. You sweep it up, put it in the dumpster, then drive it away to the recycling dump. Koala dung is popular with the area's gardeners; apparently it is as mild as the animals themselves.

I was stowing my shovel in the cart when I spied Lex Yarnell, one of the zoo's park rangers, hurrying along the path. He had a worried expression on his face, but when he saw me, he turned on a smile. A spectacularly handsome man—even better-looking than the new river otter keeper—Lex fit the old description of tall, dark, and handsome. Black hair, mahogany-colored eyes, olive skin, and broad shoulders that seemed to go on forever. With his looks he should have been able to get any woman he wanted, but his track record didn't bear that out. Several months ago he had been dumped and he still hadn't recovered.

"Nice show today, Teddy. Some of us watched it in the employee lounge and got a big laugh out of Samuel's stunt. Ariel Gonzales is sure something, isn't she? Big improvement on the wuss last year who screamed every time an animal looked at her cross-eyed."

I was about to defend the ex-anchor's honor when Lex's smile faded. "That Booth guy, can't say I'm sorry about what happened to him." He paused, then added, "Oh, ah, gee… you're engaged to Sheriff Rejas, right? What did he tell you?"

Sidestepping the question with a semi-fib, I said, "Joe never discusses his cases with me, Lex." True, up to a point; not true in that Joe was always telling me to leave the detecting to the San Sebastian Sheriff's Department.

"The newspaper said you're the one who found the body."

For what had to be the tenth time today—even Ariel had quizzed me about "finding" Booth's body while I was packing up at the TV station—I set Lex straight. In doing so, I unfortunately let slip the part about the water-resistant Zeno-7, which Joe had expressly forbidden me to mention.

"You're telling me you knew there had been

a…a murder just because you saw an otter swimming around with a cell phone? Give me a little more credit than that, Teddy. I may not be a college grad, but that doesn't mean I don't know which way the wind is blowing." The usually even-tempered Lex sounded irritated.

"What do you mean, 'which way the wind is blowing'?"

"A few minutes ago I got a call from Amberlyn, and she told me Sheriff Rejas was at her apartment door, trying to get her to accompany him to the station. The only reason she's not down there now is because she had enough sense to call me first. I told her to stay the hell away from him."

Amberlyn Lofland was the college student who had dumped Lex earlier this year. She was every bit as gorgeous a young woman as Lex a man. I had met her briefly at a Fourth of July barbeque he threw at the trailer court he lived in with his extended family, and had marveled at the sight of the two "Tens" together.

"Why in the world would Joe want to talk to your ex-girlfriend?"

Lex pretended to study the sleeping koalas, but it didn't work. His eyes kept shifting back to me. "She, um, knew Booth. And, uh, there were nude photos of her on Booth's phone."

Pictures of Amberlyn on that Zeno-7? Maybe they'd been taken clandestinely. "Was she one of his students?"

"Nah, she goes to UC Santa Cruz. It was more of a…um…personal thing."

"Personal? Like how?"

"That's kind of the reason I came up here. Amberlyn wants to talk to you."

"Whatever for? I only met her once, Lex, and if memory serves, we only talked about the weather. Besides, Sheriff Rejas told me to stay out of the Booth business and that's what I intend to do. If Amberlyn is in any kind of trouble, she needs a lawyer, not me. One of the best attorneys I know of just happens to be married to my mother, and I'll be happy to give you his number if you wish." I reeled off the number but he didn't write it down. "Now, sorry, but I'm due at the polar bear enclosure and I'm running late."

I jumped into my cart and drove away.

By the time I reached Colder Climes— renamed from Northern Climes after one of the zookeepers pointed out there were no penguins in the Arctic nor polar bears in the Antarctic—I was beginning to feel guilty about being so short with Lex. But when I made my way to the polar bear enclosure, I forced myself to forget about Amberlyn's odd request. If those pictures of her on Booth's cell were X-rated, I didn't want to know about it.

Magnus, the orphaned cub I'd picked up during my recent trip to Iceland, was splashing around in his pool, knocking a large red ball back and forth as the crowd cheered. Since he was still too small to be of any danger to humans, I needed no extreme safety measures, just entered the enclosure through the keeper's gate at the rear of the big artificial iceberg. For a bear, Magnus was surprisingly neat, so cleaning out the enclosure didn't take long.

When I emerged from the plastic iceberg into the more public pool area, he spotted me at once. With a squeak, he hauled himself out of the pool and bounded over, shaking off enough water to drench me. I didn't mind. With his snow-white fur, and big black eyes and nose, the cub was every bit as adorable as a stuffed teddy bear. My heart gave a little flutter when he nosed my hand.

"Fish? Magnus want fish?"

Yes, Magnus wanted fish.

The cub was still on a fortified milk regimen, but for the benefit of the large crowd, I tossed a few pieces of fish onto a plastic snow mound and watched as Magnus chased after them.

More cheering from the crowd.

While he was busy scarfing up his treat, I let myself out of the rear gate and walked over to the puffin exhibit, which had been placed next to the penguin enclosure. In their black-and-white outfits, puffins and penguins appear to be members of the same avian family, but they're not. Emperor penguins, which make up our group, can grow up to forty-eight inches high and weigh almost a hundred pounds, whereas puffins are little more than a foot long and weigh less than a pound. The other major difference between the two species is that penguins can't fly, where puffins are champion flyers, often winging all the way from Iceland, where I'd picked these two up, to Maine. Sometimes even further south.

Sigurd and Jodisi were also shyer than their much-larger penguin cousins, because unlike the penguins, the puffins had been hatched in the wild and still retained their feral nature. They did, however, approach when I showed up with a small pail of herring. To my dismay, when I exited their enclosure I found Lex Yarnell waiting for me.

"Listen, Teddy, I just got off the phone with Amberlyn and she's desperate to..."

I was saved from breaking my promise to Joe when the radio on my belt squawked, "Keeper Four, come in. Over."

It was the voice of Aster Edwina Gunn, president of the huge Gunn Trust which ran the zoo, making her my *de facto* boss. Being summoned by her was never a good thing.

Ignoring Lex, I snatched the radio from my belt and pressed the talk button. "Keeper Four here. Over."

"Where are you, Theodora?"

"Colder Climes." Just to goad her, since the enclosure's original name had been her idea, I added, "You know, the one you wanted to name 'Northern Climes.'"

"Very funny. Get up here now."

Here meant her lair at Gunn Castle, the moldering pile her father had shipped over from Scotland stone by stone, including the torture chamber, which, I often suspected, was still being used.

"But I'm working," I whined.

"I've already radioed Zorah to send over a replacement for you, so get a move on. I expect you here in no more than ten minutes."

Without another word, she killed the call.

"Guess you'd better go," Lex said. He didn't look happy.

Nor did I.

Gunn Castle has never been a cheery place. Ignoring the light-filled beauty of Randolph Hearst's San Simeon a few miles down the road, the dark stone structure looms over the surrounding vineyards like a vulture waiting for something to die. With its six towers, crenellated roof, and series of archer's windows, it looks like the setting for a horror film, which isn't far wrong. God only knows how many humiliations I've suffered there from childhood to adulthood, and the horrors just kept coming. Today would probably deliver another to add to my collection.

Eunice Snow, the maid Aster Edwina had hired away from my mother, led me down the long entry hall to the library. Bad sign. My boss always chose the library when delivering bad news.

"How are things, Miss Theodora?" Eunice asked, as our footsteps echoed along the cold floor stones.

"Same old, same old. How's it going with you and Bucky?"

Her smile couldn't have been broader. "They're expanding his television segment to a full half hour!"

Bucky Snow, father of Eunice's twins, Bucella and Bucky Jr., was an ex-con who had at long last landed on his feet. Always a film buff—yes, they screen movies in prison—he had parlayed the job I'd gotten for him at the San Sebastian CinePlex into a segment as film critic for KGNN on *Bucky Goes Hollywood*.

"Is he enjoying the work?"

"He says it's even more fun than boosting cars."

"How nice."

"Well, here we are." Eunice opened the two-hundred-year-old oak doors and ushered me into the library, where Aster Edwina sat at a long table, spider waiting for fly. Then Eunice wisely made tracks.

"I want you to keep me updated on this Booth thing," Aster Edwina said, moving aside the stack of legal documents she had been going through.

No hello, no how-ya-doing. Why bother with social niceties when you can go directly to scaring the hell out of your employees?

"Sorry, Aster Edwina. I promised Joe I'd keep my nose out of it this time."

"You work for me, not him."

"Hmm." I looked around, saw an empty chair. Several of them, actually. "May I sit down?"

"Why? You've got your orders, now hop to it." To signal the meeting was over, she picked up another document.

I sat down anyway, as close to her as I could get. "That's impossible."

"Choose a chair farther away from me. You smell of offal."

I remained put. "One of my job's perks. Anyway, why do you care who killed Professor Booth?"

She put the document down and glowered at me. Although well into her eighties, she was still a terrifying woman with her narrowed eyes and hawk-like nose. They say she had once been a great beauty, but as often happens with the elderly, her fierce soul was now showing through.

"I'm worried about Blue Seas Marine Laboratory," she said.

"Why? From what I hear, they're doing well. I was talking to Preston Morrell the other day and he sounded pretty happy."

"Happy is as happy does. The problem is this thing with that despicable Booth person. I'd hate to see any blowback about his time at Blue Seas, understand?"

"Not really."

As usual, she ignored my bafflement. "You need to keep a lid on that ruffian's days with the organization. We can't have its reputation smeared."

Ruffian? It was all I could do not to laugh. "But Aster Edwina, today's article in the *San Sebastian Journal* mentioned Booth's association with Blue Seas, so that cat's already out of the bag."

"He only worked there for a couple of months, yet still created a mess. After he left, I made certain his employment file was sealed, so don't you let that sheriff of yours get it unsealed."

Aster Edwina was so used to everyone dancing to her tune—no matter how discordant—she forgot that the rest of the world didn't always want to dance along. To remind her of reality, I said, "Sealed or not, Booth's already in the public record as a former employee of Blue Seas. Come to think of it, he made the local paper when he first got hired over there. I was in San Francisco at the time, but Caro sent me a copy of the article. You know how the *San Sebastian Journal* always writes about anything having to do with Blue Seas."

She pursed her lips, which made her look even meaner. "Two inches on B-4. Big deal."

"Oh, but when he left, they followed up with a longer article stating that he left to 'pursue other interests.' Caro sent me a copy of that one, too. It was at least six inches. On the front page."

"But below the fold," she snapped. "And ancient history, nothing to do with that sordid business down at the Slough. You have your marching orders, Theodora. Let me know if Sheriff Rejas starts nosing around about Booth's former connection to Blue Seas."

Although Aster Edwina was usually a cautious person, she had erred badly in referring Booth to Blue Seas. In a way it was understandable. Booth had been a good-looking man, adept at schmoozing elderly, wealthy women like her. Nevertheless, almost as soon as his new office furniture had arrived at Blue Seas, he was gone.

"But Aster Edwina…"

She pursed her lips into such a tight line they almost disappeared. "Good-bye, Theodora."

Resistance being futile, I left.

Lex Yarnell ambushed me again as soon as I got back to the zoo.

"Amberlyn's headed to class now but she'll be home in a couple of hours. And all day tomorrow." He handed me a slip of paper. "Here's her phone number."

Lex's determination to have me contact his ex-girlfriend was puzzling, and I told him so. "She broke up with you months ago, so why do you still care about whatever's going on with her? And why should my relationship with the sheriff get me involved? Like I told you earlier, I really don't know the woman."

He didn't answer right away, and when he did, it was in a voice so low I had trouble hearing him over the trumpeting of a nearby elephant. "It's complicated."

Hardly a clarification, but it aroused my curiosity. "Does she live in one of the dorms?"

"Um, off-campus, in Point Deem."

That took me aback, since Amberlyn's family didn't have Point Deem-style money. Like Lex's family, they scratched out a living near Castroville, picking crops on other peoples' farms. Then again, maybe Amberlyn shared digs with several other young women, the common housing solution for cash-strapped students.

"I'll give her a call tomorrow."

"Thank you, Teddy. I appreciate it."

He walked away quickly, as if afraid I'd change my mind.

The rest of the day passed without any more trouble, unless you count the snarl-fest between two pumas in California Habitat, or the kick-a-thon several Grevy's zebra mares in Africa Veldt got into when one grazed too close to another mare's new colt. Walking by the eastern end of the Veldt, I noticed that even the giraffes acted snappish, slinging their long necks against each other in irritation.

After the angst of the last two days I decided to visit the elephant sanctuary. Elephants always have a calming effect on me. Herd animals, they delight in each other's company. Today was no exception. Reba, Sheena, Indu, Mbutu, Carolyn, and Aliah—all rescued circus performers—were splashing around in the big pond when I arrived. When my old friend Aliah saw me, she trumpeted a hello, but didn't leave the others. I continued on toward the other end of the five-hundred-acre sanctuary where a group of eight basked in the shade of a big eucalyptus. They ignored me, too. Well, except for Mary. She flicked her trunk at me, then returned to swatting flies. I watched them for a while, allowing their gentle contentment to soothe my frazzled nerves.

Workday finally over, I went home to Gunn Landing Harbor, where I found Lila Conyers waiting for me next to the *Merilee*.

"I thought you'd never get here, Teddy," she said, as I approached on the floating dock. Her face was drawn, making her look more like forty-four than thirty-four. Unless I was mistaken, her second-hand blouse was on backwards, too. Maybe they didn't notice things like that at the day care center.

"Are you okay?" I asked.

"Yeah. No. Oh, hell, I don't know. Can I come aboard?"

At my nod Lila followed me below deck, where DJ Bonz greeted her with a stumpy tail wag. Miss Priss ignored her. All the cat cared about right now was being fed, which I proceeded to do.

"Tell me what's going on, Lila."

She slid onto the kitchenette bench and watched the cat and dog beg for more. "It's just that, well, Sheriff Rejas has been bugging me."

"What do you mean, 'bugging'?"

Priss mewled for seconds, but the last time

I had given her seconds she'd barfed on my dolphin-print duvet, so I hardened my heart.

"He's stopped by my houseboat twice."

"Twice? Joe did?"

"That's what I'm trying to tell you."

I didn't like the sound of that. "Was he alone, or did he have someone with him?"

"The first time he was alone. The second time he had a deputy with him."

That meant Joe wanted a witness to the follow-up conversation, never a good sign. "What kind of questions did he ask you?"

"Like, well, stuff."

"Stuff?"

Priss started to yowl, so I relented and gave her another scoop of Friskie's Classic Tuna Paté, her current favorite. She gobbled it up between purrs while Bonz left his now-empty bowl to scramble into Lila's lap. Lila had been a volunteer at the animal shelter when he was brought in with his hind leg mangled beyond repair. She had talked the shelter vet out of euthanizing him, promising that if he couldn't find a home, she would adopt him herself. Then she had called me and asked if I wanted to adopt the best three-legged dog in the whole wide world.

Bonz never forgets.

Neither do I.

"Who's the good boy?" Lila cooed to Bonz, ruffling his ears.

Arf!

"Yes! You're the good boy!"

Arf! Arf! He gazed at her lovingly.

"Lila, what did you tell Joe about Booth?'

"I, uh, I told the sheriff and the guy with him that I hadn't seen Professor Booth since I was his student." Her cheeks flushed red.

Rule Number One in dealing with the police: never tell them a lie you can be caught in.

"Oh, Lila, why did you say that? Everyone in the harbor knows about the time you vandalized Booth's boat. Several witnesses spotted you running away covered in paint. You're lucky none of them reported you."

"Well, somebody did, because the cops showed up thirty minutes later."

"From what the newspaper article said, you still had paint under your fingernails."

She looked down at Bonz, who wouldn't have cared if she'd defaced the Statue of Liberty. "That spray stuff's hard to get off."

When the tagging incident happened, I had been living in San Francisco. Lila's harassment complaint about Booth was ancient memory, but Caro, ever the gossip, had phoned me to yak about the fallout over Lila spray-painting LIAR!!! in Day-Glo Orange along the side of Booth's brand new ninety-seven-foot Azimut Motor Yacht. Before her visit, the yacht—a wedding present from Booth's filthy rich bride—had been a pristine white. At the time I'd been experiencing marital troubles, so I wasn't as interested in Lila's woes as I normally would have been.

"You were charged with criminal mischief," I pointed out.

"The charges were dropped. Besides, I didn't *see* Professor Booth while I was spray-painting his boat, so I wasn't actually lying."

Maybe not, but Lila's earlier sexual harassment charges against Booth, followed by the vandalism, did give her a motive for murder. "My source said you vandalized the boat because you were jealous over him marrying Harper."

"How can you be jealous about a man you hate?" Then her shoulders slumped. "Nobody ever believed me about him, the school, the lawyers, not even my own mother. She thought… she still thinks that I, that I… that I made everything up."

"I believe you, Lila."

She gave me a grateful look before her face crumpled. "Oh, Teddy, I know you do. But I'm so scared!"

Bonz, who I sometimes suspect of being a telepath, looked at her face and whined.

I slid onto the kitchenette bench and put my arm around Lila's shoulders. Since I couldn't think of anything comforting to say, I said nothing.

I was still hugging her when Joe showed up for the dinner date I'd forgotten about.

Chapter Six

The date didn't go well.

Joe had made reservations at Brownlee's, a San Sebastian gastropub specializing in nouvelle French/American cuisine and beers I had never heard of. The food was okay, but the house brew was sweet enough to pour over ice cream. To add to my discomfort, I was still wearing my zoo khakis, along with the scent of Eau de Mammal. Joe didn't mind—he never does—but the well-groomed couple at the next table kept throwing nasty looks my way. And then there was the conversation, which started out okay, then took a dive.

"Colleen watching the kids?" I asked him.

After the children's mother's death, Joe's widowed mother had moved in with him, providing a comforting presence for Antonio, nine, and Bridget, four. They were great kids, so I wasn't worried about my upcoming role in their lives. I was worried about something else.

"Yep, babysitting as usual," Joe answered. "When I left, they were all playing that new child's version of *RISK*, and Bridie had just invaded New Jersey. By the way, Teddy, what were you doing, talking to Lila Conyers? Didn't I tell you to stay out of the Booth case?"

Just what I was afraid of. Joe hated it when I got involved in a murder case. In an attempt to give myself time to think up an explanation, I said, "I wonder why there isn't a salt shaker on our table?"

"Ask the chef about the salt, not me. This Booth thing, it's more complicated than you realize, so for your own safety I…"

"I prefer beer that tastes like beer, too. Not Coke."

"Then don't drink it. What did Lila tell you?"

Evasion wasn't working, so I gave up and confronted the issue head on. "It's okay to talk to Lila as long as I report the conversation to you? That's hardly fair, Joe."

"Okay, I'll admit that I might have been out of line there, but I'm begging you, please stay away from Lila Conyers."

Evasion time again. "I'm getting us some salt."

"Salt is bad for your blood pressure."

"My blood pressure's fine. Waitress, can we get some salt over here?"

Joe sighed. "You're being difficult."

"And you're prone to exaggeration." I smiled to take the sting out of my words. I did love this man, but sheriffs are so used to bossing people around that they sometimes forget to leave that kind of behavior at the office.

"Are you kidding me, Teddy? You're a veritable danger magnet. Why, look at what you do for a living! You're out there daily with lions, tigers, elephants, and all kinds of lethal animals. Any one of them would kill you as soon as look at you."

"The animals I work with are quite nice. Most of them, anyway."

He ignored my fib. "Not only that, but you keep getting yourself mixed up in murder cases, which scares me more than the lions." He put his fork down. "*Promise* me you'll stay away from Lila Conyers."

Just then the waitress arrived with a salt shaker, which I used sparingly, the burger having been fine without it. "Ah, that's better. It just needed a little boost."

Joe snorted. "Stop changing the subject. Don't you remember almost getting killed the last time you meddled in a murder case?"

"I try to remember only the good times. You know, I'm beginning to suspect that couple over there doesn't like me. You think maybe it's because I didn't have time to shower before we left the *Merilee*?"

"You smell fine. Look, I admit choosing this restaurant was a bad idea. Any place that calls a burger *Boeuf Grillé Entre Pain* should probably be avoided. Maybe we should just drive down to Gunn Landing Beach and neck."

"We'd never find a parking place. All those teenagers."

"Then how about the *Merilee*?"

"With Bonz and Miss Priss watching? Anyway, I'm too tired. And I need a shower."

"I have a shower at my house. Two, actually."

"You also have a mother at your house. And Tonio and Bridie."

"Mom's more broad-minded than she used to be, and the kids are asleep. Speaking of your facility for subject-changing, when are we getting married?"

That caught me off guard. "Next summer, maybe?"

"Last year you said *this* summer. It's already June."

"Oh."

"Yeah, 'oh.' We need to talk about your boat, too, but every time I bring it up, you change the subject. Like you're doing now."

And there it was. The unresolved issue that kept me from setting a firm wedding date. Ever since a killer had ambushed me at the harbor, Joe's feelings about the *Merilee* and the harbor had changed. He now believed the *Merilee* was not only dangerous, but a needless expense, and had been pressuring me to sell her. I didn't want to sell my floating home. Yes, boat slips, even at the south end of the harbor weren't cheap, and neither was upkeep. But regardless of Joe's continued urging, I couldn't imagine a future without her.

Or without Joe, for that matter.

I understood his concerns about my safety—after all, his first wife had been murdered and her killer was still out there somewhere—but he couldn't spend the rest of his life being overprotective. Or could he? The problem was, an overprotective man often came across as a controlling one. I already had two control freaks in my life—my mother and my boss—and I didn't need a third.

But I loved Joe so much…

Suddenly, the recent demands of others—Caro, Lila, Aster Edwina, Lex, and dear, dear Joe—became too much. Feeling miserable, I said, "Oh, Joe, I'm just too tired to talk about the *Merilee* right now."

He placed his napkin carefully on the table. "Then perhaps I should take you home."

I didn't sleep well that night, because every time I started to drift off, the image of the *Merilee's* empty berth rose up before me. If I sold her, would her new owner keep the keel-eating barnacles scraped away? Keep her brass fittings shined, her teak deck varnished?

Would her new owner love her like I do?

Chapter Seven

The next day I was eating lunch in the staff lounge with Zorah when I saw Lila on the TV screen. She was walking between two uniformed deputies and looked terrified. The crawl at the bottom of the screen blared in capital letters, MURDER SUSPECT TAKEN INTO CUSTODY.

I felt sick.

"Teddy, are you all right?" Zorah asked. "You look like you've seen a ghost and it didn't resemble Patrick Swayze."

Waving at the TV, I said. "She's a friend." And Bonz's savior.

Zorah turned around to face the TV. "Her? The suspect? Hey, and there's your boyfriend! He's terrific looking, isn't he? Oh, well, from what I've been hearing about that Booth guy, he had it coming. But I'm sorry about your friend."

Having once been a murder suspect herself, Zorah's compassion was genuine. "Poor thing," she added. "At least she'll be treated okay. Maybe not as well as your mother was last year when she ran into her bit of trouble, but… Wait. Isn't your new stepdad a lawyer? Why don't you…"

My phone was already in my hand, my finger punching in the number of Hamilton, Lawler, and Grissom, attorneys at law. Evelyn, Al's secretary, recognized my voice and put me through immediately.

"Teddy! How nice to hear your voi…"

"Joe just arrested Lila Conyers for Stuart Booth's murder!"

A moment of silence followed, so long that I was about to speak again before Al beat me to the punch. "Interesting. Would I be wrong to guess that Ms. Conyers is a friend of yours?"

"We're closer than sisters," I fibbed. "She needs a good defense attorney."

"And I'm the best, which is why you're on the phone to me right now." He sounded gratified. "Well, there's not all that much going on here at the office, so I'll mosey over to the county jail and see what's happening. One thing. How's she fixed for money? You know I don't come cheap."

"She works part time at Tiny Tots Day Care."

Al sighed. "Pro bono case then."

"But maybe I can, you know…"

Al understood what I was hinting at. Right after my father's flight to Costa Rica with his embezzled funds, he set up a secret account for me in the Cayman Islands. It was of impressive size, but it included his ill-gotten gains, so I never touched the money. Well, almost never. Once I had withdrawn funds to help a friend in need. Now Lila fit that category.

"No, no, no, Teddy!" Al near-shouted. He, of all people, knew the trouble I'd be in if caught using the account. "Your mother would never forgive me if I charged you a dime, so let's have no more of that. You hear? And let's not discuss the… the *thing*, okay? I'll take care of what needs to be taken care of."

"You're a saint, Al."

"Naw, I'm just crazy about your mother."

When I ended the call I felt better, but I knew enough about Joe to know he would never arrest someone without good reason.

"Grissom's going to help her, then?" Zorah asked, startling me.

I nodded. Al was such an ace criminal defense attorney that Lila could have shot Booth point-blank while Booth's entire Marine Science 101 class stood around capturing it on their smartphones, yet still convince a jury of reasonable doubt. But even if found not guilty, Lila's reputation would be tainted. Having her declared innocent wasn't enough; the real killer had to be brought to justice.

An hour later I was driving my zebra cart toward my next group of chores when Bernice Unser, the volunteer who usually accompanied me to the TV studio, hailed me at the crossroads of Tropics Trail and Friendly Farm. Besides wearing the zoo's standard khaki uniform, she sported heavy gloves and clutched a wicked-looking pair of gardening shears.

"Teddy! I hoped I'd find you here."

I braked. "Hop in. I'll bet you want tell me about your daughter's wedding. How'd it go?"

"Without a hitch. I am now the proud occupant of an empty nest. But that's not what I wanted to talk you about. It's my niece. She's in trouble."

For the first time I noticed the worried

expression on Bernice's usually jovial face. She had been a zoo volunteer longer than I had been working there, and during my first few months had helped me over the rough spots. Since then I had seen her drop fifty pounds and her muscles tighten to near-teenage firmness.

She hopped into the cart without the aid of the safety rail. "My niece has been arrested."

"Your niece's name wouldn't be Lila, would it?"

"How'd you know? We don't have the same last name. Lila's my sister's girl."

"She made the noon news."

While opening and closing those lethal-looking gardening shears, she said, "You still engaged to the sheriff?"

I could see another request for aid coming. Why is it people believe that just because you're going to marry someone you have any influence over them? "Yes, and I've already done what I can. I called my stepfather and he…"

"Al Grissom?"

It was a good thing I hadn't started the cart up again or I might have run into the family of five that suddenly stopped in front of me to study their zoo map.

"You know Al?" I asked Bernice.

"My sister had to…" She stopped. "Well, that's water over the bridge. But, yes, I know him. From even before."

"Even before what? Are you talking about the sexual harassment complaint Lila once filed against Booth?"

"You can start the cart now."

Having found the spot on the map they were looking for, the family had moved on, so with Bernice beside me, we hummed along the trail to Down Under, where we climbed out. Me, to shovel poop in the Wallaby Encounter, Bernice to trim overgrowth.

Before we went our separate ways, I asked, "C'mon, Bernice. What is it you're not telling me? Was Lila in trouble even before she spray-painted Booth's boat?"

She squinted her eyes as if the sun hurt them although a huge cumulonimbus cloud was blocking it. "The teen years can be rough on girls, especially the pretty ones. That's all I'm going to say. But please do what you can for her. And for my sister, who doesn't need any more trouble in her life right now."

With that she charged into the underbrush, gardening shears at the ready.

In Down Under, the wallabies took my mind

off the accumulation of demands being made on me. Feed a wallaby, it's happy. Pick up droppings, it's happy. Put a wallaby on TV, it's grateful for the exercise.

"How you doing, Abim?" I asked the largest wallaby, who had once led Bernice and me on a merry chase through the KGNN-TV studio when he'd gotten loose during a live segment of *Anteaters to Zebras.*

Abim was doing well, and scratched at my pocket for any treat that might be hidden there. He soon found the piece of carrot I'd stowed away, and after I'd handed it to him, he leaned on his tail and munched happily.

"How are the girls today?"

The "girls," five female wallabies traded to us by the San Francisco Zoo in exchange for one of our Andean bears, were doing well, he let me know, and hopped after me as I approached the eucalyptus tree where they were hunched, waiting for their own treats. I scattered more carrot pieces around, along with lettuce and alfalfa pellets—wallabies are herbivores—and left them to it while I scooped up pellets of another kind.

After taking care of the wallabies, I did the same for the koalas, although they were too sleepy to let me know how appreciative they were. Why can't people be more like animals? Eat, defecate, sleep, mate. No worrying about the seesawing stock market, what Congress is doing, or keeping up with the Joneses. Actually, humans are animals, too, but somewhere along the way we've forgotten our true natures in our rush to complicate our lives. Thus the need for lawyers.

I fished my cell out of my pocket and called Al again.

This time he didn't sound so happy to hear from me. "What is it now, Teddy?"

"Have you seen Lila yet?"

"I walked over to the jail the minute we hung up."

"How's she doing?"

"As well as can be expected."

"How does it look for her?"

"The case, you mean? You know I can't talk about that."

"Can't you give me a general idea?"

"Technically speaking, your friend is in deep doo-doo. Bye."

Ring tone.

I seldom leave the zoo as soon as my shift is over—I enjoy my work so much I'm loathe to leave it—but today I clocked out at six sharp. After calling Linda Cushing, who lived on the *Tea 4 Two* next to the *Merilee*, and obtaining her promise to feed DJ Bonz and Miss Priss, I left for the San Sebastian County Sheriff's Office.

Joe and Deputy Emilio Gutierrez were talking to the Dispatch officer when I walked in. Joe's face lit up when he saw me, making me feel guilty because I wasn't here to see him, so before he could say anything, I blurted out, "It's visiting hours, right?"

His smile dimmed. "I'm not even going to ask who you're here to see, because I think I know."

"I need to talk to Lila."

"I'd rather you didn't."

"It's a free country, Joe."

"And a dangerous one at times, especially when people stick their pretty noses in places they don't belong."

At least he'd said my bumpy nose was pretty. "I still want to talk to her, get her side of things."

"Her attorney already did that."

"Joe. *Please.*"

The worry line between his eyebrows deepened. "Sometimes you scare me, you really do." But he turned to Emilio and said, "Take her on back, but don't let her in the cell with the prisoner. And you stay right there with her, hear? Keep her safe."

Emilio nodded.

"Hey, wait a minute, Joe. How about some privacy? Or a little compassion? The conversation might include some girl talk, too, and we can't do that with Emilio hovering around."

Without waiting for Joe's answer, Emilio said, "I'll stay far enough away that you two can say what you need to say."

Joe raised his hands in surrender. "Oh, go ahead, then. But if anything happens to you, I don't know what I'll…" He looked down at the cement floor. Not finishing his sentence, he walked away.

Jails aren't comfy places. They're not meant to be. This one, divided by gender, provided the basics and little else. Cement floor, pillowless bunk, blanket, toilet, sink. Because of the bare bones philosophy, the acoustics were raw but loud. Someone was crying, her sobs reverberating off the cinder block walls, echoing along the corridor. Lila? As I clattered along, I realized the sobs came from a granny-aged Hispanic with a large bruise on her face. When Emilio and I neared her, she stifled her cries and turned her back.

Lila wasn't exactly jumping for joy, either. Looking sallow in her orange jail jumpsuit, she sat on her bunk, her honey-blond hair hanging down in lank tendrils across her face, as if she was using it to shield herself from the ugliness of her surroundings. True to his word, Emilio stopped ten yards from her cell, giving me plenty of room to ask what I'd come to ask.

"Hi, Lila."

No answer.

Keeping my voice low, I said, "I heard Al Grissom stopped by to talk about your case."

When she looked up, I could see she had been crying, too, only silently. "Yeah, he was here." Her own voice was little more than a whisper.

"He's the best defense attorney in Central California."

"Whatever."

This new apathy alarmed me, so I tried some lighthearted chat. "I saw your Aunt Bernice today and she told me your cousin's wedding went off beautifully. That was in Chicago, right?"

The Otter of Death   95

A nod.

"Nice town, Chicago, but I wouldn't want to live there. The winters are brutal. Ever been?"

Head shake.

"They say the summers are pretty, though. And the Field Museum is extraordinary. My dad took me there once, before he..." I stopped myself. Jails weren't the place to discuss my felonious father's flight from justice. "Anyway, I got to see Sue, you know, the big T-Rex skeleton?"

Nothing.

This wasn't working so I what-the-helled it and dove in. "Lila, did you get into some kind of trouble when you were a teenager?"

"Who told you that?"

"A little bird."

"A little bird named Bernice, I bet." There was bitterness in her voice, but it was preferable to her earlier apathy. Contrary to popular opinion, apathy can kill.

"It slipped out while we were talking about the...." What should I tell her we'd been talking about? The anteater? The wallabies? "Uh, talking about the koala."

"I apologized for what I did. Doesn't that count for something?"

"It kind of depends. Tell me what happened, and what it has to do with you winding up here."

She stood up and approached her cell door with a suddenness that made me take two steps backwards.

"Scared of me, Teddy?"

"Of course not. You just startled me."

She vented a sound that could have been either a laugh or a sob. "You will be, when I tell you."

"Give me a little credit, Lila. And by the way, keep your voice down because Deputy Gutierrez is standing by the door."

"Have they found the gun yet?"

I almost asked what gun, but then I realized she had to be talking about the murder weapon. "Not as far as I know."

"Well, at least that's something, anyway." Some of the edge left her voice.

"Why so interested in the gun?"

"Since you were asking me what kind of trouble I got into as a teenager, here it is. I shot someone."

"You what?!"

Ignoring my reaction, Lila continued. "It was back in high school, and there was this big guy, Jake, one of the seniors. I was just a freshman, fourteen years old and small for my age. One day in the lunchroom Jake asked me out and I said no, because I'd heard some nasty stories about him. I didn't tell him that, just gave some vague excuse that I was too busy. Jake didn't like that. Before, he'd only picked on guys, especially the shorter ones, but then he started in on me. He'd follow me home after school, even though he didn't live in our neighborhood. He'd grab me and tell me what he was going to do if he ever caught me alone. Then he started hanging out around my house, throwing rocks at the windows. Mom said I must have done something to make him mad, but when I told her what had happened, she just kept on blaming me, saying that every girl needs to learn how to say 'no' nicely."

She paused for breath. "Then he started leaving dead things on the porch. It started with lizards, then a snake, then a little…"

Not wanting to hear about more dead things, I raised my hand. "Don't tell me. I get the picture."

"That's when I…Well, I got my mother's gun."

"Your mom owned a gun?"

"It belonged to my grandfather. A .38 revolver. She kept it in a lockbox with some ammunition and jewelry, but I'd seen her open it and knew where she kept the key. The next day after the dead ki..."

"I *said* don't tell me!"

"Sorry. Anyway, after I saw the...the dead thing I went into my mother's bedroom, got the gun, loaded it—I'd seen how to do it on TV—and put it in my backpack. After school Jake started following me like he always did, telling me he was going to do to me what he did to the ki...uh, the dead thing. Before leaving school I'd gone into the girls' restroom and hidden the gun in my loose leaf binder. I was carrying it in my arms when he grabbed me, so I took it out and shot him."

When I finally replied, I hated the quaver in my voice. "How seriously was Jake hurt?"

"He almost lost his arm. The one he grabbed me with."

"What happened afterwards?"

"I spent some time in juvie."

"Oh, no!"

"Think your boyfriend found out about that?"

As soon as I left the jail I called Albert Grissom.

"Lila Conyers is in big trouble, isn't she?"

"Like I said earlier, deep doo-doo. But I enjoy a challenge."

"Did she tell you what happened when she was fourteen?"

"Kids always know where the guns are, which is why I believe in stricter gun control laws. These days people could keep an entire armory in their garages and no one would blink an…"

When my stepfather got started on gun control he could talk all day, so I interrupted him. "How are you going to defend her?"

"You know I can't discuss the case with you."

I was about to hang up when I remembered something. "Uh, Al?"

"What is it, Teddy?" He sounded suspicious, as well he should.

"There was an older woman in the cell next to Lila. She had a big bruise on her face."

"Shot and killed her husband during a domestic dispute last night, which proves my point about the need for gun con—"

"Is there anything you can do for her?"

He didn't answer right away, and when he did, he said, "You know, there are times I wish I'd never met your mother. Not many, you understand, but it does happen. And it's always at times like this."

"Please?"

A resigned sigh. "Oh, Teddy. You know I can't say no to Caro's only child."

That evening Maureen swam up to the *Merilee* for the first time since Booth's murder. The otter must have finally recovered from the grudge she'd held against me for taking away her new toy because her furry little face looked up at me with a sweetly pleading expression when I leaned over the rail.

"Maureen want herring?"

Her body English answered *yes, yes, yes.*

I had prepared for her eventual visit by stocking up, so I went down into the cabin and took a small herring from the refrigerator. When I tossed it to her, she caught it in her paws, took a bite, then flipped her tail at me as if to say thank you, and swam away.

Too bad humans aren't so easy to please.

Chapter Eight

Autopsy completed, the medical examiner released Professor Stuart Booth's body in time for a Sunday morning burial in the Betancourt family plot. Aster Edwina had allowed me time off to attend both the funeral and the après-funeral reception. As I stared across the big hole in the ground, I noticed that although Harper Betancourt-Booth was dressed in deep black, she wasn't crying. No one else was, either.

The non-denominational minister, who obviously knew nothing about the dead man, spent far too long extolling his nonexistent virtues, then mercifully shut up and let the casket be lowered. Afterwards, the sparse crowd trooped back to the Betancourts' place for a brunch buffet.

The walled Betancourt compound—comprised of four houses, several garages, a horse barn, and numerous other outbuildings—perched atop the steep hill in the most expensive part of Gunn Landing's Old Town. Harper and Stuart Booth had been given the smallest house to live in, but the reception took place at Harper's parents' mansion, a twenty-something-room pseudo Gothic stone pile that rivaled the gloom and grandeur of even Gunn Castle. As a child I had never cared for the house, imagining it inhabited by Dracula and his blood-drinking minions, but now I simply found it pretentious. Too many cars were already parked inside the matching stone-walled compound, forcing me to park my rattletrap pickup truck at Mother's house and hike the rest of the way up in the three-inch heels I'd been foolish enough to put on that morning. Once I reached the compound, I was confronted by an armed security guard who demanded to see my ID before letting me through the iron gate where more of his brethren roamed, most accompanied by Rottweilers.

Cranmore, the Betancourts' aged English butler, showed better manners as he ushered me inside. "Such a sad occasion, Miss Bentley."

Since it's never appropriate to tell the truth at a funeral, I agreed.

Given the gloominess of the house's exterior, the décor inside would come as a surprise to anyone entering for the first time. The recent generation of Betancourts had replaced the original Jacobian furnishings with Chippendale and switched the old black-burgundy-and-gold color scheme to a more welcoming butternut and azure. The only thing that ruined the décor—to my mind, at least—was the profusion of hunting trophies scattered throughout the house. The heads of dead animals were everywhere, including the large salon where the reception was being held.

Trying hard to ignore the glass eyes of the elephant, Sumatran tiger, and African lion peering down at me from the salon's walls, I found the Betancourts and told them how sorry I was. Then I made a beeline for the groaning board, where a feast fit for starving kings was laid out.

On the way, I checked out the star-studded crowd. Among those paying their respects were my mother, dressed in a Donatella Versace little black dress; several gazillionaires; two state senators; the publisher of the *San Sebastian Journal*; the president of Betancourt College; a passel of judges, some of them even honest…

And my boss, Aster Edwina Gunn.

For a brief moment I hid behind old school friend Frasier Morgan, who was now a mid-level exec at Prime Pacific Oil, the Betancourts' company.

"Who are you hiding from, Teddy?" he whispered.

"My boss."

Frasier grinned. With his dark brown hair, hazel eyes, and marathon runner's build, he should have been handsome, but Mother Nature, enjoying one of her private jokes, had not only bestowed on him the round-cheeked face of a baby, but also a rosacea-caused red nose. If he'd had white hair, a beard, and been fatter, he would have looked like Santa Claus. Still, he had been able to snag a wife, although the marriage ended months ago.

"Oh, Aster Edwina's not that bad," he said.

"Try working for her."

He snorted a laugh, then forced his baby-face into a more serious expression. "Need a lift home? I'd be glad to oblige."

"Not necessary, but thanks. My truck's parked at my mother's place."

Out of the corner of my eye I saw Aster Edwina follow one of the senators into the

Betancourts' double-doored study. One of them probably wanted to get a million bucks or so from the other.

"The coast is clear," Frasier whispered. "But my offer still stands."

"Rain check." I said, and slipped away to the long buffet. While helping myself to the canapés, Caro sidled up to me. "The casket was a bit over-much, don't you think? All that brass."

"He wasn't a subtle man, Mother, so he would have liked it."

"You know I don't like it when you call me 'Mother.'"

"To rephrase, then, he probably would have liked that brassy casket, Caro."

"Don't get smart with me, Theodora."

I popped another pâté-smeared cracker into my mouth and mushed, "Sorry."

"Don't talk with your mouth full."

"Sorry again." I swallowed.

"Did you hear that Miles made Harper move out of the little house?"

"The place she shared with Booth? Where is she supposed to live now?"

"Here. At least until the next sucker shows up with a wedding ring."

Most people take it for granted that the

children of great fortunes lead lives of great freedom, but that isn't always true. Especially not in Harper Betancourt's case. One time, when she'd had too much wine at a mutual friend's wedding reception, she had blurted out a confession. All her pretty trinkets—the sports cars, the jewelry, the black American Express card—had been bestowed upon her with the caveat that she would do whatever her father ordered her to do and when to do it. If not, all those pretty trinkets would disappear.

"I don't envy her," I told Caro.

My mother shocked me by saying, "She could certainly use a little of your independent spirit."

Then she walked away to speak the Betancourts.

Smiling to myself, I pushed through a gathering of black-suited pall bearers to the shrimp platter to celebrate those rare words of maternal admiration. I was still eating when Lex Yarnell approached. Used to seeing him in his park ranger uniform, I almost didn't recognize him in his black suit.

"I didn't know you knew the Betancourts," I said, before realizing how that might be taken. Lex's family came from the other side of the tracks.

He didn't miss my clumsy inference. "I used to date Harper before her parents broke us up—you know how she's always been under her father's thumb. He's not real thrilled I'm here today, either. You know, trailer trash." Seeing my wince, he added, "At least it's a double-wide."

Despite my embarrassment, I had to laugh. "So how's Harper holding up? She seemed fine when I saw her earlier."

"That's because she never loved Booth in the first place. Her dad told her to marry him, so she did, leaving me in the lurch."

Before I could respond to his wowser of a comment, he asked, "Why didn't you call Amberlyn? Not that there's any reason to now, with Lila's arrest."

I took a couple of deep breaths. "I didn't call because Joe told me to stay out of it."

"But you visited Lila Conyers in jail."

Word sure travels fast in San Sebastian County.

"And I haven't heard the last of it since."

Lex's frown marred his handsome face. "That's funny, and I don't mean funny hah-hah. I never pegged you for a woman who'd let her boyfriend tell her what to do. Or not do."

"You don't understand. Joe doesn't tell me…"

"I understand more than you realize." Looking deeply unhappy, Lex drifted away.

I spent the next few minutes guilt-eating. Somewhere around my tenth shrimp, Harper herself wandered over. The new widow's demeanor proved the truth of Lex's bald statement. Her blue eyes held no hint of tears.

"Nice spread, hmm?" She waved a diamond-encrusted hand at the long table. "We used that new caterer over in Carmel."

"La Pièce de Résistance? Caro used them for her last party. You and Stuart were there, I seem to remember."

"I love your mother's house. It's so tiny and cute."

Tiny? Cute? For an eleven-room—not counting the kitchen and six baths—antiques-stuffed mansion on a shaded hillside overlooking the Pacific? Only a Betancourt could make such an outrageous statement.

I let the insult slide. "I'm so sorry about Stuart."

"You've already told me, Teddy. Twice. Once at the cemetery, and again when you first arrived at the house."

"Well, I'm still sorry. I'm sure Stuart's students are grieving, too. I've seen several of them here."

"All females, you'll notice. And blond."

Harper wasn't making conversation easy, but the Betancourts had always been like that. When your hide is insulated by your daddy's mega-millions, you're free to say whatever pops into your head—at least to anyone other than the check-writer.

"Stuart did have a way with women."

"He ever make a play for you, Teddy?"

I almost choked on a shrimp. "You're kidding, right?"

"Before we got married, I mean. Obviously you weren't his type, not with your fuzzy red hair and freckles, the bump on your nose, and the fact that you often smell of manure. Which you do now, as a matter of fact. Showers broke again at the zoo? Anyway, Stu only went for good looks, but then you never know what a man is thinking, do you? Sometimes they like to 'slum it,' as they say. Anyway, Daddy took care of writing the prenup. Part of it said that the minute Stuart started fooling around with his students again he'd be out on his ear with no alimony. So let me tell you, he cleaned up his act *post haste*. Daddy says men like Stuart need a firm hand. By the way, you never answered my question."

Surprised I could still speak after that insulting speech, I swallowed the rest of the shrimp
and stuttered, "Ah, ah, what question was that?"

"Did Stuart ever make moves on you?"

"No. It was probably the bump-on-the-nose
thing."

"You really ought to have it done." Smirking,
she walked away.

Not caring that I might have trouble getting
into my zoo uniform the next morning, I left
the shrimp platter and returned to the pâté.
It didn't make me feel any better, but it was
delicious. I was still eating when I heard a
familiar voice.

"Skip breakfast this morning?"

Joe. Dressed in civvies and looking gorgeous.
My heart went bumpety-bump.

"I didn't see you come in."

"You were too busy feeding your face." But
he smiled.

I stopped eating and smiled back. "I'm so
sorry about the other night."

"I'm sorry, too."

He touched my cheek, making my heart go
bumpety-bump again.

The sweet moment ended when he followed
up with, "Looks like the strings you pulled the
other day paid off."

"Strings? What are you talking about?"

"Your stepfather managed to get Lila Conyers released on bail this morning."

"Al did that? But…but wasn't her bail set at a million dollars or something like that?"

"Somewhat short of a million, but yeah, pretty steep. So she's out. At least she has to wear an ankle bracelet and can't leave San Sebastian County."

I thought for a moment. While wearing an ankle bracelet, Lila wouldn't be able to work, either, because what day care center wanted an accused murderer on their payroll? But maybe they were broad-minded. Whatever, I decided to whip up a big casserole and take it over to Lila's houseboat, along with the bottle of 1973 Gunn Vineyards Merlot I'd been saving for a special occasion. Getting sprung from the San Sebastian County Jail certainly fit that description.

Since Joe appeared to be in a good mood despite his prisoner's release, I took a chance and asked, "Did you guys ever find the murder weapon? Was it a handgun? A rifle?"

All good humor left his face. "Oh, Teddy…"

"To get a conviction you'd need to trace it to Lila, right?"

"Stay out of it, Teddy." When he walked away he looked more sad than angry.

A movement to my left showed Miles Stephenson Betancourt IV heading toward me. The CEO of Prime Pacific Oil looked chipper for a man who had just returned from his son-in-law's funeral.

"Nice seeing you again, Teddy." Miles was handsome in the sleek way some wealthy men are, with a five-hundred-dollar haircut and a bespoke Brioni Vanquish suit. He had always been light on the charm, though.

"Nice seeing you, too," I lied. After all, this man was responsible for every dead animal "decorating" the Betancourt walls. "So sorry it has to be at such a sad occasion."

"Sad, my ass. The man was a slug."

So much for not speaking ill of the dead.

"I was just talking to your beautiful mother. What's this I hear about you being engaged to the sheriff? Given your aristocratic background and the old Bentley family money, I would have thought you could do better."

When I finished grinding my teeth, I turned on my three-inch heels and got the hell out of there.

As I wobbled downhill to my truck, I hauled my cell out of my third-hand Michael Kors handbag and called Amberlyn Lofland, Lex Yarnell's ex-girlfriend. She picked up on the second ring.

"It's Teddy Bentley. We met a couple of years ago at Lex's place. He told me you wanted to talk."

"Oh! Gee!" Her voice was high, almost child-like. "Now that there's been an arrest, it may not be necessary."

Now that there's been an arrest? Had Amberlyn feared she might be questioned about Stuart Booth's murder? Curiouser and curiouser.

"Well, you never know," I said. "These things can go sideways on you. Sometimes the police arrest Person A just to lull Person B, their real suspect, into a false sense of security. Given the fact that Person A is already out of jail, I'm thinking that's what's going on. Maybe we should get together and see if there's anything you need to worry about."

She gulped. "You think?"

I tried to sound tough and worldly-wise. "Yeah, I think."

Twenty minutes later, still wearing my all-purpose black dress, I was sitting in Amberlyn Lofland's Point Deem condo located three short blocks from the Pacific Ocean. Not the usual student digs. Although small—a one-bedroom furnished with a queen-sized bed, which I figured ruled out a roommate—the apartment's location alone must have cost Amberlyn a tidy sum. The light from the large, west-facing picture window revealed that the furnishings weren't student-salvage, either. Besides a chic chrome-and-glass dinette set, they included two matching peach-colored sofas separated by a large gnarled-oak coffee table. Over one of the sofas hung a brightly colored, signed and numbered, Manfred Rothmore litho, the artist *San Francisco Style Magazine* had crowned "California's Reigning Post-Modernist."

All this for a UC Santa Cruz sophomore who hailed from the wrong side of the tracks.

Since I'm a slob, I turned down the glass of merlot she offered, fearing for the life of the pale beige Berber carpet.

"You don't mind if I have one?" she asked.

"Have at it." *In vino veritas.*

Instead of sitting on the sofa across from mine, she settled herself next to me. "It's awfully nice of you to do this for me, Teddy."

I gave her what I hoped was a kindly smile. "I haven't done anything yet, but I'm here and I'm ready to listen. We girls have to stick together, don't we?" Especially since the boys so often tried to boss us around.

"They're not all as nice as you."

Yes, Amberlyn was a beauty with her naturally pale blond hair and eyes such a deep blue they looked almost lavender, but she was also naïve. Surely she didn't believe that our brief meeting a couple of years ago made me trustworthy. Maybe she didn't have any close girlfriends. That often happens with beautiful women.

But not wanting to get sucked into gender politics, I went straight to the point. "Lex said you had something you wanted to discuss."

She moved closer, her shapely leg almost touching my less attractive one. "It's about Stu."

"Stu?"

"You know, Professor Booth."

"Oh. *Stu* Booth." Where the heck was this going?

Taking a deep breath, she said, "The police saw those pictures of me on his phone. I thought I was okay when they arrested that Conyers woman, but now that they've let her go, I'm afraid they might come after me. Should I talk to an attorney? Somebody like your stepfather, 'cause he's so brilliant? I want to make certain the checks continue to be sent to the realtor like Stu promised or I'm up shit creek. See?"

I shook my head. No, I didn't see.

"Lex didn't tell you?"

I shook my head again. "What was Lex supposed to tell me?"

"That I was Stu's Sugar Baby."

Sugar Baby? Despite her tone, I almost laughed at her use of the old-fashioned term. But after a moment, the import of what she said sunk in, so I asked, "Amberlyn, are you seriously telling me that 'Stu' was, ah, helping you pay your rent?" I gestured with my hand, taking in the big picture window, the nice furnishings, the signed litho.

When she crossed her arms across her spectacular chest, metallic gold nail polish winked at me, helped along by a couple of diamond rings. Not Harper Betancourt-Booth-sized diamonds, but impressive enough.

"Helping? As if!" she humphed. "Stu pays for the whole thing as well as my tuition, and a little extra on the side so I can have nice clothes. That's how the Sugar Baby thing works, you know. So what am I supposed to do now? The new semester starts in a couple of months and I need to find out what he's already paid and what he hasn't, and what kind of legal arrangements he's made for me. The last time he was over here, that's what he said he was going to do, see? He loved me so much he wanted to make sure I'd be taken care of if anything bad ever happened to him. But I'm kinda scared now that the cops might start looking at me as a suspect, which of course I couldn't possibly be, because it would be stupid to kill the goose that laid the golden eggs, right? But sometimes the cops aren't smart enough to figure that out." She stopped, took a breath, and added, "Your fiancé excepted, of course. I'm sure he's super-smart. Like me."

Oh, dear Lord. After I recovered from my shock, I remembered reading about the "Sugar Baby thing" in the *San Sebastian Shout*, the area's free alternative newspaper. According to the article, sharply rising tuition rates— more than a thousand percent in the past four decades—had necessitated unusual financial arrangements for an increasing number of coeds.

It worked like this:

An attractive young woman needing tuition

assistance posted her picture and a brief bio on websites such as SeekingSugarDaddy.com, then waited. Once a well-heeled man responded, the so-called interview process began, ending in a trial run at a nice hotel. If the trial run proved to be to both individuals' liking, the financial arrangements were finalized, usually by contract. According to the article, approximately two to three million coeds were already reaping the benefits of debt-free education, thanks to their Sugar Daddies. In turn, the Sugar Daddies received unlimited companionship from beautiful coeds. The article's writer had interviewed one of them, a sophomore at UCSC who preferred anonymity but, for the article, wanted to be referred to as "Dolly."

Singing the praises of the Sugar Baby/Sugar Daddy arrangement, "Dolly" said, "It's not just about sex, because you don't really have to sleep with them, not if you don't want to. But gee, you want to make them happy, don't you, because what young woman wouldn't want to have a really, really wise older man in her life? My Sugar Daddy—I'll call him Jim, but that's not really his name—he's, like, my best friend, so of course I sleep with him."

I must have been frowning because Amberlyn said, "It's not just about sex. Stu and I really, really respect each other. He's, like, my best friend."

Suspecting that I was talking to the mysterious "Dolly," I said, "Respected. And was."

"Huh?"

"Past tense, since he's dead."

"Well, you know what I mean. Really, what's the difference between me and your mom, because she…?"

I stood up. "Don't. You. Dare."

She flinched. "Well, uh, I'm sorry, it's just that… it's just that…I…I really, really miss Stu, you know? And now, what am I going to do about next semester?"

"Accumulate a mountain of debt like everyone else."

"But then I'd be working for something, like, ten or twenty years just to pay it off! You know my parents can't help out, and God knows I don't want to wind up like them, working on some artichoke farm until my arthritis got so bad I couldn't work anymore."

I'd been about to leave, but sat back down.

Despite Amberlyn's nasty crack about my mother, I saw her point. The Sugar Baby article had pointed out that the national student debt load had crept past one-point-five *trillion* dollars, to my mind an obscene amount. Yet it was almost impossible to get a decent job without a college degree, so what was a young person to do? Only the best and the brightest were able to get full ride scholarships, which meant that most either had to work part-time jobs or rack up a terrifying amount of debt. Unless, that is, they were lucky enough to have wealthy, or at least middle class, parents. Which Amberlyn didn't. What she did have was beauty.

After thinking over everything she'd told me, I said, "You said Stu promised he was going to make some sort of financial arrangement for your, ah, protection. When was this?"

"Last week."

"What day last week?"

"Tuesday, I think."

Eight days before he was killed, enough time for him to have seen a lawyer. Then something else struck me. "Wait a minute. You're saying he paid your tuition and your rent, plus gave you a little extra besides, but you hadn't seen him in over a week. Considering your arrangement, doesn't that sound strange to you?"

She flushed again. "We talked on the phone a lot."

"What's 'a lot'?"

"Almost every night."

"Last week, too?"

She looked out the big picture window. Over the top of the next condo and off into the distance, you could see a thin sliver of the blue Pacific. "He, uh, he didn't call me last week."

"You didn't call him?"

"He told me never to call him. See?"

I saw. God forbid Stuart Booth's wife, Harper Betancourt-Booth, intercepted her call and found out about the Sugar Baby/Sugar Daddy arrangement.

"A wise policy, I'm sure. But Amberlyn, Lex told me Stu's phone had pictures of you. In the nude."

No blush. Instead, she gestured toward the Manfred Rothmore litho "Stu had an eye for art."

Which brought up another topic. "I'm sure Stu had a nice salary at the college, but not enough for him to do the things he likes to do, collect art, etc., and support you as well, so where'd the extra money come from?"

"The Betancourts gave him an allowance. That's the way rich people do things."

Somehow I was able to hide my smile, because

sometimes they did, and sometimes they didn't. These days Caro was rolling in dough, but I supported myself—although I had to admit it was over her objections. The thing was, once you took money from someone, you pretty much had to do what they wanted you to do, and there was no way I would ever let myself in for such servitude. Then I remembered Aster Edwina Gunn's many demands and the fact that I'd kowtowed to almost every one of them. So who was I to judge?

Dismissing my own semi-servitude, I asked, "That financial arrangement you said Stu promised to make 'just in case.' What's his attorney's name?"

She shrugged elegant shoulders. "If I knew, I wouldn't be having this conversation, would I? I'd just call him."

"Or her."

"Huh?"

"Some lawyers are women. But okay, I'll make a couple of phone calls, see what I can find out. In the meantime, I'm curious about something."

"Yeah?"

"Is the Sugar Baby thing what broke up you and Lex?"

She gave me a look of disbelief. "Of course not! And we're not really broken up. When Stu's not here..." She paused. "When Stu, uh, *wasn't* here, Lex would come by and we'd...Uh, you know. Because Lex is the love of my life."

Of everything I had heard today, that comment shocked me the most "Really?"

"Swear to God! We've been together since we were twelve, grew up in the same trailer park. I'll never love anyone like I love Lex. See?" She crossed her heart with that diamond-encrusted hand.

Yep. I saw. Kinda.

Eager to flee this ethics-challenging conversation, I sighed, stood up, and headed for the door. Just before I reached it, I turned around. "By the way, Amberlyn, what's your major?"

Her smile didn't travel all the way to her lavender eyes. "Finance. I need to make money. A *lot* of money. Because you know what? In fifteen years I'll be almost as old as you and I'll start losing my looks. Who'll want me then?"

Chapter Nine

I made it to the Gunn Zoo by two-thirty, where I found a note taped to my locker telling me all my charges in Down Under had been fed, watered, and cleaned up afterwards by other zookeepers. After radioing Zorah to thank her for making that happen, I changed into my uniform and made my way to Colder Climes to see how Magnus was getting along.

Quite well, apparently.

The little polar bear cub was sitting on his artificial ice floe, basking in the oohs and ahhs of his admirers. After giving me a brief *huff* in recognition, he stood on his hind legs and waved his paws, eliciting even louder oohs and ahhs. What a ham.

Assured that Magnus was settling in well, I headed over to Tropics Trail to take care of Lucy, the giant anteater. I had just finished sweeping up a pile of anteater dung when my mother showed up, still clad in her snazzy funeral attire.

As I loaded a sack of dung into the zoo cart, she said, "Sometimes I despair of you, Theodora."

No news there, since Caro was always despairing of me.

"You could have behaved better during the Betancourts' funeral reception! What were you thinking, eating so much? You acted like you were half-starved."

I didn't answer, just heaved another sack of dung onto the cart. I was still smarting over Amberlyn's final words to me.

Usually, I'm not happy to have my mother visit me at the zoo, but today was different. Caro had great social connections and I saw a chance to benefit from them.

"You know Frasier Morgan, don't you?" I asked her. "He was at the reception."

She raised professionally plucked eyebrows. "Well, of course. Everyone knows Frasier. That red nose of his, he should have something done about it. Cosmetic surgeons can work wonders these days. Speaking of noses, why don't you and I take that cosmetic surgery cruise to Spain

I was telling you about? My eyes need work again, and that bumpy nose of yours needs a total rebuild. You get the work done in New York two days before you embark, and recover while you're…"

"Do you have his private number? I used to, but somewhere along the years I lost it."

"Whose? The surgeon's? I can vouch for…"

"Frasier Morgan's."

She blinked thick artificial lashes. "Why?"

"I just…wanted to talk." Frasier being close to the Betancourts, there was a chance he knew the name of Stuart Booth's attorney. Among other things.

"You just want to talk. Hmm." When Caro gave me that sideways look, I knew what she was thinking. *Frasier Morgan, MBA Stanford. Currently working his way up the corporate ladder at Prime Pacific Oil. Not handsome, and he'll never be a gazillionaire, but he still has better prospects than that lowly county sheriff she's engaged to.*

Barging in on her web-spinning, I said, "How did Frasier happen to be at the funeral reception? None of the other Prime Pacific execs were there."

"I imagine it was because his father was so

close to the Betancourts. They were hunting buddies. Don't give me that look, Theodora. I know how you feel about hunting, and I can assure you that at least on that one issue, Frasier does *not* take after his father. He wouldn't dream of killing an animal. But after his father's passing, Frasier inherited the membership in the Carmel Oaks Country Club, so now he and Miles Betancourt have a standing Sunday foursome."

"With their wives?"

"Don't be ridiculous. Men can't do business with their wives hanging around. The other two men are also executives with Prime Pacific."

Although I hated myself for what I was about to do, I did it anyway. "You know, I seem to remember reading something in *San Sebastian Style* about Frasier going through a divorce."

"Yes, and I think it was very bad form of them to write about it, especially the part where Evelyn threw him out of the house just because he…Well, never mind what he did. Men are men. They do things that make women unhappy. Anyway, just so you know, the divorce is final. But why so curious? You never paid any attention to Frasier before. Oh, wait a minute. Didn't you date him once before you met...before you met that..." she seemed to be having trouble saying the word. "...*sheriff?*" She made the word sound like a cat coughing up a hairball.

Frasier's Santa Claus nose had never bothered me, but our first date had turned out to be the last because it had been the most boring evening of my life. All he could talk about was finance, which I wasn't interested in. When I'd brought up my own job at the zoo, his responses proved he couldn't tell a crocodile from an alligator.

But to my mother, I pretended otherwise. "Things have changed since then," I told her, "and I was thinking that maybe he's lonely. So about that phone number. Do you have it or not?"

Hope glittered in Caro's eyes. "I have everyone's phone number. Everyone who counts, that is." She plucked her cell phone from her sleek Hermès handbag, and after a couple of thumb motions, reeled off the number.

"That's his personal cell, Theodora, so you don't reach Evelyn by mistake. She got the house, you know, including the landline, but she's still bitter. God knows what she'd tell you about Frasier if you started talking to her."

I didn't care. I only wanted to find out if he knew anything about Stuart Booth.

Desperation thy name is an unattractive, newly divorced man. Frasier was pathetically eager to meet me for drinks at Fork, San Sebastian's minimalist-except-for-its-prices eatery. Since I didn't get off work until six, I had to rush home to the *Merilee* to shower and change into a somewhat less elegant dress than the little black number I'd worn to the funeral. At least this one was clean.

Seven p.m. found me standing at Fork's crowded bar, trying to enjoy the glass of Gunn Vineyards Chablis that Frasier ordered for me. Given my guilty conscience over using the poor guy like this, it tasted like vinegar.

"...and so you see, regardless of what you might have heard, Teddy, that's what actually happened," Frasier finished, after a long and no doubt fictitious, tale of what had happened between him and his ex-wife. He was freshly shaved and showered, the strong scent of his lemony aftershave struggling mightily with the L'aire du Temps worn by the woman standing behind him, and the Eau de Muget on the woman next to me. All in all, the bar smelled like a flower garden that had been watered with Chivas Regal.

"Evelyn always was difficult," I commiserated, my fingers crossed behind me once more. I'd only met Evelyn Jennings Morgan twice, and both times she had seemed pleasant.

Frasier nodded. "You wouldn't believe the bitchery. Why, even now, she's telling people…"

Another long, boring tale of the Evils of Evelyn. When he finally wound down, I leaned forward, and said, "Yes, yes, that's terrible, but tell me more about you, Frasier. I've always found you to be a fascinating, although very mysterious, man."

I expected a thunderbolt from Heaven to strike me dead any second, but it didn't happen. Instead, Frasier—thrilled, as any man would be to be called fascinating and mysterious—started talking about his job. It was almost, but not quite, as boring as his wails about his blood-sucking ex-wife. Oblivious to my disinterest, he harangued me about BPDs, CCSs, CBMs, resbots, gigajoules, and God-knows-what-else having to do with the oil industry. When he finally got around to grumping about the restrictions imposed on his employer by the vile Environmental Protection Agency, I finally found my opening.

"Environmental Protection Agency?" I near-shrieked. "Oh, my God, they're just awful! I know how much Prime Pacific Oil cares for the environment and the lengths you people go to protect it. We here in San Sebastian County are so, so grateful."

Still no thunderbolt. Encouraged, I continued, "Stuart Booth was of immense help there, wasn't he?"

Frasier gave me a blank look. "Huh?"

I tried again. "Well, you know, helping with the otter count."

"Otter count?"

Granted, any man who's just been taken to the cleaners by his ex-wife had things other than sea otters on his mind, but still, how could he be that dense? "Frasier, otters are like canaries in coal mines. They're first to die when the environment goes bad, which is why keeping count of their population numbers is so important. I would think you'd know all about that since Prime Pacific is working on getting clearance to start offshore drilling again."

Maybe it was my imagination but I thought his red nose just got redder. "My degree is in

Business Administration, Teddy, not Ecology, and I don't know anything about otters. Please don't tell me you're one of those Otter Conservancy nutcakes who blames Prime Pacific every time an otter burps."

Making haste not to alienate him, I said, "No, no, you've got me all wrong. I was wondering, just *wondering*, mind you, that given Booth's own environmental activism..."—no thunderbolt yet? "... if he might have gotten into an argument with one of those crazy Conservancy folks and, well, you know."

Frasier's eyes goggled. "Are you telling me you think Stu Booth was murdered by an eco-terrorist? Over *otters?*"

"As the old saying goes, lie down with dogs, get up with fleas."

The alarm left his face. "I don't know any-thing about dogs, either. Never had one."

Oh, Lord, this man was literal. Eager to keep the conversation on topic, I said, "Doesn't Evelyn have a Schnauzer?"

"Her dog, not mine. If I were to ever get a dog, not that I will, mind you, because I travel too much and it wouldn't be fair to the animal, I'd want one of those dogs like the Betancourts have."

"Rottweilers."

"Right. One of those things. With a spiked collar."

"Speaking of the Betancourts, poor old Harper, eh? Losing her husband like that."

He pulled a long face. "Very sad. But she's a brave girl and I know she'll bounce back."

I let the "girl" business slide. "Did you two ever date?"

"Are you serious? Harper never gave me the time of day. Besides, she had a thing for older men. Daddy issues, you know."

"Stu was about twenty years older than her, wasn't he?"

"Seventeen. From what I heard, her mother had a fit when she and Stu returned from Vegas already married. She didn't even know Harper was out of town." His voice dropped to a near whisper. "Then again, they say she drinks."

"Harper does?"

"No, no. Gloria Betancourt. Her mother. I imagine Gloria was too drunk to notice Harper was gone until a week later when she showed up again wearing a wedding ring. I mean, good Lord, they were all living in the main house at the time! This was before Harper's father moved her and Stu into the old game keeper's cottage at the rear of the property, you understand. Just think of it, Teddy. A mother living in the same house as her daughter, and not knowing she'd just gotten married. What kind of family is that?"

With a sad shake of his head, Frasier stared at his now empty wineglass. He tried to get the bartender's attention, but the bartender was busy serving four men at the other end of the bar.

"It's a pretty big house, so it's understandable you might not see another person for days," I countered, more in Gloria Betancourt's defense than Harper's. I had heard the rumors about Harper's mother, too, but I was after bigger game. "Stu sure liked them young, didn't he?"

Frasier leaned forward and reduced his voice to the point where I could barely hear him over the cacophony of the drinkers surrounding us. "Of course he liked them young, who doesn't? Although there's a legal limit to that, isn't there? Just between you and me and the lamppost, I think it's a good thing Harper came along to settle him down, because the way he was going with his students, he was about to screw himself right out of a career." He blinked. "Oops. Pardon my French."

Like I'd never heard the term before. "But with everything you've told me, and Harper's Daddy issues aside, why do you think she actually married Stuart Booth? Compared to the guys she usually dated, he was fairly tame. Remember that sketchy French race-car driver? And the supposed Italian 'count,' who turned out to be a phony?"

The bartender brought over a fresh glass of Chablis, which quieted Frasier for a moment. After taking a sip and pronouncing it blah, he said, "Easy answer. Harper's father finally got tired of her behavior and told her that if she didn't settle down, he'd disinherit her. And then—get this!—he shoved Booth at her. Can you believe it? I guess he thought Booth was the lesser of evils."

Since the French race-car driver was rumored to have once killed a track rival, and the phony "count" had been outed as a drug dealer, Harper's father might have been right. But as for teaching old dogs new tricks...

"Did you ever hear any rumors of Stu's, ah, licentious behavior with his students after they got married?"

"Nah. Miles nipped that in the bud. Say, how about after we finish these..." Frasier nodded at our wineglasses, "we go into the restaurant and get something to eat? At the reception this morning Miles kept me so busy talking about the opening in Prime Pacific's Research and Development department that I never made it to the buffet. I've been wanting to get into R&D for a long time, so I just stood there and listened. Now my stomach's growling."

Hoping to learn more, I followed him into the dining room. As we ate in the under-decorated, cream-on-white restaurant, Frasier tortured me with another long harangue about California's "bitch-friendly" divorce laws. As he rambled on, the thought occurred to me that if the man wanted to have any sort of après-Evelyn love life, he needed to step up his game. By the time I was only halfway through my *Ragout de Boulettes et de Pattes de Cochon*, otherwise known as sausage roll-ups, I was near comatose from boredom.

I snapped out of it, though, when Joe and his mother walked in.

Unfortunately, Frasier picked that very moment to grasp my hand and ask me if I would like to go to his rented condo and share a bottle of Chateau Lafite Rotschild 2008 he had rescued from Evil Evelyn's grasping hands.

Before I could pull my hand away, Joe spotted us.

He froze for a moment, then turned on his heel and ushered his mother out of the restaurant.

Two hours later, while lying in my bunk at the *Merilee*, I tried for the third time to get Joe to pick up his phone. He wouldn't. Maybe it was just my imagination, but I thought his voice mail salutation even sounded frosty.

In honor of the Three Strikes, You're Out rule, I gave up.

Around three in the morning, a hissing sound woke me from a deep sleep. At first I thought it might have been a holdover from the dream I'd been having about Sssbyl, the Gunn Zoo's one-time-runaway Mohave rattlesnake, but then I noticed Bonz sitting at attention on the edge of my bed with his ears up and head cocked.

No dream.

In a harbor, middle-of-the-night hissing sounds are never good news. There are all sorts of power and fuel lines trailing around, and a break in any of them could create a serious problem. Concerned, I slipped my bathrobe over my PJs, grabbed a flashlight, and started topside. Three rungs up the galley ladder, I heard another sound: someone running. Then Bonz began to bark. Always a friendly animal, his alarm worried me enough that I halted my climb and listened until the steps faded away.

When all was quiet again, I made my way to the stickier-than-usual deck, only to discover that a heavy fog had rolled in during the night, dimming the harbor lights to a tenuous glow and the nearby boats to gray shadows. Whoever was roaming around had disappeared into the fog.

The "hissing" sound had stopped, making me suspect a less dangerous and more earthy cause: a passerby using the harbor as his emergency urinal.

Ugh.

Sometimes too-hearty partiers, such as Kenny Norgaard, managed to fall overboard, thus ingesting an unintended gulp of already-filthy harbor water before struggling back on board.

Double ugh.

Since there was nothing I could do about it now, I was ready to return to my snug bed. But then my flashlight's glow revealed the reason the deck felt so sticky.

In bright red letters spangled with gaudy gold-ish flakes, someone had spray-painted MND YR OWN BIZ in foot-high letters on the teak. Underneath the letters was a crude drawing of a skull.

Chapter Ten

I had just finished gathering up my acetone-soaked rags to take to the harbor's hazardous waste facility when Caro showed up. Leave it to her to know that Mondays were my day off.

"Pack," she said, plunking down her Louis Vuitton suitcases on the dock where she stood, tapping a Jimmy Choo-shod foot. She was wearing a lime-green silk Céline jumpsuit, which didn't go all that well with the red luggage, a rare slipup for her.

"Please don't start that again, Mother."

"What's that awful smell?"

"Paint remover."

She looked down at the *Merilee*'s deck. "Why, you've ruined the teak!"

"I'll re-stain and re-varnish, but first things first."

"What are you talking about, Theodora?"

Not bothering to answer, I stood up and stretched. To a certain point, Caro was right. Paint remover played merry hell with teak, but I needed to get the graffiti off before it set up permanently. Once that was accomplished I would refinish the planking, which I'd been meaning to do, anyway. Poor old *Merilee* was looking more than a bit weathered.

I said, "You can follow me to the hazardous waste facility if you want." I picked up the rags and stepped off the boat, DJ Bonz at my heels.

"Then you'll pack. Right?"

No need to answer. I wasn't going anywhere.

As I handed over the rags to the facility manager, the harbor began to wake up. A clear morning now, fishing boats headed out into the Pacific while early-rising liveaboarders hoofed it toward the community showers. Above, seagulls screeched. Somewhere nearby, a harbor seal barked. My mother could nag me all she wanted, but I wasn't leaving this place.

Then I remembered Joe.

Joe wanted me to sell the *Merilee*, too.

Same problem, different person.

On the way back to the *Merilee*, Caro kept up with my every step. How she could do that in five-inch heels amazed me.

"Did you hear me, Theodora? Pack!"

"Why are you starting this all over again? I'm staying here and that's that."

She gave me a look. "You haven't heard the news, have you?"

"What news? More gossip from Kenny Norgaard? Or Darleene Bauer, who's almost as bad?" To make the dig even deeper, I added, "Better stop hanging around those harbor bars, Mother. They'll rot your mind as well as your liver."

She didn't take the bait. "It was on Al's police scanner."

"What was?"

"The body."

"Stuart Booth's body? Old news."

"No. The girl's."

With five yards yet to go to reach the *Merilee*, I halted. "What girl?"

"The one they found shot to death on the jogging trail near Point Deem this morning. That's only six miles up the coast, and it's getting too dangerous for you to live here by yourself on that rickety boat and…"

I grabbed Caro's arm. "What was her name?"

She shook off my hand. "For goodness sake, Theodora, you're stronger than you realize, so stop the manhandling. All that lifting and shoveling and whatever else you do over at the zoo makes you behave in a decidedly unfeminine manner. Next thing I know you'll be lifting weights and joining that nasty women's wrestling organization, what do they call it? WWF? WTF? Anyway, the police scanner didn't give a name, only that the joggers who called it in recognized her as a student at UC Santa Cruz."

"*Shot*, did you say?"

"That's what the police scanner said. At least I think it did." She looked puzzled for a moment. "Yes, yes. I'm pretty certain it did mention a gunshot wound. Look, if you need me to, I'll even help you pack. I've always been a better packer than you. The secret is to roll, not fold, and…"

I felt sick. "Just stop. Please."

Surprisingly, she did. Peering at me closely, she said, "Are you all right, dear?"

"I didn't get much sleep last night."

Behind us, Bonz whined. He wanted us to either continue his walkies or reboard the *Merilee*. Thankfully, his behavior took Caro's mind off me for a second.

"Bonzie wants fed?" she baby-talked at him.

"He's already been fed. And thanks for stopping by and your kind offer, but I have to be someplace in a few minutes and I need to get going."

She looked at me in outrage. "Like that? You smell like turpentine!"

"Paint remover."

"Same thing. Whatever, you need to pack." She pointed to the suitcases sitting on the edge of the dock.

"Good-bye, Mother." I quickly closed the distance to the *Merilee*, bypassed the suitcases, and jumped on board. After a moment of indecision, Bonz joined me.

Since it's not right to take a civilian dog to a crime scene, I had to disappoint Bonz and leave him to Puss' tender mercies. After that, it didn't take long for me to drive to the start of Point Deem's jogging path, where what appeared to be every police car in Santa Cruz County sat in the trail's parking lot. Several yards away, two plainclothes detectives were interviewing a group of young men wearing UC Santa Cruz Track Team sweatshirts. One of the students, who looked as sick as I felt, sat on the ground with his head slumped forward. The others remained standing, pretending they were fine.

It was a particularly attractive area, an eight-mile-long asphalt path that looped through a sprinkling of live oaks and Monterey pines. At night lamplights lit the path, lending it an eerie beauty. Apparently not a safe one, though.

I positioned myself downwind from the breeze blowing in from the Pacific. As I hoped, I was able to catch a phrase here and there.

"... saw a guy with a beard running."

"...black beard."

"...beard was dark brown because..."

"Blue sweatshirt or..."

"He wore running pants...."

Finally, I heard the name of the victim.

Amberlyn.

The drive back to Gunn Landing was a sad one.

Amberlyn had wanted an education to lift herself above the poverty that had stalked her family for generations. Granted, her method of doing so was hardly traditional, but did it deserve a death sentence? As for me, I was a believer in that old Native American saying about walking a mile in another man's moccasins before judging him. Or her. If I had been raised in poverty and saw a paid-for college education as my only way out, who knows what I would have done.

I never use my cell while driving, so I pulled over and called the zoo. As soon as Zorah picked up, I went straight to the point. "Has Lex Yarnell clocked in yet?"

"Funny you should ask. He just called in sick."

Popular belief notwithstanding, differing law enforcement agencies are usually quick to share information with each other. The Santa Cruz authorities would be well-aware that two gunshot deaths within a week—even one was rare in this area—had been separated by less than six miles. It was my guess they had already reached out to Joe. Only one question remained: had they found Amberlyn's phone yet? The one with Lex Yarnell's number on it?

Zorah's voice snapped me back to the present moment. "What's going on, Teddy?"

Before I could rethink the wisdom of my next question, I asked, "Did you ever meet Amberlyn Lofland?"

"Lex's ex-girlfriend? Sure. He brought her to a couple of zoo dos. Gorgeous girl. Smart, too. Why do you ask?"

"How did Lex sound when he called in?"

"Like he had a bad cold. Now, c'mon. Tell me what's going on?"

Since she would find out soon enough, I told her.

"Oh, crap."

"Exactly. As soon as I get off the phone I'm driving over to Lex's place, see if he needs anything."

"Do you think that's a good idea?" Zorah asked.

"Why wouldn't it be?"

"Maybe you're forgetting, but he took their breakup awfully hard, and it might be smarter if you eased off. For a while, anyway."

I couldn't believe what I was hearing. "Don't tell me you suspect Lex!"

"He was awfully torn up, Teddy. And men can…"

"Lex Yarnell doesn't have a violent bone in his body." At that point, a battered, slow-moving pickup piled high with gardening equipment almost sideswiped me, so I pulled even further off the road.

A tsk-tsk came over the phone. "Either you've got a bad memory or you're in denial. Don't you remember that fracas in Monkey Mania last year? The guy who grabbed one of the squirrel monkey juveniles by the tail and swung it around? Lex broke his jaw."

"That was in defense of the monkey. The poor thing wound up needing surgery."

"So'd the guy. We're just lucky there were witnesses or we'd be up to our eyeballs in lawsuits. Take my advice and stay away from Lex for a while."

"You sound like my mother."

"Has it ever occurred to you that sometimes your mother is right?"

With that, she hung up.

I wasn't going to let Zorah's paranoia affect me, so when I rejoined the traffic I stayed on Highway 1 when it bypassed Gunn Landing and followed it southeast until it took me to Castroville. Then I turned onto SR-156, where I continued to the trailer park on the eastern end of town. During the drive my phone had signaled several new calls and texts, so I switched it off. Too distracting, especially since I needed to concentrate on how to deliver the bad news to Lex.

California is blessed with many quality mobile home communities offering happy residents a plethora of community pools, saunas, and in some cases, even gyms. Babbling Brooks wasn't one of them. The place where Amberlyn had been raised and Lex still lived sat on a crumbling asphalt street behind a construction equipment storage yard, and consisted mainly of rusting relics at least thirty years old. The park's one communal offering was a gravel-covered oval which featured a swing set, several benches, two barbeques, and a red-and-yellow-striped trash barrel that didn't appear to have been emptied lately.

A favorite with local farmworkers, Babbling Brooks was pretty much deserted, with most of its inhabitants busy in the fields. The only voices I could hear came from a couple of elderly women overseeing three young children on the swings.

"Not so high, Susan!"

"*Perdiste el zapato, José!*"

"Push harder, Bennett!"

After parking, I sidestepped a few beat-up toys littering the walkway and made my way to Lex's double-wide.

Casa Yarnell faced the trailer park's "park."

With square-footage almost as large as some tract homes, it was nonetheless in terrible shape. Paint-peeled on one side and blistered on the other, the metal trailer's original color could only be guessed at. One of the windows was broken, and some enterprising soul had taped up a cut-to-fit piece of cardboard cannibalized from a box, which informed me that PAMPERS KEEP YOUR BABY DRY.

After I knocked on Lex's unscreened door, a muted voice from inside called that he would be with me in a moment. Seconds later the door opened, revealing Lex in a bathrobe. He clutched a wad of tissues in his hand.

Giving me a puzzled look, he rasped, "I'd say thanks for stopping by, whatever the reason—Zorah's big mouth, maybe?—but I might be contagious." As if to prove his point, he sneezed.

So Lex really was sick. Judging from the jovial note in his voice, he didn't know about Amberlyn yet. But I felt it best to find out for certain.

"I wanted to see how you were doing. It's my day off, so I have the time. Uh, have you been watching TV, by any chance?"

He shook his head. "Just sipping chamomile tea and reading Ian Fleming, you know, one of those James Bond things. Dated now, but still fun to read. Amberlyn likes them, too, and we used to trade them back and forth. Hey, you're welcome to come in and share some tea—I just made a fresh pot—but you'd be taking a chance on getting what I've got, so I don't recommend it."

I gave him a strained smile. "Where's the family?" Meaning his mother, father, grandmother, and the three younger siblings he helped support.

"Out in the fields, where else? You know how it is."

Yes, I did, and thank Heaven not from personal experience. "Think they'll be back for lunch?"

A double sneeze. "Nah, they're brown-bagging. This week they're over at Clemento's, helping with the bok choy and carrots. Might even stay the night, save on gas, work there again tomorrow. And the next day. They took their sleeping bags."

The gigantic Clemento Farms, which raised practically everything edible, was located seventy miles away. And while the Yarnell family's patched-together Volkswagen bus didn't use much gas, to them a penny saved was very much a penny earned. Now I had a choice. Keep my mouth shut about Amberlyn and return to Gunn Landing, leaving Lex to find out the bad news on his own, or woman up and deliver the news while at least he had a friend to comfort him.

I heaved a sigh and said, "Maybe I could use that tea, after all."

Three hours later I was on the *Merilee*, having spent one of the most miserable mornings of my life. Lex had proven the lie of the old saying *Big boys don't cry*. He had cried so hard I worried he might harm himself, but he finally settled down to the point where I felt it safe to leave. Just to be safe, on my way to my pickup I alerted the toddler-watching grannies, who each promised to look in on him.

Love. Who could fathom it? Tenderhearted Lex had loved avaricious Amberlyn, but although I had grudgingly liked the young woman, part of me wondered if she had deserved Lex's depth of emotion. Then again, is love something that needs to be earned, or should it be freely given?

"Who do you love?" I asked Bonz, since dogs have all the answers where love is concerned.

Walkies, he thought at me. *And you.*

So I took him for walkies.

The stroll through Gunn Landing Park helped take my mind off Amberlyn. Bonz made a couple of new friends—identical teacup poodles wearing matching pink rhinestone collars— but after much tail-sniffing and tree-visiting, it was time to return to the *Merilee*.

As we were walking by the *High Life*, Kenny Norgaard called out to me, "The cops were looking for you!" which made Ruth Donohue, sunbathing on the deck of the *Clear Light* look up in alarm.

Knowing Kenny's penchant for exaggeration, I asked, "When you say 'cops,' do you mean Joe?"

"Who else, dear heart?"

Maybe plenty of 'elses,' such as plainclothes detectives from Santa Cruz. They might be curious once they found my number on Amberlyn's phone.

"Did Joe say what he wanted?"

"We didn't talk, although methinks he looked a wee bit unhappy. And, ah, your mother was with him."

"What!?" The idea of Caro and Joe on a mission together stunned me.

"Yes, and they were *très* buddy-buddy. Have they finally buried the peace pipe? I mean, *smoked* the peace pipe, since it's hatchets we bury, isn't it, and usually in someone's back. I was wondering if you could have been doing something to annoy them both. Hmmm? As an aside, I must say that was a lovely dress your mother was wearing. A Missoni, if I am correct. And those strappy Francesco Russo heels were to die for. She looked like she'd just walked off a Paris runway. Say, want a drink? I have a pitcher-full here. Be thrilled to share."

He waved his Mai Tai at me. At least it looked like a Mai Tai, cute little umbrella and all. Grumping a no-thanks at him, Bonz and I continued on our way while I did some deep thinking. Earlier this morning, Caro had been wearing a lime green jumpsuit, but was now in a Missoni dress (Kenny was never wrong about these things). Could she possibly have changed into a more serious outfit in order to drive to San Sebastian and ask Joe for help in making me decamp to Old Town? All this while I was comforting Lex Yarnell? No, the idea of a Caro/Joe partnership was too bizarre even for my mother.

But Kenny's report made me so uncomfortable that it was only when Bonz and I were passing Lila Conyers' *Just In Time* that something floating around in my unconscious finally swam to the surface.

Graffiti.

On a boat.

After Lila's harassment case against Stuart Booth was dismissed, she had spray-painted LIAR on his Azimut Motor Yacht.

I didn't want to believe that Lila would do such a thing to my beloved *Merilee*. After all, she had chosen Day-Glo Orange for her handiwork on Booth's boat, whereas last night's vandal had used red with goldish metal flakes.

Still…

Once I'd returned Bonz to the *Merilee*—no sign of either Joe or Caro, thank heaven—I made a beeline to Lila Conyers' houseboat. She was home. No surprise there, since while in jail she had lost her part-time job at Tiny Tots. She looked fairly upbeat, considering. A healthy glow had returned to her cheeks, and her blue eyes were lively again.

"How are you doing?" I asked, after being invited on board and settling myself onto a rickety deck chair.

Lila pointed at her ankle monitor. "Can't say this is a nice addition to my wardrobe, but thanks to you and Al, all I have to complain about right now is the County's taste in accessories."

"Does it chafe?"

"Just against my nerves."

I hated to take away her supposed good mood, but I had no choice. "Lila, someone spray-painted the *Merilee*'s deck last night. Did you hear anything around three a.m.?"

She didn't answer right away, just stared at me. Finally, she said, "And you came to see me because I have a history of vandalizing boats."

"Since you're the only tagger I know, yeah. May I ask where you bought the paint? The stuff you used on Booth's boat, I mean, not mine."

"Then you don't suspect me?"

"Of course not, but I'm thinking it might have been someone inspired by your own past exploits. Send me a warning, and at the same time, throw suspicion on you."

"Warning?"

"In text-type spelling, it read, 'Mind your own business.' In bright red, with iridescent gold flecks."

Another pause, then, "Jake's Hobby Shop in San Sebastian has the best color selection, but you can buy that stuff—it's called Candy Apple Red—all over the place these days. Heck, they even sell it at Costco."

"So, again, did you hear anything weird around three a.m.?"

"Weird how? This is a marina, for Pete's sake. There's all kinds of weirdness going down all the time. Kenny's parties, for one. Did you know that a couple of weeks ago when you were up in San Francisco for that conference on otters, he hosted a birthday party for his cat Roger? Made everyone wear a cat costume. Darleene Bauer cheated and wore a dress she swore was manufactured in Thailand when it was still called Siam, as in Siamese cat. Kenny said that didn't count and they got into a whopping big argument. Over a dress."

"Too bad I missed it. But I mean 'weird' like somebody running down the dock at three in the morning."

"Sorry, I was catching up on all the sleep I lost while I was in jail. It's noisy as hell in there. All those clanging doors." In a lower voice she added, "And the crying."

I leaned forward so that the freshening Pacific

breeze didn't carry away what I was about to say next. "Have you watched the news today?"

"No, why?"

"A friend of Booth's was found shot to death on a jogging trail in Santa Cruz."

After Lila caught her breath, she said, "A female friend, by any chance? Like, a student?"

"Right on both counts."

She turned her face away so I couldn't see her expression. "So the bastard never stopped. Wonder if your boyfriend's going to arrest me again?"

That's what I had been worrying about. "She wasn't one of his own students. She goes to… uh, *went* to UC Santa Cruz. Amberlyn Lofland. Did you know her?"

When Lila faced me again, I saw her earlier liveliness had disappeared. The pink was gone from her cheeks, replaced by a sickly pallor.

"Never even heard the name." Before I could react, she jumped out of her deck chair and rushed inside the houseboat. A few seconds later I heard her vomiting.

For a moment I didn't know which action to take: rush to her aid or stay where I was. Deciding that most people prefer to vomit in private, I chose a compromise between the two. I went into her galley kitchen, poured her a glass of water from the tap, and stood at the ready outside her miniscule bathroom. While I waited for her to empty her stomach, I couldn't help but notice the disarray. Her unmade bed revealed dingy sheets, half-eaten food crusted the unmatched dishes piled in the sink, and cheap clothes lay strewn around what little floor space the houseboat offered. Depression? Or evidence of a seriously disordered mind?

A few minutes later Lila emerged, smelling worse than I did after a shift at the zoo. I handed her the glass. "Gargle. Brush your teeth. And wash up." I'd have put her in the shower if she had one, but she didn't. Like most liveaboarders, she used the public showers next to the laundromat.

When she disappeared into the bathroom, I picked the clothes off the floor and stripped the bed. I was scraping the dishes when she reemerged.

"What are you doing, Teddy?"

"Helping the woman who helped Bonz."

"He needed help. I don't."

Sayeth the woman wearing an ankle bracelet courtesy of the San Sebastian County Sheriff's Department. I ignored her and continued scraping a plate marred by a crack down the middle. It was a miracle the thing didn't fall apart on me.

"Teddy, please stop."

I put on my "stern" voice, the one I used whenever a zoo animal tried to get frisky with me. "Get some fresh air. I'll come out and talk to you after I've finished up in here."

She opened her mouth as if to say something, then changed her mind and went on deck.

Since the houseboat was so small, it didn't take long to instill some semblance of order, but at the end I was left with a pile of dirty sheets and clothes that smelled faintly of mildew.

Emerging into the sunlight I asked, "Where do you keep the clean sheets?"

"I only have the one set."

How long had this been going on under my nose? I hauled two pillowcases full of dirty laundry onto the deck. "See you later," I told Lila. "Unless you want to come with me."

"Look, you don't have to do that."

"You'd do the same for me if I were in your shoes."

It was true. Lila's compassion didn't confine itself to injured dogs. Many was the time she had taken over a casserole to a fellow liveaboarder laid low with the flu, or babysat for free when someone needed to go on a job interview.

"Lila?"

A sigh. "Just let me sit here alone for a while, okay? And I'm…I'm sorry I snapped at you. You're a good friend, Teddy." She didn't turn around, just kept staring at the Pacific, where the late afternoon sun had hidden behind a cloudbank. But I could tell she was crying.

Shouldering the heavy pillowcases, I headed for the group laundromat.

Two hours later I stopped off at the *Merilee* to pick up an extra set of sheets and pillowcases to give to Lila, but before going below I found a polite note from Joe taped on the hatch, asking me to call him. Caro had left a note, too, but hers was more strident. What in the world…? Then I remembered switching off my phone just before arriving at Lex's trailer. Oh, well. First things first. With Bonz following my every step, I rummaged through my closet and pulled out everything I thought might fit Lila. Then I collected the bed linens and left.

Since Bonz was so insistent, I allowed him

to accompany me this time. A good dog can heal the heart, as Bonz had certainly healed mine after my divorce. When we arrived at *Just In Time*, I at first thought Lila had not moved from her deck chair since I'd left for the laundromat, but when I went inside to make up her bed, leaving Bonz curled up her lap, I saw that she had opened a couple of the houseboat's windows, allowing enough fresh air in to chase away more unpleasant odors.

I stowed the clean clothes and made up her bunk.

"Feeling better?" I asked her, when I was done.

She gave me a wan smile. "Who wouldn't feel better with a dog in their lap?"

Chapter Eleven

The rest of the day passed without another major incident, partially because of the rare mercies of voice mail. Once I'd turned on my phone and saw so many messages—mostly from Joe and my mother—I didn't know where to start first. When I did, all I got was voice mail. Joe was "away from the phone but I'll get back to you as soon as possible." Same with Caro, whose message said essentially the same thing, but snootier. Relieved, I spent the afternoon reorganizing the *Merilee*'s storage compartments, then rewarded myself by playing Capture the Devious Red Dot with Miss Priss. Bonz had long ago learned the Devious Red Dot was located in my laser pen, so he enjoyed watching Priss make a fluffy fool of herself.

When Priss had tired herself out, I returned

some calls, but I ignored the five phone messages Frasier had left. That fact-seeking dinner had landed me in enough trouble already, and I didn't need more. Besides, there were enough single women in San Sebastian County that all he had to do was find one who didn't mind listening to his tales of the Evils of Evelyn. As I deleted his messages, I wished him well.

At six I visited the harbor's community shower, then dressed in something more appropriate for an Otter Conservancy meeting than sweats and jeans.

The group met at the Unitarian Universalist Church in Santa Cruz the first Monday of each month, so by seven I was sitting in the church's basement listening to a talk by Dr. Isabell Morrison, a scientist from the veterinary school at UC Davis. She didn't tell us much more than we already knew, that the problem toxoplasma gondii was getting worse, not better. Feral cat colonies, which shed the parasite in their feces, were suspected, but other sources of pollution were being studied as well. The popularity of flushable kitty litter meant that the parasite was winding up in the nearby sewage treatment plants, but so far the plants' current treatment methods had failed to kill the flushed parasite.

Dr. Morrison forecast that the numbers of sea otter deaths from toxoplasma gondii would continue to climb.

"Well, that was cheerful," said Darleene Bauer later as she, Frank Owens, and I put the chairs away and returned the church room to its normal setup.

As we stacked the chairs, the river otter keeper wondered aloud about something that had been bothering me. "Don't you think it's odd that the increase in sea otter deaths hasn't been reflected in the reports from around here? According to the statistics Dr. Morrison quoted, we sound almost like a toxo-free zone, but I myself reported two deceased ones."

"Same here," Frank said. "I e-mailed pictures of three carcasses."

"You're not telling me anything I don't know since I had to retype *both* your reports," Darleene reminded us, sounding cranky. "Neither of you can type worth a damn."

I let that pass. "But what about Booth's count? He was covering the north side of the Slough. Surely he found carcasses."

Darleene shrugged. "No clue there, 'cause I didn't get his latest report, did I? Somebody killed him before he could send it to me for retyping. Anyway, I was planning to have a conversation with Booth about his methods if he didn't report any deaths this year, but alas…" She mimicked an exaggerated expression of grief. "Say, either of you know where I can pick up another printer and fax combo? Cheap? Half my office equipment's down for the count."

A discussion followed on the merits of stand-alones as opposed to combo machines, and which chain offered the best prices. Darleene being no friend of conglomerates—she was especially Starbucks-averse—took Frank's advice to check out the offerings at Buffalo Bob's Electronics Emporium in Monterey Bay. Higher prices, but a sole proprietor.

Halfway back to Gunn Landing, I began to wonder.

Did Booth have the completed otter report on him when he died?

And if so, was it still on his phone?

Lex Yarnell wasn't at the zoo when I arrived the next morning, no surprise there. Wisely or not, he'd loved Amberlyn and preferred keeping his grief to himself. But when I stopped by the employee lounge for a cup of coffee, I found the *San Sebastian Journal* being passed from zookeeper to zookeeper. When it finally reached me, I found that an "unnamed source" had leaked the entire Sugar Baby story.

Zookeepers aren't saints. Myra Sebrowski, for instance, gloated, "A kept woman, can you *believe* that? I mean, how sordid can you get, whoring yourself out to some old fart for tuition money?"

"At least the poor woman was trying to better herself." This from Robin Chase, who was rubbing hand cream on a new tattoo. "Last week you were carrying on about Booth being such a nice guy, and you weren't referring to him as 'some old fart' then."

"That's before I found out…" Myra stopped abruptly.

"Found out what?" I asked.

Myra gave me a withering look. "Nothing. It's just that he was pretty old, wasn't he? For sure too old for that Amberlyn person. What was she, like nineteen or something? Pathetic, if you ask me."

Robin, who had never liked Myra, snapped, "From what the *Journal* said, that 'Amberlyn person' was only five years younger than you.

And his age sure didn't stop you from drooling over him, did it? Not that he ever drooled back." Robin narrowed her eyes. "Or did he?"

Looking flustered, Myra stood up. "I'm not going to waste any more time with petty gossip. Gotta get to my apes."

She flounced out.

I finished my coffee, wondering briefly whether there might be a connection between Myra and Booth she didn't want me to know about. But she was a brunette, where Booth had famously preferred blondes.

Still wondering, I left to load some animals for a trip to the TV station.

Bernice and I breathed a sigh of relief when for once, *Anteaters to Zebras* went smoothly, at least where the animals were concerned. Alejandro the llama hammed it up for the live cameras and didn't spit on anyone. As for Charlemagne the hedgehog, he fell so in love with anchorwoman Ariel Gonzales that he didn't curl up in a self-protective ball. After scuttling up and down her arm a few times, he settled himself on her shoulder and played with her bejeweled earlobe. Carlos, my favorite Collie's magpie jay, was so thrilled at being out and about with me that he perched on my knee and delivered an oratorio of joy.

Teeteeteeteek: Long-billed Dowitcher.

Buzzy dzzt: Green-breasted Mango.

Churry chorry chorry: Mourning Warbler.

He didn't even sulk when I popped him into his birdcage/carrier. He just sat on one of the crossbars and pretended to be a meadowlark.

But then a human began misbehaving, and wouldn't you know it was a human being I'd always trusted. Which just goes to show.

With Carlos providing background music, Ariel leaned forward on the set's faux-leather sofa, the hedgehog moving with her. "We here at KGNN always appreciate your stopping by with the Gunn Zoo's wonderful animals, but I would be remiss if I didn't ask you to say a few words about the double murder case the police are investigating in your area. I hear you actually found one of the bodies."

"The only thing I found was a cell phone," I said firmly. "Certainly no body. And as for the so-called 'double murder case,' those two events happened several miles apart, and as far as I know, are not connected."

"And yet the newspapers reported the victims knew each other."

"I wouldn't know anything about that."

"I also hear you've been questioned by the authorities. Several times, as a matter of fact."

"Cite your source, Ariel."

She glanced at Carlos, still in full trill. "A little birdy told me."

Oh, Ariel, and here I thought we were friends. Determined to keep my voice steady, I replied, "Well, it's untrue."

Carlos picked that moment to shut up. After the glory of his solo concerto, the silence felt ominous. Even the hedgehog stopped playing with Ariel's ear.

"But you knew both victims, didn't you, Teddy? Professor Stuart Booth, head of the Marine Science program at Betancourt College, and Amberlyn Lofland, a student at UC Santa Cruz? Professor Booth kept a boat at Gunn Landing Harbor. Surely you two interacted at some point."

Bernice, who had been standing just out of camera range throughout the interview, looked at least as uncomfortable as I felt. At my signal, she made a big show of carrying Carlos' cage away, but in the rush, left Charlemagne behind.

Not that he cared. The hedgehog merely returned his attentions to Ariel's ear.

Trying not to let the TV host's questioning shake me, I explained, "Professor Booth's boat was moored in the expensive section of the harbor, next to the yacht club. My boat is docked in the, ah, *discount* area, so there's no way we would normally run into each other." I wasn't about to let slip the info that Booth and I were both involved in the recent otter count.

"How about Amberlyn Lofland, then? The same little birdy told me you were seen visiting her apartment the day before she was murdered."

It was time for redirection, a skill honed to perfection by every zookeeper. Forcing myself to look chipper, I said, "Did you know that miners' cats aren't really cats? They're actually related to the raccoon family! They came by that inaccurate name because they were always slinking around silver miners' camps, looking for table scraps! As for myself, I've always thought they look like a cross between a ring-tailed lemur and a fox, but some people..."

"Do you deny visiting Miss Lofland?"

"Come to think of it, another fascinating fact about animals few people are aware of is that koalas hardly ever drink water! I'll bet you didn't know that either, did you, Ariel? Koalas get most of their moisture from the eucalyptus leaves they eat, and thus are beautifully suited to their desert environment, so the move from Australia to Gunn...."

"According to my sources, this isn't the first time you've been involved in a murder case. Don't you think that's odd?"

The camera's red light was still on, but unless my waterproof, pee-proof Timex was wrong, we had less than a minute to go before my segment was finished. Then the red light would go off and I could take my animals and vamoose.

I gave Ariel a bright smile. "The Gunn Zoo is especially proud of Sssybil, our Mohave rattlesnake. She's an especially intelligent reptile and is quite active on social media. She's on Facebook, Snapchat, has her own website, and tweets several times a day, frequently about her children, many of whom have gone to other zoos. Sssybil is also widely known for her..."

The red light blinked out.

"Shame on you!" I snapped at Ariel, plucking the hedgehog off her neck. "*Anteaters to Zebras* is supposed to be all about animals, but you turned it into the *Agatha Christie Hour*."

She spread her hands. "Sorry, Teddy. Orders from on high. The station manager handed me that list of questions and told me to ask them or else. And we gals both know what 'or else' means, don't we? Kudos to you for handling the situation so well. And give Sssybil my regards."

Still feeling betrayed, I put the hedgehog on my own neck and left.

"Told you so," Bernice said, as we drove the van out of the parking lot while the animals snuffled, chirped, and squeaked in the compartment behind us.

"Did not."

"Well, I meant to. At least she didn't bring up my niece."

"Even Ariel wouldn't do such a dastardly thing," I insisted. "She's a Marine. They're all about honor."

"But she's a TV personality now, and you know what those folks are like."

There was nothing to say to that, so I remained silent for the rest of the drive.

When we arrived at the zoo I found a note on my locker asking me to stop by the office. Certain that the zoo director had been watching the disaster on *Anteaters to Zebras,* I walked down to the Admin Building and into the head office, where Zorah peered at me over an intimidatingly tall stack of papers.

"Nice show," she cracked.

"A laugh a minute. But it's good to know you always follow my TV adventures."

"So does Aster Edwina, who called and told me to keep you off the air until this thing blows over. I hope that doesn't upset you."

"Are you kidding? I don't want to ever go through that again. Do you have any idea what it feels like to be cross-examined on live TV?"

"No, and I don't want to. Now go ahead and do your zookeeper thing. I have to finish filling out these forms re those cheetahs we've applied for. If we don't act fast, the San Francisco Zoo will get them. Or the San Diego, which is always one-upping us."

I was almost at the door before she added, "Another thing. Kabuki's been flinging feces at the visitors."

"Again?"

Zorah made a face. "He usually misses, but today he's already hurled a couple near-hits and it's not even noon yet. If this behavior continues, we might have to take him off exhibit. Think you might be able to do something?"

"Why not ask Myra Sebrowski? She's his keeper."

"Nothing Myra's tried seems to work. Kabuki's always had a soft spot for you. Just give it a try, okay?"

Although I didn't relish having to work alongside the surly Myra, I agreed and headed toward Kabuki's enclosure. As I drove my zebra cart along the zoo's pathways, it occurred to me that I could use the occasion to find out why Myra had been so quick to come to Booth's defense.

But first things first.

Before Kabuki had been sent to us by another zoo, the Japanese macaque—commonly known as a snow monkey—had once observed a group of chimps flinging feces at an obnoxious teenage boy, and apparently thought it looked like fun. Before coming to us, he'd indulged in a few fastballs of his own. Now separated from the naughty chimps by three states and five years, Kabuki still went through periods where his old behavior reemerged.

Like elephants, monkeys never forget.

Kabuki's enclosure was located between

Tropics Trail and Verdant Veldt, a large enclosure strewn with boulders to climb on, ropes to swing with, and shaded by tall eucalyptus trees. A flowing stream added to its tranquil ambience. Several times a year the zoo trucked in snow for the macaques to play in.

While many people view macaques as unappealing animals, I found Kabuki rather handsome with his silvery coat, pink face, and deep-set eyes. As macaques go, he was quite the screen idol. This morning I found him sitting in lonely splendor atop the largest boulder in the enclosure, staring intently at three young men pointing at him and making rude remarks. The rest of the monkey troop were busy picking through the rocks at the far side of the enclosure, hunting for tasty insects.

With the exception of the famous Koko and a few other super-socialized gorillas, it is doubtful monkeys can understand human language. They're intelligent, yes, but their minds don't work the same way as ours. However, there is no question that most animals are sensitive to *tone*, the way certain words are pronounced. You can call a macaque an idiot, but if you say the word softly and sweetly, the word sounds tender. But if you overlay the word with the scorn with which it's usually uttered, the animal picks up on that.

The three men made no effort to hide their scorn. They laughed, they pointed, they made insulting noises. Not only did they make fun of Kabuki himself, but they went on to disparage his mother, his father, his aunts and uncles, and any children he may have sired. While Kabuki couldn't understand the words themselves, he knew he was being mocked.

I looked around for Myra, wanting her to step in and break up the insult session—there were children nearby—but she was nowhere in sight. Before I could go in search of her, Kabuki took care of the matter himself.

The macaque climbed down from the boulder, ambled casually toward the edge of the moat that separated him from the fence, and squatted.

Knowing what was about to happen, I yelled, "Duck, guys!"

Too late.

Having produced a fresh weapon, Kabuki hurled it toward the men, and before they could scramble out of the way, the turd hit the most vocal of them square in the face.

Kabuki had been practicing.

"Restrooms are that way," I said to the man, somehow managing to hide my grin. "You can wash up in there. Some advice, though. Teasing an animal is never a good idea. The blowback can be excruciating."

No answer from the victim, just gagging sounds. Monkey poo isn't pleasant.

As soon as the trio hurried toward the restrooms, I approached the fence. Spotting me, Kabuki gave a little dance and moved even closer to the moat. He couldn't get to me, though, so instead of staying there, I walked around to the rear of the enclosure where the keepers' entrance was hidden behind strategically placed fake boulders. There I found Myra cleaning out the macaques' night cages.

"Kabuki just hit a visitor in the face with a turd."

She pulled her beautiful face into a frown. "I thought his aim wasn't all that good."

"It's improved."

"Oh, crap. Literally. Think the visitor will sue?"

I recalled the man's muscle shirt, his Cleveland Indians baseball cap, his half-laced high-tops. "He didn't look like the litigious type."

Although Myra can be unpleasant with

humans, when it comes to her monkeys and apes, she's all care and concern. "At least that's something. But geez, Teddy. I've been wracking my brain, yet still can't come up with anything to stop his behavior. What about you? Kabuki's not the easiest macaque to work with, and believe me I've tried, but maybe you can try?" Her face crumpled into a plea. "I'd hate to see him go off-exhibit."

In zoo parlance, to go "off-exhibit" could mean one of three things: the animal in question would be given some extended R&R time in a non-viewable area; the animal would be traded to another zoo in hopes a change of scene would stop the negative behavior; or the animal would be euthanized, something the Gunn Zoo never did unless the animal in question was so ill it could not be saved.

R&R with Kabuki had already been tried and it hadn't worked, which meant he was in danger of being traded. Neither Myra nor I wanted to see that happen. Neither would his harem.

"Have there been any changes in his habitat in the last couple of months other than the new baby? Seems to me I remember four females." Yet all I could see were three grown females, one female adolescent, and one male infant riding on its mother's back.

"Aster Edwina had us send Akemi to St. Louis last month. They lost their one female macaque last winter and the male was grieving."

"Well, now we're the ones with a grieving male. Kabuki had two babies with Akemi, didn't he?" I waved toward the adolescent and the infant. "You say she left last month. When exactly did Kabuki start pitching practice?"

Light dawned. "Three weeks ago."

"Sounds like he needs a new love interest. I'll call Aster Edwina."

Only later did I remember that I'd forgotten to ask Myra about her possible interaction with Stuart Booth.

As it turned out, I didn't have to call Aster Edwina. She called me.

"Teddy, stop whatever you're doing and come up here."

Up here, meant Gunn Castle. "What if I'm in the middle of running from an escaped lion?"

"Then change direction."

End of call.

I checked my watch. Just after four p.m. I would miss the glut of late-arriving visitors trying to squeeze their visit to the Gunn Zoo's three hundred acres into two hours, always a busy time. After calling Zorah and telling her what was happening, I parked my cart and headed for the castle.

"Teddy, you promised to keep me informed about the Booth situation, yet I haven't heard a word from you," Aster Edwina said the moment I walked through the library door at Gunn Castle. "Why not?"

"I've been busy."

"You had a whole day off Monday and could have contacted me then."

It would never occur to the old harridan that anyone had a life that did not revolve around her orders. Nevertheless, I told her what I'd learned since we last met.

When I was done, she groused, "That's all? The SOB had a kept woman?"

"They're called Sugar Babies these days, as long as they're in college."

"Disgraceful. And what about that Lila girl, the one your boyfriend arrested?"

"Lila has been released from custody." I left

out the part about the electronic monitoring device she was wearing on her ankle.

Those eagle eyes burrowed into mine. "You think she did it?"

"Not really. She was the first student to accuse him of sexual harassment, but that was years ago. If she was going to kill him, she'd have done it then." I also left out the part about Lila vandalizing Booth's boat in the aftermath. Maybe Aster Edwina had forgotten about the incident.

"Hmm. If you…"

The library door opened and Eunice came in bearing a tray laden with a teapot and a sole teacup. She gave me a guilty look and shook her head.

"Thank you, Eunice," Aster Edwina said. "That will be all."

Eunice looked at the solitary teacup and hesitantly began, "Uh, don't you think Teddy…?"

"I *said*, that will be all!"

Eunice scampered.

"Now where were we?" Aster Edwina said, lifting her teacup. From its smoky scent and dark color, I gathered it was Lapsang Souchong, a tea I've always been partial to. My mouth watered.

"I was telling you Lila Conyers had nothing to do with Booth's murder. Or Amberlyn's."

"Too bad. That would have tied everything up neatly. The faster this thing is solved, the better for all of us."

"You don't think getting to the truth is more important than neatness?"

She sniffed. "There asks one who doesn't understand the complexities of life."

"Perhaps. But I'm pretty sure you can relax about the murder being tied to Blue Seas Marine Laboratory, so your connection to the case is in the clear."

She slammed her teacup down so hard I was surprised it didn't break. "My connection? What the hell do you mean, *my connection*?!"

I had been about to remind her that she was the one who had advised Blue Seas to hire Booth in the first place, but I'd already angered her so much I held my tongue. Still, the fact that she had given the licentious creep a glowing reference gave rise to an interesting question: why had she done it in the first place? A possible explanation occurred to me. Despite Booth's preference for young female students, he had also been slick with elderly women, especially when there might be the prospect of financial gain for one of his many marine projects. I did some quick math in my head. Booth was something like twenty years younger than Aster Edwina, and when she had referred him to Blue Seas, he would have been in his thirties as opposed to her fifties. Not that uncommon a coupling when money and/or power were involved.

"Oh, I didn't mean what you obviously thought I meant," I backtracked. "Just that you did send him over to Blue Seas, so maybe your name was on some of the paperwork."

"All the Human Resources paperwork is sealed. I made certain of that."

But easily accessed by a search warrant. "Well, that's a relief. Can I go now?"

"Nothing would make me happier."

Although I had wanted to discuss the problem with Kabuki, this wasn't the time, so I left Aster Edwina to her Lapsang Souchong. And it was just as well. When I arrived at the macaque's enclosure, I found him winding up with the dexterity of a major league pitcher, if not the grace.

"Kabuki, no!" I yelled. "Bad monkey!"

Startled, Kabuki stopped his windup, but the naughty little boy who had been chosen as the recipient of his latest slimy projectile didn't appreciate the save. Seeing my approach, the boy hid the rock he'd been about to throw in his jeans pocket.

"We was just playin'!" he whined. He looked to be around eight, and his mother—who was old enough to have known better than allow her son to pitch rocks at an animal—looked unhappy at my interruption.

"That monkey doesn't play nice," I said, stretching out my hand. "Give me the rock."

With a surly expression, the boy complied.

"Thank you. Now why don't you head for California Trail and visit the river otters?" On my way from Gunn Castle I'd seen Frank Owens cleaning out their pond. He wouldn't put up with any nonsense from the two. "The otters are much more polite. But before you go, I'd like to inform you that California Penal Code 597 calls for an up to twenty-thousand-dollar fine and a year in jail for molesting wildlife."

"Those monkeys aren't wildlife, they're tame," the mother said, jutting her chin forward. She was overly madeup, and the thin black line she'd drawn to serve as eyebrows gave her a clownish look, but I didn't find her casual cruelty amusing.

"PC 597 doesn't differentiate. Please move away from this enclosure."

In the classic stance of defiance, the mother placed her clenched fists on her broad hips. "We paid our admission and we'll see what we want to see. I'm not going to let you push me and my kid around."

Emboldened by his mother, her son picked up another rock.

No otters for them.

Matching her aggression, I said, "You need to leave the zoo now. Do it peacefully or I'll call the park ranger and have you escorted out."

"You wouldn't dare," she huffed.

"Try me." I held out my hand to the boy. "Rock."

Displaying more sense than his mother, the boy gave me the rock. Like the first one, it was almost the size of Aster Edwina's teacup and could have hurt Kabuki badly if it had landed on him.

I pointed down the hill. "The exit's that way."

The witless mother was still miffed. "You told us we could go see the otters!"

"I changed my mind."

With a stream of invectives that would have made a gangsta rapper blush, the woman grabbed her son by the arm and headed toward the exit. I stayed where I was until they rounded a clump of coffeeberry bushes and drifted out of sight. At that point, I unhooked my radio and opened the channel to whatever park ranger was nearest.

"Rock-thrower boy, around eight years old, red-and-white-striped tee-shirt and jeans, heading south on Tropics Trail from macaque enclosure. Accompanied by mother, blond, late twenties, pink-flowered dress. If the mom refuses to attend our seminar on safe animal/ human interaction, take photograph for REFUSE ADMISSION bulletin board. Keeper Four, out."

During all this, Kabuki had watched quietly. I leaned over the rail and called out, "See the trouble you caused?"

He smacked his lips and cooed, macaque for "Oh, you sweet thing, you."

Although he was a handsomer-than-usual macaque, I answered, "Sorry, guy, I'm engaged to a human." Then, given the events of the past couple of days, I added, "At least I hope I still am."

By now, Myra had moved onto the Great Apes enclosure, where I found her cleaning out the mountain gorillas' night house. After warning her about the rock-thrower, I shared my idea about a way to resolve the Kabuki situation.

"I heard through the grapevine that the National Zoo has a grieving female macaque who lost her mate and won't socialize with the new alpha male. There've been a couple of nasty fights between them and her keepers have had to isolate her."

Myra looked up from the pile of dung she had been transferring to a trash can on rollers. Her Hollywood starlet face, so unhappy earlier, now looked hopeful. "Are you talking about Clarabelle? They say she was pretty attached to old Shinzu, more so than the rest of the troop. Unusual, isn't it?"

Yes, it was unusual in that female macaques weren't known for their fidelity. The females were known to mate with as many as four males during mating season and seldom showed favorites. But there are always exceptions to a rule, and Clarabelle appeared to be one of those exceptions. Not good. Because of the destruction of their native environment, the population of Japanese macaques was in freefall. The species hadn't yet reached "threatened" status, but was verging on it, so a fertile young female who disliked a new alpha male was a problem.

"I'll talk to Aster Edwina about calling the National to see if it's possible to bring Clarabelle out here," I said. "Maybe a new environment will help her. And you know Kabuki. There's never been a female macaque who didn't find him irresistible."

Myra actually smiled. "Yeah, he's a stud."

Finally. Here was my opening. "Speaking of studs, how well did you know Stuart Booth?"

The smile faded.

"Mind your own business, Teddy."

With that, she resumed sweeping.

As I drove my zebra cart toward Friendly Farm, I thought about Aster Edwina and our uncomfortable conversation. Looking back, I realized she had always been touchy on the subject of Stuart Booth. The more I thought about it, the more I suspected that her touchiness did not stem from her unwise reference letter on his behalf to Blue Seas. It hinted at something more personal.

In a painting over one of the Gunn Castle's massive fireplaces, the artist had portrayed the then fifty-year-old Aster Edwina was still a beauty, although a severe one. Her gray eyes, now flinty, were large and direct; her cheekbones high, her jawline as magnificent as a young Katharine Hepburn's. And her hair! Masses of deep black curls only partially held in check by a diamond-encrusted tiara. The woman looked like a queen, and in some ways, still did. When the portrait had been painted, decades before she had written the Blue Seas letter, she'd been beautiful enough to attract numerous suitors.

I put Aster Edwina out of my mind as I drove onto Friendly Farm, where Alejandro's hippity-hop display in the paddock proved how happy he was to see me. Hardly camera-shy, the llama had enjoyed his stint under the hot lights of *Anteaters to Zebras* because it meant he would get to spend extra time with me. We had once gone through hard times together at the local Renaissance Faire, making our already close bond even stronger. The llama's only disappointment was that no child sat in the zebra cart with me when I drove up. He was a sucker for kids.

"Things going well with you, Alejandro?"

"*Mmmm.*"

"That's nice. Any kiddies stop by to see you today?"

"*Mmmm.*"

"Good! Now how would you like some alfalfa pellets?"

"*Mmmm!*"

Llamas being tidy animals—they preferred to defecate in the same spot every time—it didn't take long to clean his enclosure. Afterwards, I spent a few extra minutes with him, nuzzling and ear-scratching, until he dozed off.

While I was driving by the Sumatran tiger enclosure, I spied Janet Hewitt leaving the keepers' area with Robin Chase. I'd been meaning to talk to the keeper trainee ever since she'd had her weeping spell over Stuart Booth, but somehow she always managed to evade me. Determined not to miss this opportunity, I braked the zebra cart.

"Hey, Janet!" I called. "I need to talk to you!"

"Can't!" Her face was rosy from the hard work big cats required. "Robin and I are on our way to clean out the ocelot's night house."

The excuse didn't work. Turning to her, Robin said, "Naw, we're fine. I'll meet you there in ten." Off she went down the trail, her animal tattoos striding along with her.

There was no point in being subtle, so after climbing down from the cart, I said to the trainee, "You realize, don't you, that there's been another shooting death?"

At first she seemed reluctant to answer, but then muttered, "That thing in Santa Cruz, right?"

"That 'thing's' name was Amberlyn, and she was only a couple of years younger than you. She was a…" I searched for the right word. "…a *friend* of Booth's."

Janet's eyes widened, and for a moment she looked much younger than she was. "That's… that's sad. But what's it got to do with me? All I did was take a couple of classes with him, and despite all the junk that's being whispered about him, Professor Booth was a great teacher."

"Do you know what a Sugar Baby is, Janet?"

Her rose-cheeked face grew pale. "No." Talk about a bad liar.

"Are you familiar with the website SeekingSugarDaddy.com?"

Her face grew paler until she was almost the color of the zoo's albino tamarin monkey. "Never heard of it."

"Well, I think…"

"Gotta go!" Without another word she pushed past me and trotted down the trail after Robin.

There being nothing else I could do, I let her go.

An hour later I clocked out. My working day—as frustrating as it had been—was over.

My planned return to the *Merilee* was cut short when I was detained by the police in the zoo's parking lot.

"Who was that man and why was he kissing you?" Joe grumped.

Wearing those awful mirrored sunglasses civilians like myself hate, he leaned against his blue and white SAN SEBASTIAN SHERIFF cruiser with his arms crossed. He couldn't have looked more intimidating.

But time had taught me Joe was more bark than bite.

"His name is Frasier Morgan and he's an old school chum. As for why he was kissing me— on my hand, I'd like to remind you—he just got divorced and he's lonely. Not that I'm going to do anything about it. For your information, I jerked my hand away immediately, but you and your mom had already taken off, so you didn't see that." I took a breath. "By the way, I have a couple of questions for you, too."

"Uh, Teddy, I can't…"

"What in the world were you and my mother doing, leaving me notes on the *Merilee*?"

"We'd both tried to call you and didn't get an answer. So we were worried."

"'We'? Since when are you and my mother in cahoots?"

The mirrored sunglasses couldn't hide his flinch. "She came by my office in a panic, convinced that you were in immediate danger. Frankly, I'd been worried about the same thing. Anyway, she begged me to help convince you to move up to her house, so I went along with it. If I overreacted, I'm sorry. My only excuse is that case is...is…" He stuttered to a halt.

"One more question. Could you please take off those awful sunglasses? I don't like talking to mirrors."

When he complied, his eyes were the same sweet blue I'd always known, but today they were crinkled with worry. "Honey, has it occurred to you how much danger you may be in? Two people are dead and you knew both of them."

"I didn't know Amberlyn Lofland."

"Her phone says you did. You called her the day before she was killed."

There was no point in denying the obvious

truth. "Sounds like you've been in touch with the Santa Cruz Police Department."

"They reached out to me, yes. Why were you at Ms. Lofland's apartment shortly after that phone call?"

Maybe I had some wiggle room here. "Who says I was there?"

"The lady in 4A said she saw a woman with fuzzy red hair wearing, and I quote 'one of those all-purpose little black dresses' visit Ms. Lofland the afternoon before the murder."

"Every redhead has one of those things."

"She also described the bump on your nose. Haven't I warned you about getting mixed up in serious cases? It's bad enough that you visited one of the suspects in jail, but now you've actually been seen with the killer's other victim."

"*Other* victim? So ballistics has tied the same firearm to both murders?"

"I didn't say that."

"Not in so many words."

Joe stepped away from the cruiser and stood so close to me that I could smell fresh after-shave. Aha! He'd primped before stopping by. "You know what, Teddy? I think your mother is right. Why don't you move in with her until this case clears? That way neither of us will have to worry about you."

I closed the few inches left between us. "I'll take it under consideration, Sheriff. In the meantime, why don't you follow me home in that great big cruiser of yours?"

He caught his breath. "You're impossible, you know that?"

"Yeah, and you love it."

Chapter Twelve

Despite the wonderful night we had shared on the *Merilee*, the next morning Joe refused to give up any information about the investigation.

I nibbled at his earlobe, which he'd always enjoyed. "Did the same gun kill Booth and Amberlyn?"

"No comment." He kissed me on the neck for the hundredth time.

"Rifle or handgun?"

"No comment."

"Any suspects? Besides Lila, I mean."

"No comment."

"Besides the nude pictures of Amberlyn on Booth's phone, were there pictures of any other naked females?"

"No comment."

"You're the one who's impossible!"

"Said the pot to the kettle."

"Oh, Joe, please!"

"'Oh, Joe, please,' what?" he asked.

"Oh, please, do that again."

He complied.

An hour later, while leaving the *Merilee*, Joe said over his shoulder, "Phone your mother."

I did, but waited until my lunch break at the zoo. Then I hit speed dial on my cell and steeled myself to eat a generous helping of crow.

Caro answered immediately. "It's about time you called." Her voice was so loud it could be heard several tables away.

"Look, Mother, I…"

"*Caro!*"

"Sorry, Caro. I know you've been worried about me, but it's not necessary. I've promised Joe I won't involve myself in the Booth investigation."

"Do you have your fingers crossed behind your back, Theodora?"

"No," I lied.

Several snickers from nearby zookeepers who could see my crossed fingers.

"You realize you could get killed," Caro continued. "After all, you were almost killed the last time. And the time before that."

"People exaggerate."

"The sheriff person doesn't!"

The lunchroom fell ominously silent.

I lowered my voice and hissed into the phone, "Could you please stop shouting?"

"Don't you tell me what to do!" she yelled.

"I didn't 'tell' you anything, I asked. Politely. I even said 'please.' And as for that 'sheriff person,' you mean Joe? The *person* you've been hanging around with all week?"

"We weren't 'hanging around,' we were on a mission."

A vision of the Blues Brothers popped into my brain; they'd been on a mission, too. "And that was?"

"To save you from yourself."

"I don't need saving."

"Yes, you do, you foolish girl. If something happened to you…" Her voice trailed off for a moment, and unless I was wrong, I heard sniffles. Caro being Caro, she recovered immediately. "Well, enough of that. You need to come up here and stay where you're safe until this murder investigation is over." A gasp. "What's that? Is someone shooting at you?"

"I'm in the zoo's lunchroom and the bear keeper just put popcorn in the microwave." Within seconds the air reeked of run-down movie house. I covered my nose, but it didn't work. How could something so delicious smell so bad?

"Well, it sounded like gunshots, Theodora."

"I'm perfectly safe here at the zoo, Caro. We have armed park rangers. If worse comes to worst, I can hide in the tigers' night house." I chuckled to make sure she knew it was a joke. "And as for my moving in with you, sorry, but I prefer living at my own place."

"That awful, leaky boat?"

"The *Merilee* doesn't leak. She's not awful, either. In fact, she's in great shape for her age. Maybe you need to come spend the weekend at the harbor with me and learn what a pleasant boat she is. You'd wake up in the morning and smell that fresh sea air…" There was no way Caro would even spend a night on anything less than a five-star yacht, but the longer I talked, the easier it was to lead her away from her favorite subject. Me. Back home. Where she could spend her life making my life miserable.

It worked.

A sniff. "I'm sick of hearing about that boat, but there's something you can do for me."

Here it came, a second helping of crow. This time with giblet gravy.

"I'm in a bit of a fix," she said. "You remember my old friend, Miriam Haight-Smitherton? From San Francisco? Well, she and her family just moved down here permanently, and she encouraged me to join Keep Our Shoreline Clean with her. The things we do for our friends, eh? The upshot is, I promised to host their monthly dinner meeting Friday. For the speaker, I booked that nice vet at UC Davis to discuss the otter situation, which as you know, I'm very concerned about. But this morning she called and said she couldn't do it, that she'd all of a sudden remembered she had to be somewhere else that evening. Hmph! People these days! Anyway, that leaves me with you. All you need to do is give a brief talk about otters or harbor seals or whatever it is you're into these days, just as long as it lives in the ocean. Oh, and make it educational. From some of the things I've heard the other members say, they're a bit clueless about wildlife."

When I recovered from my shock enough to speak, I yelped, "*You joined KOSC? You have got to be kidding me!*"

Upon hearing me speak the infamous

acronym, the other zookeepers started paying attention again. The bear keeper, even turned off the microwave so he and the others could hear better.

"I just told you I did. Weren't you listening?"

It was my turn to shout. "You said you joined an ecology group!"

Despite its name, Keep Our Shoreline Clean had nothing to do with keeping litter off the shoreline; it had everything to do with keeping people off. That is to say, certain kinds of people, such as teachers, hairdressers, bank tellers, and farm laborers. As far as KOSC was concerned, God forbid a gazillionaire had to share the beach with riff-raff.

Caro sounded offended at my tone. "What's wrong with you? Of course I joined KOSC. I care what's been happening to our shoreline. Empty beer cans, plastic bags… Horrible! Besides Miriam, of course, I don't know the members well at all, but they're some of San Sebastian County's finest people. This county has been good to us Bentleys and it's time we returned the favor. The dinner will be a nice start."

"Nice start?" I snorted. "I'd rather help a giraffe through a breech birth than sit through a Keep Our Shoreline Clean function."

"I'll pretend I didn't hear that. If you'd prefer not to, you don't have to eat with us. Just give your spiel about otters or something, and I'll make certain you're in and out in less than an hour."

Ignoring my protests, Caro reeled off the guest list, some of whom surprised me, some of whom didn't. But when she got to Harper Betancourt-Booth I snapped to attention. "Does Harper know you want me there?"

"She thinks the UC Davis vet will be there, but what does it matter?"

It was a good thing my mother couldn't see my sour smile over the phone. "We've never really gotten along."

"She was perfectly nice to you during the funeral reception."

Observant, my mother is not. But I surprised her by agreeing to give a talk. "I'll even shower for the occasion," I added.

"Smarty pants!" But she giggled. Being obeyed always put Caro in a good mood.

On that note, she hung up.

"You're actually going to attend a KOSC meeting?" asked Jack Spence, turning the microwave back on. The bear keeper sounded outraged.

"Hasn't anyone told you it's not polite to eavesdrop?"

This brought a communal laugh from the other zookeepers, eavesdroppers all.

"But honestly, Teddy," said Robin Chase, only slightly less outraged than Jack, "if those snobs get their way, the entire coastline of California will be reserved for property owners only."

Ah, nothing like being the winner in a love triangle to turn a shy gal bold. But even though it looked like the Sumatran tiger on Robin's arm tattoo was snarling at me, I stood my ground. "I have my reasons for going."

My explanation, vague as it was, convinced no one, so a few minutes later—leaving behind a chorus of frowns—I headed for Down Under and the less judgmental koalas.

It was a day for miracles. The koalas, all three of them, were actually awake when I arrived, and Wanchu wanted to get picked up. I complied.

"Who's my sweet girl?" I cooed as she wrapped her furry arms around my neck.

"*Awwharl, awwharl!*"

A koala's voice isn't nearly as cute as the animal; it sounds like an aggrieved grizzly bear clearing its throat. In fact, the noise was so startling that it made Wanchu's joey pop his head out of her pouch and study her.

"*Eeep?*" he asked.

"*Awwharl, awwharl!*"

Satisfied that all was well, the joey pulled his head back in.

Since Wanchu was used in the zoo's popular "Name That Animal!" children's production, being carried around had become part of her daily routine. So with her cuddled in my arms, we paced the enclosure together until she grew tired and began to look longingly at the fake tree where her mate had just dozed off.

"Nighty night," I told her, handing her over to a friendly tree limb. Before I could walk away, she was snoring.

The only thing bad about working at a zoo is that the days pass by too quickly. After saying good-bye to Wanchu, it seemed only minutes before I was on the *Merilee* watching Bonz and Miss Priss eating their dinner. Once they were through, I gave Bonz a long walk through the park, but when we returned I didn't feel like sitting around and watching *Animal Planet* reruns, as was my usual evening pastime. Besides, I hadn't done any grocery shopping for a week, and my cupboard was almost as bare as Old Mother Hubbard's. Hoping to snag an invitation to dinner, I called Joe, only to reach his voice mail. He wasn't still angry with me—last night had proven that—but a county sheriff's hours were more irregular than a zookeeper's. Something had happened somewhere and he was out trying to fix it.

Reminding myself to shop on the way home from the zoo the next day, I gave up trying to make a meal out of nothing but flour, sugar, and mustard, and walked down to Phil's Fish Market, where the Wednesday special was always *Frutti Di Mare*, bits of sea food served on angel hair pasta.

The hostess who led me to my table turned out to be Lila Conyers, wearing an ensemble of my castoffs: a navy blue dress with pink pin-striping, snazzed up by a pair of strappy pink sandals. Although she looked better in the outfit than I ever had, the court-ordered ankle bracelet somewhat spoiled the effect.

Happy for her, I congratulated Lila on her new job, but she shook her head.

"It's only temporary. Phil's full-time hostess got called for jury duty."

"Maybe it'll be a long trial."

"Petty theft. Word is, there's a plea deal coming."

"Oh. Sorry."

Reverting to her hostess persona, she asked, "Do you prefer an indoor table or an outside one?"

I scanned the dining room and found it even more crowded than usual, but the patio overlooking the harbor still had two empty tables. One table in particular, although occupied, interested me. "Outside is fine, and why don't you seat me with Dr. Morrell?"

"You know him?"

"He used to date my mother."

Lila looked impressed, as well she should, since her original life plan had been to work at Blue Seas Marine Laboratory.

With a hopeful look on her face, she led me to his table, where Preston proclaimed himself happy to make room for me.

"We have to stop meeting like this," he said, giving me a wink. "People will begin to talk."

"They already are," I smirked back. As I settled myself down, I gave Lila my order, and once she handed it off to the nearby waitress, she returned to the hostess station to help someone else.

"Did you know that our hostess majored in Marine Science," I asked Preston, "and that she's looking for a job?"

A kindly smile. "Beauty *and* brains, an unbeatable combination. So why is such a paragon of the female gender working as a hostess?"

By the time my dinner arrived, I had talked Preston into giving Lila an interview the next morning. Aware her police record would show up on her background check, I also gave him her reasons for spray-painting Booth's boat.

Preston was all sympathy. "That man was a menace. If there's a Hell—and when I hear stuff like this I hope there is—Booth's frying there right now. But before you ask, his file at Blue Seas is still sealed. Although…" He paused for a minute, looking down at his mostly eaten *Frutti Di Mare.* "….when I interview her, I promise that I'll take all that into account. But it's too bad she didn't finish her education. The person she would be replacing was already working on his master's, and I was hoping for someone with similar qualifications."

"If I remember correctly, Blue Seas fronted his tuition."

"Only because we'd received a large grant. Given this administration, though…"

I wasn't about to talk politics with him, so I interjected, "May I ask how much the grant was for?"

He named a six-figure amount that reminded me of Amberlyn's desperation before a killer had ended her dreams. "All the woman needs is a chance."

"I'll tell my secretary to put her on the interview list. Can't promise anything, though."

"Couldn't ask for more."

Good deed done for the day, I stopped hyping Lila as soon as my *Frutti Di Mare* arrived. It was delicious.

The first thing I did the next morning was stop by Admin to discuss the Japanese macaque situation with Zorah.

She listened carefully, then nodded in agreement. "Clarabelle sounds like the perfect solution. A new female would keep Kabuki busy enough to stay out of trouble. And he'll be good for her, too. He's always been a big hit with the ladies. If Aster Edwina approves, I'll call the National today and see what we can do. They've owed us a favor ever since we took that cockatoo off their hands. The darned thing can cuss in six languages!"

We spent a few minutes discussing the difficulties of re-training foul-mouthed fowl before Zorah said, "Why don't you call Aster Edwina yourself about Kabuki? You two have always been thick as fleas."

"Not lately, we haven't."

She raised her eyebrows. "What's she ticked off about now?" A longtime resident of San Sebastian County, Zorah had known Aster Edwina almost as long as I had. And anyone who knew the old harridan, however slightly, had at least once been burned by her scorching temper.

With a sigh, I explained, "She's demanding that I keep her abreast of the murder investigation, but Joe won't cooperate. Not only that, but my mother's convinced I'm about to be murdered and is strong-arming me to move in with her up at Old Town."

Zorah made a face. "Sucks to be you. Okay, I'll call Aster Edwina myself and see what kind of deal we can work out with the National. As for now, don't you have places to go, animals to feed? I've got a busy morning ahead."

She waggled her hand toward the door, where

a half-dozen zookeepers waited in line, each carrying a large manila file folder with a picture of an animal on the cover. From the looks of things, the first zookeeper wanted to talk about a wildebeest.

That evening I tuned into some more *Animal Planet* reruns while waiting for Joe to call, but after watching the late edition of the local news, I realized it wasn't going to happen. A smiling news anchor reporting from the scene of an accident said that sixteen-year-old twin brothers, thinking it was a great idea to drink and drive, had wrapped their father's Lexus around a tree. The camera zoomed in on Joe and his blood-splattered uniform. He was holding one boy's hand as the EMTs carried him toward an ambulance to join his brother. The boy was sobbing, and from the expression on Joe's face, I could see he wasn't happy, either.

Unfazed by this backdrop of misery, the news anchor chirped, "And in yet another accident on the PCH, but this one has a happier ending! The EMTs on the scene say the eighteen-year-old girl who was texting while driving suffered no major injuries from her drift into the water-filled ditch. She might even be released from the hospital tomorrow morning."

I turned off the TV and asked Bonz if he wanted another "walkies." Taking his tail-wagging for a yes, I grabbed his leash and off we went.

Usually Bonz and I take the Gunn Landing Park's coastal pathway, but this time I chose the East Fork, which wound inland. Always well-lit by streetlights designed to look like carriage lamps, the path boasted gravel walkways lined with irregular-shaped rocks, most the size of softballs. Because of the area's lush vegetation—chaparral, evening primrose, Pacific silverweed, and coyote bush—East Fork provided a nice break from the constant view of the ocean.

Tonight was no exception. As we ambled along under the moonlight, we met up with several of Bonz's favorites, most importantly the tiny poodle he'd enjoyed a celibate romance with for the past year. Tonight, MiouMiou had on a pink rhinestone-studded jacket that matched her painted toenails. The two dogs sniffed and nipped and danced like old lovers, but for obvious reasons it came to nothing. Sara and Jake Montini, MiouMiou's owners, who lived on the *Rising Sun*, a sixty-five-foot trimaran moored at the ritzy north end of the harbor, were volunteers at the San Sebastian County No Kill Animal Shelter. Both understood the need for keeping the dog and cat population under control.

All sweet assignations must end, so when the Montinis led MiouMiou back toward the harbor, Bonz and I continued our walk. It was a peaceful night, warm and pleasant, and other harbor-dwellers had turned out in full force. We even ran into Kenny Norgaard, taking a rare off-boat amble.

"Shurprised to see you, dear heart," he slurred. "You too, Bonz."

Not bothered by Kenny's poor enunciation, Bonz wagged his stump of a tail and sniffed at Kenny's Topsiders.

"Why surprised? I walk Bonz every evening."

He gave me a tipsy grin. "Oh, you know, becaush of the murders, and you being a woman living all by yourshelf. Don'tcha think you oughta be more careful?"

"Thanks for your concern, Kenny, but Bonz and I are fine. And as you can see…" I gestured toward another group of liveaboarders coming along the path, "…we're as safe here as we would be at Food 4 Less."

"Heard they had a robbery there las' week."

"Kids stealing beer. Hardly Bonnie and Clyde."

"Theresh coyotes, too." Here he vented a gaseous burp. "They come down from the hills, eat little bunnies."

Mother Nature; red in tooth and claw. "We haven't seen coyotes this close to the harbor in months. Now, you take care getting to the *High Life*, okay? I wouldn't want to see you fall into that nasty harbor water."

My own warning delivered, Bonz and I moved on.

But as we walked along the trail, I remembered hearing a report of a possibly rabid coyote loose in San Sebastian County. Local wildlife officials hadn't been able to confirm the sighting but in his booze-addled way, Kenny might have had a point. Deciding to cut our walk short—just in case—I let Bonz water one more tree, then turned around.

It was only later, when I'd plunked myself in front of the TV again, that I began thinking about Kenny's warning: *You being a woman living all by yourshelf. Don'tcha think you oughta be more careful?*

Did he know something I didn't?

Chapter Thirteen

Friday evening finally rolled around, and with it Caro's dinner party for the detestable Keep Our Shoreline Clean high-muckity-mucks. I incurred Caro's wrath by arriving late—strawberry crepes were being served—but her good humor returned when we moved into the sitting room where I launched into my speech about the necessity of an unpolluted seacoast.

Pretending to listen were mother's San Francisco friend, Miriam Haight-Smitherton, wearing a red Chanel; recently widowed Harper Betancourt-Booth, sporting a non-funereal pink Gucci; Harper's more somberly clad father, Miles Stephenson Betancourt IV; Angus MacPherson, the publisher of the *San Sebastian Journal*; several local millionaires, whose names I didn't bother to memorize; and—irritatingly enough—Betancourt lackey Frasier Morgan, whose pesky phone calls I had never returned.

The dull glaze on everyone's eyes sparked into anger when I gave my summation.

"So there you have it. Our beautiful Pacific is in trouble. Not only do we still have the cruel and continuing practice of shark-finning, but we're seeing increased numbers of whale strandings, deaths of sea lions from eating fish poisoned by comoic acid, otters dying from toxoplasma gondii, and the kelp forests—upon which so many marine animals rely on for food and shelter—are being destroyed. Global warming? You betcha! The oceans are getting warmer, and that's hastening the destruction. If those problems aren't enough, the ecosystem of the Pacific is being further harmed by the oil platforms along the seacoast. Platforms such as Prime Pacific's own Pacific Pride, right off Gunn Landing Harbor."

During this last I glared at Miles Stephenson Betancourt IV, CEO of Prime Pacific Oil. He glared back.

Satisfied, I added the *de rigueur*, "Thank you for your kind attention. Now enjoy your brandy. Or port. Or whatever."

The only person who clapped was Caro.

My attempt to coax Harper Betancourt-Booth into a conversation failed. She had instinctively loathed me before tonight, and now I'd gone and given her a reason. Oh, well.

After bolting down the remains of my Pedro Ximenez Triana Hidalgo, I gathered my things to leave. I had almost made it to the door when Frasier approached, his red nose leading the way. "I didn't know you felt that way about oil platforms." He no longer seemed as taken by my charms as he had during the dinner we'd shared at Fork.

"You never asked."

"Look, I can understand why some people are nervous because of that blowout in the Gulf, but there's no need to be. Prime Pacific itself has a flawless safety record. And the need for oil and petroleum products is universal. Without it, you wouldn't have gas for your pickup truck or lipstick for that pretty mouth of yours. And, uh, why haven't you returned my calls?"

It was time to bite the bullet, which frankly, was preferable to being drawn into another argument about off-shore drilling. "I'm sorry, Frasier, but we have nothing in common. Besides, I'm engaged. Didn't my mother tell you?"

He shook his head. "But then why would she…?"

"Caro doesn't like my fiancé."

"Could the lucky man be someone I know?"

"Joe Rejas."

"You don't mean Sheriff Joe Rejas!" His eyes widened. I hadn't noticed before, but they were nice eyes.

"Yeah, him."

Frasier stood there blinking for a few moments, then leaned forward and gave me a quick peck on the cheek. "Well, congratulations, then. But if something happens to change your mind, you have my phone number."

With that, he rejoined the Betancourts, who were still glaring at me.

The next day—Saturday—was a whirlwind of activity at the zoo. Four church buses dropped off seventy-five young parishioners and their parents to attend our "Name That Animal!" show, where various zookeepers trotted out their less-lethal charges. The avian world was represented by a singing macaw (her favorite song was Beyoncé's "Single Ladies"); big cats, by El Capitan, our leash-trained ocelot; marsupials, by Wanchu, the huggy koala; and various examples of other species, including a hedgehog, a tortoise, an iguana, and even a hand-raised penguin who, like the macaw, "sang" on cue.

Much laughter and cheering all around.

Saturday was a great day for weekday nine-to-fivers, too, and they formed long lines to see Magnus, our polar bear cub. Business was also booming on Tropics Trail, where anteater pup Little Ricky entertained his admirers by jumping on and off Lucy's back.

It was especially crowded over at the Japanese macaque enclosure, partially because of the rumors about our shit-slinging monkey. Those who wanted to see the action were disappointed, because Kabuki had been moved off-exhibit to a smaller habitat in hopes the semi-isolation would calm him down. In the meantime, Zorah had received an agreement from Aster Edwina to begin negotiations to procure Clarabelle from the National Zoo in D.C. Love, we hoped, would conquer all.

Feeling sorry for the off-exhibit monkey, I visited him in his night house, where he gazed at me with sad eyes.

"See what happens when you don't behave?"

Grunt.

"But I do have some good news for you."

Grunt.

"You may be getting a new girlfriend soon."

Grunt?

"Her name's Clarabelle."

Grunt!

"Oh, quit bothering him, Teddy," snapped Myra Sebrowski, who had entered the night house area while Kabuki and I were having our scintillating conversation.

"He's lonely."

Looking crankier than usual, she snapped, "Of course he's lonely! Who wouldn't be, sitting here alone all day? Zorah and I discussed the possibility of bringing one of the females over to keep him company, but in the end we decided not to because…"

Her radio crackled. "Keeper One to Keeper Eight, come in." Zorah.

Myra snatched the radio off her belt. "Keeper Eight here. Over."

"Clarabelle's a go. We'll receive her Tuesday after next. I've already alerted Quarantine. Over."

"Thanks for letting me know. Over." Myra sounded pleased, as well she should.

"And just so you know, Myra, Jack Spence came in to talk about Magnus, so if you see Teddy, tell her..."

Keeper Four—me—interrupted. "There's nothing wrong with him, I hope! Over."

"Who? Jack, or the bear?" Zorah's laugh told me that whatever Jack's news, it wasn't serious. "Both are fine. What I was going to tell Myra before you so rudely cut in, is that on the way to Admin, Jack ran across your mother. She's looking for you, so consider yourself warned. Keeper One, over and out."

Crackle, hiss, silence.

As Myra had listened to the news about Clarabelle, the crankiness left her face. Not caring a whit about the Caro situation, she turned to Kabuki, and said, "Hey, handsome, you hear that? A new love's on her way to light up your life. And you, hers."

Putting the discomfort of Caro's looming visit aside, I figured Myra's lightened mood gave me the chance to dig for some information. "Speaking of love, Myra, I've been checking around and found out that you once took a class from Stuart Booth. Did you ever notice him display untoward behavior with his female students?"

Some of the crankiness returned. "Didn't I tell you to mind your own business?"

"Oh, did you? Sorry, can't remember."

She made a guttural sound similar to those I'd heard Kabuki make, but instead of stalking away, she stayed put. "You are just so...so..." Another guttural sound. "All right. Since it's obvious you're not going to stop hounding me about this, here's my answer. No, I *never* noticed Professor Booth 'display untoward behavior' to his female students. And since you're all set to follow up by asking, hell, no, I did not have an affair with him. But I'll tell you this. I happen to think that in the past he got a raw deal, instigated by a bunch of whiners who couldn't take being rejected and filed harassment complaints out of revenge. Now go piss off to your koalas and leave me alone!"

On my way to Down Under, where I hoped Caro wouldn't find me, I replayed what Myra had said. A "bunch" of whiners, meaning more than one.

Lila, I already knew about. As for Amberlyn, there was no way she would have made a complaint about Booth; their relationship was too financially rewarding. Besides, Amberlyn had never been his student. Who else?

After doing some quick math in my head, I came up with a name. Then, to confirm my suspicion, I reversed course and headed for the big cat enclosure. But I never made it. Before I reached the top of the hill, my luck ran out.

Caro spotted me.

And she was waving a newspaper.

"Did you read this?" she demanded, when I reached her. She looked chic as usual, but the teal Fendi jumpsuit clashed terribly with her rage-red face.

"What is it now, Mo… Caro?"

Instead of answering, she asked another question. "Why didn't you tell me what that awful group was actually into?"

A group of zoo visitors made a wide circle around her. For all they knew, she was just another nut on a rampage. Come to think of it, they may have been right.

"Are you talking about the Keep Our Shoreline Clean people?" I asked Caro.

"Of course I am!" She flapped the newspaper at me again. It was the *San Sebastian Journal*.

To give myself a chance to think, I looked up at the sky. Clear blue. Not much happening there. Sighing, I returned my gaze to my mother's furious face. "Thanks to Miriam

Haight-Smitherton, you'd already joined, so what did you expect me to do? Demand you drop your membership? You know I don't work that way. Now, is there something in that newspaper you want me to see, or are you going to paddle me with it?"

Her face grew redder. "I *never* paddled you! Neither did your father." She narrowed her eyes. "Maybe that's where we went wrong." She shoved the newspaper at me. "Read and weep!"

Since it was already open to the Op Ed page, it didn't take long to find the article that had upset my mother. Over an unflattering picture of me with my mouth open ran the headline:

ZOOKEEPER BITES HAND
THAT FEEDS HER

An editorial by Angus McClusky,
Publisher of the San Sebastian Journal

While giving a talk at the monthly meeting of Keep Our Shoreline Clean, the zookeeping oil heiress Theodora Iona Esmeralda Bentley managed to insult every member of that illustrious board.

I looked up. "Oil heiress? What the...?"

"Shut up and keep reading."

Citing highly questionable figures from poorly researched studies, Ms. Bentley drew a parallel between oil platform production and the deaths of sea life in the Monterey Bay area.

"Hey, I didn't..."
"Keep reading."

Cooler temperaments and better educated minds know that Ms. Bentley's claims are faux science. Regardless of her pronouncements, sea life actually thrives beneath oil platforms like our beautiful platform, Prime Pride. As for global warming, that claim has also been proven to be utter nonsense. A one-degree Fahrenheit rise in ocean temperatures over the past one hundred years is hardly anything to panic about.

Perhaps instead of spewing falsehoods, Ms. Bentley—whose wealthy father bankrupted his own company by absconding with several million dollars—should stick to matters she knows something about.

I yelped a string of obscenities, making a couple of passersby frown.

"My thoughts, too," Caro said, primly. "How dare Angus write about you like that? I'm so sorry I no longer own any stock in that rag of his, because if I still did, I'd demand his resignation from the *Journal's* board."

I gave her a look. "No longer? Do you mean we, uh, the Bentleys used to own stock in that newspaper?"

"Yes, but that was before your father took off for Costa Rica."

I was almost afraid to ask the next question but I did anyway. "This 'oil heiress' thing. What's that all about?"

"I've always believed in a well-rounded portfolio."

"Please don't tell me you're one of Prime Pacific's stockholders!"

She looked down at the trail, across which a dung beetle was busily rolling its latest treasure. She put out a protective, Jimmy Choo-shod foot to keep one of the passersby from stepping on it. "Then I won't."

As soon as the dung beetle had made it across the trail unsquashed, Caro cleared her throat and added, "I dumped my shares this morning. At a loss, I might add. That was even before I cancelled my membership in Keep Our Shoreline Clean. As for Miriam Haight-Smitherton, I don't know what I ever saw in that snob in the first place."

Caro might have been many things—irritating, vain, greedy—but she had always been a fiercely protective mother. Moved, I gave her a hug.

"Phew, Teddy, you stink," she protested, once I released her.

Zoos are popular places for weddings, and by noon, two marriage ceremonies had been completed—one near Monkey Mania, the other in the middle of Friendly Farm, with Alejandro acting as best man, and a carnation-festooned goat as flower girl. A third was scheduled for three p.m. on the stone platform that jutted over the lake surrounding Lemur Island, our new red-ruffed lemur exhibit.

Animals just being animals had forced the lemurs' move from their old home, which had once been situated directly across from the howler monkeys. For some reason Chairman

Mao, the alpha male howler, had taken a dislike to Gumbo, the alpha lemur. Mao was vocal about his dislike, and either by design or accident had trained his family of four females and three adolescents to help him complain. If you've ever heard howlers—they sound something like poorly tuned jet engines—you can imagine the misery this chorus of bellows caused everyone. It irked the lemurs enough that they had screeched back. A red-ruffed lemur's alarm call isn't pretty, either, and in their own way, their decibel levels almost reach the howlers' volume.

Noisy or not, the stone overlook, just down the hill from the giant anteater enclosure, has become an increasingly popular venue for weddings. Twenty feet in diameter, the overlook can accommodate the major stars of the wedding party—bride, groom, minister, best man, flower girl, etc.—and the long cement apron in front of it can handle approximately fifty guests. Perfect for small weddings. Safe, too. There was a three-foot-high rock wall around the edge of the overlook, and the lake itself was fenced off, discouraging tipsy guests from taking a refreshing plunge.

But safety measures can only go so far, because

in any environment popular with children, accidents will happen. I had just let myself into the giant anteaters' enclosure after stowing Lucy and her baby safely in the small adjoining pen, when a boy of about eight fell while running down the hill. His own shriek almost matched the howler monkeys', who were sounding off in the distance. It looked like a nasty fall—the boy had pretty much shredded the skin across his knees—so I left the enclosure and hurried to his side. By the time I reached him, his parents had appeared. The father was telling him to "man up," while the mother held her son's hand and murmured encouraging words.

"We need to get him to First Aid," I told them. "Let me bring my cart around and I'll take you there." I hurried behind the anteaters' enclosure, jumped into the cart, and ferried the family to the First Aid Station near the zoo's entrance. By the time we reached it, the boy had indeed manned up.

"It's nothing," he told his weeping mother. "Just a little blood."

While waiting for the ambulance to arrive—several stitches were needed—I chatted with Bradley Morris, our on-staff EMT. By one o'clock, he told me, the tally at the gate had been nine thousand, three hundred and fifty-two visitors, three-quarters of them children. By two o'clock, two other children had visited the First Aid Station with skinned knees, the standard injury, and an adult male had needed a two-inch gauze compress after banging his head against a rock ledge near the cougar enclosure; he had been too busy talking on his cell phone to notice he'd veered off the well-marked trail.

"Crowded like we are today," Bradley said, "we're lucky the casualty count hasn't been higher."

"The day's not over yet," I said.

I returned to the anteater enclosure just in time to see the wedding party for the scheduled three o'clock troop by.

Like most modern weddings, the party included a videographer, and I noticed that Lucy had caught not only his discerning eye, but the flower girl's, too. The five-or-something-year-old dug in her pink patent leather heels and refused to go any further unless she was given a ride on the "long-nosed horsie."

Despite her cherubic looks—sky-blue eyes, blond ringlets, the whole nine yards—I could recognize a hellion when I saw one, so I patiently explained that an anteater's temperament was more akin to a tiger's than a horsie's, but if she wanted, after the wedding I might be able to give her a ride on a llama. If it was okay with her mother, of course.

"Alejandro especially loves young ladies in pink dresses," I told her.

Turning to a heavyset woman of around fifty, who was stuffed into an expensive but unflattering paisley print dress, the child said, "You better let me, Mommy. Or else."

Mommy murmured, "Whatever you want, darling."

Ah. A "surprise" baby, and obviously spoiled.

"Got 'em!" announced the Hollywood-handsome videographer. He had taken advantage of the wedding party's brief stop to film Lucy and Little Ricky. "Got that noisy group of monkeys, too."

"They're howlers," I said.

"And so aptly named." With that, he and the rest of the wedding party moved on.

As the very young bride passed by, I studied her dress, a frothy affair which had probably been purchased from Gabrielle's, the outrageously expensive wedding boutique in Carmel. The strapless sweetheart neckline showcased the bride's thin, fashion-model shoulders, while the belle-of-the-ball skirt encompassed yards and yards of misty tulle and hand-beaded lace appliqués. It probably cost more than my truck and boat combined. As if recognizing my state of near-penury, the bride lifted her chin and gave me an arrogant stare.

Oh, well. Good marriages aren't based on beaded lace appliqués alone.

Roughly ten minutes later, shrieks began emanating from the direction of Lemur Island. At first I ignored them because it was close to the red-ruffed lemurs' feeding time, and they always started calling for their keeper well in advance. But as I listened more carefully, I realized the shrieks were human.

I dropped my rake and ran down the hill toward Lemur Lake. Upon reaching the overlook, I saw the wedding party leaning over the stone wall, calling out encouragement to someone in the water below.

"Outta my way!" I yelled, shoving aside the mother of the little girl who had wanted a ride on the "horsie."

"My baby!" she yelled, attempting to heave her heavy bulk over the three-foot-high wall.

Baby?

I looked down at the water five feet below,

where I saw the tiny flower girl struggling in the water. She had somehow fallen in and was so mired in mud and reeds she couldn't pull herself free. Her tearless face signaled she wasn't hurt, just frustrated at her inability to move. Good. The water was only two feet deep in this area, so she was in little danger of drowning. That was the extent of her good luck, because she had landed mere inches away from the trumpeter swans' nest, where several day-old cygnets sat waiting for their parents to bring them dinner.

The cygnets peep-honked, sounding an alarm at the girl's intrusion into their territory. Their panicked calls summoned Romeo and Juliet, the zoo's mated pair, foraging less than ten yards away. Romeo, the larger of the two, jerked his head out of the water, took one look at the little girl, then began to paddle madly to take care of this perceived threat to his babies. He was in full battle mode. Honking. Wings up. Feathers bristling.

And Mama Juliet was right behind him.

Trumpeter swans may be beautiful, but they are quick to defend their babies with beating wings and slashing bills. The injuries inflicted by these large birds aren't as minor as you might think. A peck from a swan's bill can take out an eye, and a blow from an enraged trumpeter's four-foot-long wing has been known to break an adult human's leg. God only knows what one could do to a five-year-old child.

If they reached her…

I vaulted over the stone wall and landed in the lake halfway between the struggling child and the oncoming trumpeter swan. Sodden from my plunge, I had just managed to haul the child out of the swan poop-infused mud when something large and white fluttered across my line of sight. It hit the reeking water with a splash. Juliet, taking wing? Holding the girl by one arm and wiping my wet hair out of my eyes with the other, I finally managed to see what had landed in the water.

The bride.

"*My sissy!*" the former fashion plate screamed, floundering through the muck toward the child, her exquisite wedding dress collecting reeds, lily pads, and swan poop as she sloshed her way toward us. "*Don't you let that monster get my sissy!*"

Not to be outdone in the heroism sweepstakes, the groom followed his bride into the water. Now four of us—including the giggling flower girl—stood facing down the enraged Romeo. No birdbrain, Romeo honked a final threat, then paddled around us in a wide arc to reach his cygnets. Juliet, also honking, followed his lead.

Crisis averted, we slogged ashore, where I was delighted to find my radio still worked. The park ranger on the other end had just assured me help was on its way when the cute little cause of all this mess finally spoke up.

"I want my llama ride now!"

Chapter Fourteen

"Well, aren't you the media queen?" Kenny Norgaard called to me as I squished past his *High Life* in my still-soggy boots.

Due to my habit of leaving a clean uniform in my locker, I was at least wearing dry clothes, but I hadn't thought to include a spare pair of boots. Oh, well.

"Media queen?" I asked Kenny. "You mean that nasty Op Ed piece in the *Journal*?"

"That, too, and by the way I deeply deplore its tone, dear heart, but that's mere small-town stuff. I'm talking about your latest TV triumph."

I stopped. "What are you talking about? My Tuesday gig on KGNN?"

To my surprise, Darleene Bauer emerged from the *High Life*'s cabin. "No, silly. You've been all over the six o'clock news and now they're getting ready to feature you on CNN. Come and see."

Curious, I clambered aboard *High Life* to find Lila Conyers and Ruth Donohue huddled around the big plasma television set in Kenny's cabin, which at one time had been quite nice. No one's attention was on the ruined mahogany and brass fittings, it was on the TV, which at the moment was airing a deodorant commercial. "You'll smell like a flower all day," the announcer promised.

Don't I wish.

The announcer, a svelte brunette wearing a skinny black dress, disappeared, replaced by a giggling Anderson Cooper.

"And now for the hilarious video we promised you earlier. A rescue of sorts went down a couple hours ago at a Monterey Bay-area zoo."

Cooper's white-on-white face disappeared, replaced by the little flower girl's rosy-cheeked one. The videographer had caught her standing on the overlook at the lake, holding a bouquet of flowers. As the camera panned in, she climbed onto the stone wall, and said, "Watch me! I'm gonna visit the baby birdies!"

Before anyone could stop her, she jumped off the wall.

The videographer must have had excellent equipment, because the sound system picked up the splash of the girl hitting the water.

Not to mention the following screams.

The video sped up, and next thing you know, there was I, making my own leap off the wall into the lake. The camera caught my embrace of the girl and gave me a nice close-up as I clutched her to my chest and turned my back on the approaching trumpeter swan, prepared to get my butt pecked to a fare-thee-well.

Then there was another loud splash as the bride arrived, bringing much tulle and hand-beaded appliqués.

The groom's splash followed.

Here came Romeo and Juliet. Amid much honking and hissing, they thought twice about their planned attack and rejoined their peeping cygnets. The camera panned again to follow me, the bride—now clutching her "Sissy"—and the bridegroom as we struggled past the indignant swans to the shore, trailing cattails, lily pads, and the tattered remnants of a once-priceless wedding gown.

"And with that fun video, we leave you," Anderson Cooper said, still giggling. "Stay tuned for Don Lemon's report on the latest White House firings on *CNN Tonight!*"

Kenny turned off the TV and beamed at me. "The camera loves you, dear heart."

Darleene Bauer cracked, "I thought Teddy looked especially fetching with that lily pad on her head." The president of the Otter Conservancy never failed to delight in someone else's peccadilloes.

Not so, Lila. "Oh, Teddy, you're so brave. Wish I was as brave as you."

I blinked in surprise. "Are you kidding me? You were the first one who had the courage to report Booth's behavior. Only then did the others come forward."

"And look what it got me. Undereducated and underemployed."

Darleene and Ruth exchanged glances. Kenny looked down at his Topsiders.

Ignoring the shift in mood, Lila asked, "Is the zoo hiring, by any chance? You know how much I love animals."

I had to tell her no, but that I would keep trying. Since the day care center had fired her, I'd checked with Zorah every morning, but there were no openings in any of the zoo's various districts. Even if there had been, Lila's lack of a science degree—thanks to the predatory Stuart Booth—would have kept her from working directly with animals. Zorah had told me that the best Lila could hope for was service person at one of the food and beverage booths, yet all of them remained fully staffed. I made a mental note to check in with Preston Morrell to see why he hadn't yet called her for an interview.

I hoped it wasn't because the position had already been filled.

"Say, I hear they need a barista at Cappuccino & Chowder," Ruth offered. "Do you have…?"

Lila shook her head. "I don't know how to run one of those espresso machines."

For all of Ruth's sharp angles and even sharper tongue, the ex-soccer player had a soft heart. "I could teach you. I used to substitute at my cousin's coffee bar in Florida. The tips can be pretty good, even for an old crone like me."

"You're no crone, Ruth," Kenny said, leaning forward to pat her knobby knee. "And forty isn't old, either. These days it's the new twenty-five."

Lila suddenly stood up and gave Kenny a pained smile. "Thanks for letting me watch Teddy's adventures, but I need to get back to my boat. I just remembered that I left some soup simmering on the stove."

We all recognized the lie, but let her go without argument. After a few minutes of strained conversation, I rose to leave, too. That began a general exodus from the *High Life*'s cabin which, frankly, could have used a good cleaning. The rank smell of mildew more than cancelled out its once-beautiful fittings. Darleene and Ruth headed for their respective boats, Kenny went topside to his usual deck chair. He never missed a harbor sunset.

Or a margarita to toast it with.

My animals were overjoyed to see me, Bonz especially. The poor dog was all but crossing his remaining three legs in his hurry to make it outside to pee, but once he'd watered a harborside tree, he ran back into the *Merilee*'s cabin to gobble down the rest of his dinner.

"Don't worry, Bonz, you'll get a real 'walkies' as soon as you're done," I assured him.

He wagged his stumpy tail.

It didn't take long for the little terrier to finish his meal, so within minutes we were headed for Gunn Landing Park. Bonz and I had both enjoyed our walk inland on the East Fork Trail so much the other evening, we decided to repeat it.

We were less than a quarter mile along when the fog crept in.

With my back to the ocean, and heavy chaparral blocking my sightline, I hadn't noticed the fog's approach. No matter. Carriage lamps still lit the trail, their yellowish beams creating large halos through the fog. I did miss seeing the moon, though. It had risen full and silver when we left the *Merilee*, but was now swallowed by mist.

Carriage lamps or no, as the fog deepened, the path became darker than I would have wished. The dense foliage made it appear darker still, so I decided to cut the walk short.

One thing about fog. It can surprise you.

As Bonz and I wended our way back toward the harbor, we encountered a clear patch. To my delight, I saw bats fluttering around one of the carriage lamps, gorging on moths and other insects. I'm not one of those people who dislike bats. In fact, I rather like their dog-like faces and tiny, human-like hands. The only known flying mammal—sugar gliders and Rocky the flying squirrel don't count because they "coast"—bats are nowhere near as dangerous as believed. Their bad reputation has been caused by decades of *Dracula* movies, not to mention several flawed studies proclaiming that up to ten percent of them are rabid—a great exaggeration. Recent research strongly suggests that only one percent of wild bats carry the rabies virus.

This doesn't mean we should all run out into the cool night air with a net to capture bats. In their own way, bats are very much herd animals; they nest in groups, and pine away when forced to live alone. Being mammals, they also nurse their young, so if a bat aficionado inadvertently captures a mama bat, her babies will starve to death. Another reason to never capture a wild bat is because he—or she—might turn out to be among that unlucky one percent. No matter how cute, none of us wants a rabid bat in our house.

I stood there for a while, admiring the bats' sonar-assisted feeding frenzy until a rustle in the nearby chaparral caught my attention. When Bonz began to growl, I realized we had better move along. On rare occasion, coyotes came down from the hills to prey upon shore birds, and I didn't want to get caught between a hungry coyote and his supper.

"Let's go, Bonz," I said, stepping toward the park light.

He didn't budge, just strained against his

leash and growled louder, his snarls evolving into sharp, ugly barks.

I leaned over to steady him with a calming hand. "Bonz! What are you…?"

That's when someone shot me.

Chapter Fifteen

At first I didn't realize I'd been shot. I felt no pain yet—that would come later—and all I knew was that something had hit me in the left shoulder hard enough to make me fall. At the same moment, I heard something that sounded like a firecracker.

As I lay stunned on the gravel pathway trying to figure out what was happening, Bonz jerked the leash out of my hand and plunged into the brush, making a snarling noise I had never heard him make before.

Then I heard a grunt.

Followed by a yip.

"Bonz!" I screamed. "No!"

More snarling. Another grunt, then a horrible *ai, ai, ai* sound from my dog.

Fuzzy though my brain seemed to be, I began

to figure it out. The wetness on my shoulder wasn't evening dew; it was blood. I'd been shot. And my poor three-legged terrier had attacked my attacker, and whoever he or she was, was fighting back.

"Leave my dog alone!" I yelled, and added a few loud shrieks for good measure. One of the liveaboarders might still be close enough to…

More yelping. Was I going to let Bonz be killed while I lay here awaiting rescue like some wimpy fairy-tale princess?

Hell, no.

After shrieking a final plea for help—"Call 9-1-1!"—I scouted the ground for some sort of weapon, but all I could find were the white rocks lining the path. None appeared large enough to cause much damage, but they were better than nothing. I grasped a rock and lurched to my feet. The world tilted around me and my left shoulder, which had been numb up to this point, suddenly felt like it was on fire.

I shook the dizziness out of my head, and with the rock in my right hand, lurched into the bushes to save my dog. While slapping the chaparral away from my face, I could hear the attacker smashing his way through the brush, accompanied by gasps that could have been come from human or animal, man or woman.

When I reached the stamped-down area where the shooter had been lying in wait, he—or she –wasn't there.

Just Bonz.

Lying on the grass.

Not moving.

Chapter Sixteen

The scene in the Emergency Room at San Sebastian County Hospital was chaotic. Caro arrived at pretty much the same time as Joe, and once they realized my wound was minor—a three-inch gash along my left shoulder—they spent more time arguing than consoling.

Caro looked smashing in her petal pink Missoni, and Joe was handsome as ever in his sheriff's uniform, even though I detected a blood smear on his sleeve. Both shared the same angry expression.

"Teddy, you need to get out of that harbor." Joe.

"For once the man is talking sense." Caro.

"How's Bonz?" Me.

"A murder investigation isn't Amateur Night at the San Sebastian Karaoke Club." Joe.

"I *said*, how's Bonz?" Me.

"If I've told you once, I've told you a hundred times, women have no business getting involved in such tawdry affairs as homicide investigations." Caro.

"There's a killer on the loose and now he's focused on you." Joe.

"HOW'S BONZ!!!" Me.

"He'll be fine. Ariel Gonzales took him to the emergency vet hospital." Joe.

"What's a talking head doing at the harbor? She doesn't even own a boat." Me. Then, to the doctor, "Does that have to be so tight?"

"Yep." The doctor.

"Ms. Gonzales said she could hear you screaming because she was down there visiting a friend, but by the time she got to you, you'd passed out holding Bonz. The Montinis heard you, too. They reached you right after she did, and they're the ones who actually made the 9-1-1 call. Ms. Gonzales was too busy administering first aid." Joe.

"What friend?" Me.

"What do you mean, what friend?" Joe.

"The one you said Ariel Gonzales was visiting." Me.

"Oh. That. Well, it appears that Ms. Gonzales

is on, ah, very friendly terms with the zoo's new river otter keeper." Joe.

"Frank Owens?" Me.

"Yeah. Him." Joe.

While I was thinking, Caro filled the silence. "As soon as the doctor assures me you'll be okay, I'm going to the *Merilee* and packing your things."

"Oh, she'll be fine as long as she takes it easy for the next few days," the doctor said, doing something hurtful to my shoulder. "The bullet missed the bone and passed through the left deltoid. Lucky shot. Lucky for her, not the shooter."

"Packing won't take long since you don't have all that much." Caro.

"Don't touch my stuff." Me.

"Listen to your mother, Teddy." Joe.

"But I can't leave the *Merilee*. Who'd feed Miss Priss?" Me.

"I've fed that unappreciative feline before and I'll feed her again. Bonz, too, as soon as the vet releases him. In fact, both Bonz and Priss are moving to my house. Same as you." Caro.

"I'm not going to your house!" Me.

"You're absolutely right, Teddy." Joe.

"Huh?" Me.

"You're coming to *my* house." Joe.

"Really!" Me.

"If you people would shut up this wouldn't take so long." The doctor.

You know what happens when an irresistible force meets an immovable object? Someone gives, that's what.

Thirty minutes later a grumpy ER doctor released me into Joe's care with a prescription for pain pills, one of which I popped immediately. After declaring a temporary détente, Caro said she would stop by the *Merilee* the next morning to pick up Miss Priss and pack my things, which she promised to deliver to Joe's. He thanked her profusely, and after he gave me a nudge, I did, too. Before assisting me to his cruiser, he allowed me to call the emergency vet's office, where I learned that Bonz was still in surgery for a splintered rib, which was in danger of piercing a lung. His prognosis was good, I was told, and barring complications, he should heal in no time.

Relieved, I slept all the way to Joe's house in San Sebastian.

When I awoke the next morning, two children were staring down at me.

"You're supposed to ask for permission to come on board a boat," I told them.

"You're not on a boat," said the oldest, a boy of about ten. "You're in our house."

"When are you going to be our new mommy?" the little girl asked.

"New mommy?"

Stumped as to where I was and what I was doing there, I looked around and saw beige walls, thick black-and-beige curtains, and a framed, signed poster of Alexander Rossi winning the Indy 500 hanging opposite the bed. I was in Joe's bedroom. How…?

As the children continued staring at me, my shoulder began to throb. Then I remembered.

The gunshot.

Bonz's cries.

The hospital.

"Of course I'm going to be your new mommy—we'll have such fun," I told the children, who my clearing brain now recognized as Bridget, four, known as Bridie; and Antonio, nine, known as Tonio. "But first I have to find out about my dog."

"Grandma already called the vet," Tonio

informed me. "The person she talked to said he broke a rib in an extra-bad place but it's fixed now."

Bridie looked at me with pleading in her blue eyes. "Can you bring him here? I really, really, really love puppies."

"Bonz isn't a puppy anymore," I told her, forcing myself to smile at her even though it probably came across as a grimace. "He's a grown-up dog, just a bit on the small side. And he only has three legs."

I checked to see if I was wearing any clothes under the black-and-beige duvet covering me. Yep, I was wearing a Kelly green nightgown covered with bright yellow daisies. Colleen's. Being first-generation Irish, Joe's mother was partial to green.

"Only three legs? What happened to the other one?" Tonio asked.

"A car hit him years ago. He..."

The bedroom door opened slowly and Joe's mother tiptoed in. Although almost sixty, Colleen's naturally red hair and round, unlined face made her appear much younger. An acclaimed cook, she wore a well-used green apron over a paler green housedress. "You two aren't supposed to be in here," she whispered to the children, her brogue almost undetectable. "Teddy needs her sleep." Finally noticing that my eyes were open, she said, "Ah, you're up! How do you feel?"

"I was thinking about taking a pain pill."

Worry lines appeared between her blue eyes. "How bad is it?"

"Only a five or six out of ten, so on second thought, I'll hold off."

Bridie clambered onto the bed and patted my bandaged shoulder. I managed not to scream.

Colleen pried the little girl away from me. "Bridie, I need you and Tonio to help make breakfast." To me, she mouthed "Sorry."

"Don't apologize," I told her. "You've been wonderful. So have the kids. Bridie even made me smile. Um, has Joe already left for work?"

"Liquor store holdup on the west side. Clerk shot in the leg."

I winced on the clerk's behalf.

A half hour later I had washed myself as best I could in the bathroom sink, dressed in an assortment of Colleen's mostly green clothes— thankfully we were about the same size—and was sitting at the dining room table, feasting on chorizo, eggs scrambled with cheddar and scallions, a large helping of cottage fries, and homemade biscuits. Good thing eating only requires one hand.

"You look really, really, really white," Bridie said, studying me. "I can't even see your freckles anymore."

Bridie, Irish first name or no, had black hair and warm brown skin inherited from her father. Yet she had wound up with her grandmother's Irish blue eyes, creating a startling and beautiful contrast. Tonio, with his red hair, pale skin, and blue eyes, looked one-hundred percent Irish. His mother, Sonia—dead now for almost four years—had been a redhead, too. I'd seen pictures of her, and she and I could have passed for sisters. Who knows? Perhaps if I ran the same DNA tests that the zoo runs on its animals, I would find that Sonia and I shared the same long-ago Irish ancestor.

Thinking of the zoo made me drop my fork and jerk upright so suddenly it hurt my shoulder all over again. A glance at the old schoolhouse clock on the wall revealed that it was just past eight-thirty. I was two-and-a-half hours late for work.

"My animals! I have to call the zoo and tell them I won't be there!"

"I called for you," Colleen reassured me.

"The zoo director, I think Zorah's her name, was dismayed by what happened. She'd already heard about it on the morning news and shifted everyone's schedule around so that your animals are covered. By the way, when you're done eating you need to look at the flowers you've received."

Even over the chorizo's powerful scent, I could make out the mixture of carnations, roses, and lilies emanating from the living room. "From the zoo?"

"Them, too. You sure have a lot of friends. Even that old bi… uh, *witch* Aster Edwina sent you a lovely bouquet."

"Witch! Witch! Witch!" Bridie chanted.

"Guilt makes witches do strange things," I said, remembering how Aster Edwina had near-twisted my arm to keep her informed about the investigation. Maybe she blamed herself for my getting shot. "By the way, Colleen, wasn't that Joe's room I slept in last night?"

"Joe thought you'd be more comfortable there than on the sofa." A smile.

"Then where did he sleep?" The adobe house, originally built by Joe's grandfather and added onto in later years, had only three bedrooms: Joe's room, the kids' room—they double-bunked—and Colleen's.

"He slept on the porch."

The "porch" was a glass-enclosed sunroom overlooking the wooded hillside at the rear of the property. It contained a long, L-shaped settee that had often served as a guest room. Not appropriate sleeping quarters for a too-busy sheriff. Joe needed his rest.

"But Colleen, you two are doing so much! I should be the one out…"

From somewhere I heard wind chimes.

"That's the doorbell," Colleen said, rising from her chair. "Probably more flowers for you."

No such luck.

It was Caro.

With suitcases.

"Oooh, those are nice!" Colleen said, ogling the Louis Vuittons.

"I brought Theodora some clothes."

"Theo… Oh, you mean Teddy. Well, come in, come in. Want some coffee? There's half a pot left. You take cream? Sugar?"

"Black. How's she doing?"

I poked my head around Colleen's shoulders. "I'm doing fine."

Caro's eyebrows weren't quite as perfect as usual, but they still managed to express surprise. "Up and around already?"

I started to reach for a suitcase, then changed my mind when the floor tilted under me. "Yep, I'm up and around."

"But you're so pale." One side of her hastily lipsticked mouth began to tremble.

I remembered not to shrug my shoulders. "Just lost a little blood, that's all. Nothing major."

Caro's face twisted.

"Oh, get in here," Colleen insisted, holding a Louis Vuitton by one hand, Caro's arm by the other. But once she'd pulled her inside the flower-filled living room, my mother burst into tears, something I had only seen her do twice before: the day my father was arrested for embezzlement, and the day he skipped bail and fled the country.

As she sobbed against Colleen's bosom, Tonio dashed out the door and grabbed the remaining Vuitton. Ignoring the sob-fest, he dragged it into the house. "Bet these things cost a million bucks," he puffed, taking the other suitcase from Colleen, who now needed both hands to comfort my mother.

Belatedly, I moved forward, and with my good arm hugged Caro. "There, there," I said. "There, there."

An hour later I was finally able to peel Caro off me by telling her Miss Priss would be pining for her. As if cats ever pine.

Caro's exit accomplished, I talked Colleen into taking me to the vet hospital to visit Bonz.

The poor mutt was still stoned out of his doggy mind when we arrived, sporting a bandage that wrapped around his entire torso. Nevertheless, the loyal little thing summoned up enough energy to lick my hand.

"Saved my life, didn't you?" I murmured into his ear. "Wouldn't let Bad Man finish me off, would you?"

More licking.

"Gramma, I want a puppy!" Bridie demanded.

"Me, too," Tonio.

Colleen put a finger to her lips. "Shhh. Let Bonz go back to sleep."

"Want puppy." This time in a whisper.

A conference with Dr. Hope Givens, a cool blonde, reaffirmed what I already knew, that the shooter had kicked Bonz in the side, fracturing two ribs, splintering another. "But the surgery went well, and he'll be fine."

I swallowed, afraid I'd start bawling like my mother. "Yes, that's what you told me over the phone, but…"

Some of Givens' frost disappeared. "It's still true, so please relax. He's in no danger."

"When can he come home?" By that, I meant to the *Merilee*, of course. There was no way I'd let some killer disrupt my life. Then again…

I remembered Bonz's yelps when the killer kicked him.

I remembered his limp body lying on the grass.

"What did you say?" I asked the vet. "I, uh, wasn't listening."

"We'll release him in a couple of days, but don't hold me to it. It all depends on whether…"

"Whether or not there are complications. In cases like this, how often are there complications?"

"Not often. Any other questions?"

I shook my head. If more questions arose, I would check with her, although not as often as Caro and Joe had been checking on me. They had called time and time again that morning to make certain I was still alive.

As if reading my mind, Dr. Givens said, "You're welcome to call me anytime."

"Oh, I will."

Joe managed to make it home for lunch. He refused to allow me to move into the sunroom, saying he was perfectly comfortable out there. After delivering that refusal, he added, "You're not going back to the *Merilee*, either. In fact, you're not leaving this house again."

"But I have to check on Bonz."

"Believe it or not, we do have a telephone here. A landline and a plethora of cells."

"Plethoras are not the same thing as seeing for yourself."

He turned to his mother. "Make sure she doesn't stick her nose outside."

With perfect equanimity, Colleen replied, "Dear, I'm your mother, not your deputy."

"You understand what I just said?"

"I learned English even before I learned Gaelic."

"Daddy, I want a puppy." Bridie had a one track mind.

"You'll be getting one soon," Joe said. "His name is Bonz. A cat, too. Her name is Miss Priss." He gave me that name-the-date look I knew so well.

I smiled at Bridie. "Miss Priss is with my mother right now, but I'm sure you'll love her, too. The cat, I mean."

Joe's face turned thoughtful for a moment, then he grinned. "To clarify, kids, you'll also be getting a new grandma. Her name is Caro."

Tonio frowned. "I hope she doesn't cry *all* the time."

I waited for fifteen minutes after Joe left the house, then, as Colleen was holed up in the kitchen studying some recipe she intended to make for dinner, I wobbled two blocks down the tree-lined street to Bucky Snow's house.

Many of the lots in Joe's semi-rural neighborhood had acreage, but Bucky wasn't as fortunate. Still, his place was an improvement on his former digs. Since serving his time in prison for grand theft auto, the new *Bucky Goes Hollywood* TV star had moved up in the world, taking his wife and twins from a single-wide trailer to a two-bedroom adobe fixer-upper. And he also, for once in his life, drove a car he had actually purchased, not swiped. Like his house, the Honda Odyssey appeared aged, but was in tip-top condition. So was the yard Bucky was watering when I approached.

"You free this morning, Bucky?"

He turned off the water. "Hey, girl! Saw you on the news this morning. Did you see the flowers I took over? Grew them in my own yard."

I vaguely remembered seeing a bunch of black-eyed Susans sitting in a milk carton vase near the huge pile of roses the zoo sent me. "Thank you, they're lovely."

Then something alarming occurred to me. "Bucky, how did you know I was staying at Joe's?"

"It's what the news announcer said, that—I'm trying to quote here and I'm sorry if I'm getting it wrong—that 'Fortunately the victim is engaged to the county sheriff, and is recuperating at his house in San Sebastian.' There. I'm pretty sure that's word for word. I've been doing exercises to help me memorize my scripts. Doing a TV show is rougher than I guessed."

I narrowed my eyes. "Who was it?"

"Who was who?"

"The news announcer."

"Oh, her. It was that woman you're always talking to on your animal program. I forget her name."

"Ariel Gonzales?"

"Yeah, her."

I didn't like this at all. According to Joe, Ariel had been helping me when the Montinis showed up and called 9-1-1. Or at least "helping" was what it looked like. Yet Ariel was savvy enough to know the harm it could do to release my current whereabouts, so why had she done it? Orders from her producers again? Or something else?

"Bucky, I need a ride."

Bucky dropped me off at the harbor's parking lot. After asking him for a final favor, which he was happy to grant, I wobbled to the *Merilee* and found what I needed: my car keys. I also grabbed my laptop, because you never know, do you?

While I was loading up other necessities into a plastic garbage bag, a thud against the *Merilee*'s hull alerted me I had a visitor.

Maureen.

The otter was back again, demanding a treat. Fortunately there was still some herring in the galley's tiny refrigerator, and it still smelled okay.

I took two of them topside and dropped one into her waiting paws.

"*Ngh!*" Otter-speak for *Thank you!*

"Want another?"

"*Nee-nee!*" Otter speak for *Hurry up, I'm starving down here!*

As I tossed her the other herring, a crowd of liveaboarders came clattering along the dock to inquire about my health. The noise chased Maureen away.

"The doctor says it's merely a flesh wound," I assured Kenny Norgaard, Ruth Donohue, Dee Dee Pascal, Lila Conyers, and Darleene Bauer, after thanking them for the flowers they'd sent me. "I'm perfectly fine."

A bit of a stretch there. After my walk to Bucky's, the ride to the harbor, and packing things up to take to Joe's, I wasn't feeling all that great. In fact, I felt downright light-headed, but that didn't stop me from asking, "Do any of you know which boat Frank Owens is staying on?"

"The new member of the Otter Conservancy? Sure, he's on *Ring of Bright Water*," Darleene said. "It's been temporarily berthed at the far south end of the harbor for three months, waiting for a slip to open up near the yacht club. With you working at the zoo and running into him every day, I'm surprised you didn't know that."

I could have kicked myself for not making the connection since I had passed the splendid Beneteau Oceanis sloop several times on the way to the park and smiled at her name. *Ring of Bright Water* was the classic wildlife book by

Gavin Maxwell which described the wild otters near his home in western Scotland. Could there possibly be a more perfect name for an otter keeper's boat?

"If you're thinking about exchanging the handsome sheriff for Owens, dear heart, be warned that Ariel Gonzales, that TV person, has a thing with him." This, from Kenny. "They even get quite loud at times."

He was eager to tell me more, Kenny always was, but I held up a restraining hand.

"Don't need to know. Well, it's been nice chatting with you all, and thanks again for the beautiful flowers. Peonies and lilacs are among my favorites."

"I picked them out," Lila said. Her smile, along with the pink tint to her cheeks, made me believe she was finally recovering from her stint in the San Sebastian County Jail. "One of the dresses you gave me has a peony and lilac print, and I've been wearing it to job interviews."

Interviews? Plural? "Hasn't Preston Morrell called you yet?"

The smile faded. "His secretary did, but she didn't sound hopeful when I told her I don't have a degree."

"Hmm." I needed to do more work on Preston.

And I would, just as soon as I tracked down Ariel. First, to thank her for saving my life, and second, to see if she actually had.

By the time I had driven my pickup over to the veterinarian hospital to visit Bonz again, and then hidden my truck in Bucky's garage, it became clear that I had overtaxed myself, so I asked Bucky to drive me the measly two blocks back to Joe's house. When I arrived, I was so pale that Colleen hustled me straight to bed. Oddly enough, she didn't question me about my hours-long disappearance. Maybe she understood.

Whatever the reason, I fell asleep, and dreamt that I was running through a nightmare forest with a three-legged dog in my arms.

Chapter Seventeen

Monday being my usual day off, there was no need to call in sick. After last night's sleep and a hearty breakfast cooked by my future mother-in-law, I felt relatively strong. There might have been the occasional twinge from my injured shoulder, but nothing serious enough to keep me from tracking down the home address of Ariel Gonzales.

"Promise you'll take it easy today," Joe said, taking the dish towel away from me and using it himself. Colleen had raised him to be an accomplished drier.

"I promise."

"Leave the detecting to me."

"Of course."

Colleen, who was scrubbing the cast-iron skillet she had used to fry the breakfast sausage, said, "Stop fussing at the woman, Joe."

"You don't know her like I do," he grumbled.

He looked so handsome in his sheriff's uniform that I had a hard time keeping my hands off him, so I grabbed another dish towel and started to work on a serving platter.

"In fact," Colleen continued, "the most physical thing Teddy will do all day is check out that nice granny cottage you're building." She was wearing a different green dress, protected by the same green apron. Come to think of it, even the laptop she kept in the kitchen's tiny office nook had a green cover.

"I prefer the term 'mother-in-law unit,'" Joe said. "You don't look like a granny."

Colleen's smile held a note of sadness. "You inherited that sense of precision from your father."

Joe's father, who had preceded his son as San Sebastian County Sheriff, had been dead for ten years, but a picture of him remained in every room. Joe, except for his Irish-blue eyes, looked just like him.

"It's a mess back there so you gals need to be careful," Joe warned. "Rebar, loose boards, nails all over the place, a couple of ripped insulation packages, bad for the lungs. Come to think of it, don't even go near it."

Colleen's smile broadened. "Your tendency to overprotect, too."

"What?"

"Genes, dear. Genes. You're your father all over again."

Joe made a few grumbling noises, but at the end, leaned over and kissed his mother's cheek. "Whatever."

As soon as the dishes were put away, Joe and I went into the not-totally-green living room, done up in his own favored color scheme of beige-on-black. The room was now further enlivened by bouquets of fresh flowers. Bridie and Tonio were plunked in front of the large-screen TV, watching *Sesame Street*. Ever the doting father, he kissed them good-bye. After giving me a different kind of kiss, he headed to his office.

"He means well," Colleen said, waving through the window at him.

"Yeah, I know."

"Or you wouldn't put up with it, would you? His father was the same way with me. Always fussing. But it was only because he loved me and wanted to protect me. Whoever would have guessed that in the end, he was the one needing protection?" She sighed. "Well, enough of the grim stuff. Do you want to go outside and listen to the birds, or are there a few leads you want to run down? I saw you sneaking your laptop into the bedroom, by the way."

Flushing, I stammered, "I, uh, I, ah…"

"Teddy, I understand more than you'll ever know." With that she gave me a pat on my good shoulder and headed into the kitchen. Seconds later she was typing something on her laptop. Probably another recipe.

Tracking down Ariel Gonzales turned out to be easy.

Remembering the lovely bouquet of orange and yellow zinnias she had sent me, I simply called San Sebastian's Boutique de Fleur and told the young-sounding clerk who answered that I wanted to mail thank you cards to everyone who had sent me flowers.

"But Ariel Gonzales's home address is the only one I don't have, so perhaps you can…"

God bless trusting clerks. I discovered that Ariel lived less than ten minutes away in a duplex just off San Sebastian's main drag. Not only that, but the clerk also gave me Ariel's phone number.

A glance at my waterproof/poop-proof Timex showed me it was almost ten. Since Ariel anchored the six a.m. news, then *Good Morning, San Sebastian*, followed by the noon news broadcast, she would be at the TV station for at least the next three hours. As good as I felt today, I didn't want to hang around in the street waiting for her to show, so I dragged my laptop out from under my bed and fired it up.

Good thing, too.

We tend to define war heroes by only their bright and shining moments. When their light shines as brightly as had Ariel's, we often forget that they had lives before they risked them to save others.

A simple Google search brought up her official bio. Born to an ex-Marine sergeant father and an ex-Navy nurse mother, she had been the editor of her high school newspaper and hosted the school's five-minute news program on KGNN. After graduating with highest honors from San Sebastian High, she was granted a full ride scholarship to UC San Bertram, where she majored in Marine Science.

Guess who was teaching Marine Science when she enrolled at UC San Bertram?

Dr. Stuart Booth, that's who.

Further net searches revealed that a year into her studies Ariel had left UC San Bertram, transferring to Cal Poly San Luis Obispo to major in Engineering. Somehow I doubted that Ariel made that momentous decision because she had fallen out of love with the ocean.

I picked up my truck from Bucky's and spent the next hour at the vet hospital visiting Bonz again. He looked much stronger, and managed to wobble forward to greet me. Seeing him on his feet again lifted my heart.

"He's ready to go home, isn't he?" I'd asked Dr. Givens upon arriving, only to receive bad news.

"Maybe tomorrow," she said. "His temperature was a bit elevated this morning. Nothing serious, but I want to keep my eye on him for another twenty-four hours."

At least she let me sit with him until he began snoring. Then I returned him to the veterinarian's version of ICU and headed to Casa Rejas for a nap of my own. The trip had tired me more than expected.

Two hours later, I was parked on a shady street near the town center. My research had shown that Ariel had recently purchased the duplex at 472 North Hibiscus Lane, lived in one unit, and rented out the other. The exterior of the Craftsman's cottage and grounds were in immaculate condition, with the house and facings freshly painted, the lush greenery recently trimmed. Ariel either kept a handyman on retainer or was an avid do-it-yourselfer.

"Hi, there!" I bubbled, when she answered my knock. A Chihuahua-something-mix stood at her feet, snarling at me. "Just dropped by to thank you for the beautiful zinnias. And for saving my life."

Ariel's smile wasn't as jaunty as mine. "Hardly necessary since your attacker was on the run by the time I got there." Dressed in paint-spattered jeans and tee shirt, she had washed off her TV makeup. The long red scar on her cheek glared against her olive skin, which was further blemished by splatters of yellow paint. "Shouldn't you be in bed or something?"

"Bed rest is overrated. Do you have time for a chat?"

She gave me a look I couldn't quite interpret. "Sure, as long as you don't mind the smell of latex."

When I stepped inside, giving the still snarling dog a wide berth, I found the living room half Landlady Green, half Buttercup Yellow—the color of the paint on her face. "Why, you're redecorating! I like that yellow. Cheerier than the green." Truth be told, I was tired of green. And beige-on-black. Before Joe and I married, we needed to have a serious discussion about home décor.

"Would you like a drink? I have tea and I have coffee, so name your poison."

"Coffee sounds lovely."

Noticing my concerned look at the Chihuahua-something, she said, "Don't worry, Chaco's nasty, but he doesn't bite. At least not so far."

I followed her and the ill-tempered Chaco into the kitchen, noting the drop cloth-covered beige carpet, the similarly covered Danish furniture. With the walls in the process of being transformed from blah to zippy I saw no pictures or photographs other than the one sitting on a teak end table. It showed several tired-looking Marines standing in front of a helicopter loaded with a startling display of rockets. Ariel was one of the Marines.

I settled myself at the kitchen table, a daring

combination of glass and oxidized iron. "That picture in the living room, are those the Marines…?" I let the sentence trail off.

"The guys I lifted off the mountain? Yeah. I like to look at it when things get rough. Here's your coffee. Want anything in it?"

"I like it black. What do you mean by 'rough'?"

"You can take the girl out of Afghanistan, but you can't take Afghanistan out of the girl. Now tell me why you're here, and I know it has nothing to do with home improvements."

Such straightforwardness deserved an equally straight-forward answer, but I wasn't yet ready. "Did you get a good look at the man who shot me?" I took a sip of the coffee; it was strong enough to fuel that helicopter.

"Never saw him." She took a sip of her own black coffee. Looked pleased and set the cup down to cool.

"Not at all?"

"Nope. Nada. Zip. There was a lot of brush and it was as dark as Bin Laden's soul. Foggy, too." Without being asked, nasty Chaco jumped into her lap. Ariel smiled down at him. "Oooh's the good boy?"

Chaco drooled.

"Are you certain the shooter was even a man?"

"Sure as hell sounded like one."

"Sounded?"

"Heavy breaths ending in basso grunts. 'Course, it could just as well have been a woman with an unusually deep voice, but whoever it was clomped like a guy, too."

Instead of her careful television pronunciation, she had slipped into a more relaxed manner of speaking, which I took for a good sign. "The Montinis didn't get a look at him, either."

"Look, Teddy, if you don't mind my saying so, it wasn't very smart for you to go walking around out there after dark, especially after there've been two back-to-back killings in the area. You have a death wish or something?"

Stung, I said, "I had to walk my dog."

"Dogs can be walked in better-lit areas." She smiled down at Chaco again.

"Well, you were walking around out there."

"No I wasn't. I was with a friend when I heard the shot, so I…" Another shrug.

"So you ran toward it."

"That's what I do."

"Talk about someone having a death wish. Um, besides coming here to thank you for saving my life, I've got a couple more questions I'd like to ask."

She frowned. "Such as?"

"Why did you let the public know where I was staying?"

The frown grew deeper. "My producer ordered me to bring up the Booth murder. And as difficult as it can be, I still love my job, and I'd like to keep it."

"Understood. But I'm betting he—or she—didn't tell you to endanger me further."

"You're right. She didn't. It just slipped out."

"Really?"

"Really. Teddy, strange things can happen on live TV, and a momentary loss of common sense is just one of them. Next question." She reached for her coffee mug.

"Okay, since you insist. How well did you know Stuart Booth?"

Ariel's hand, in the midst of lifting her mug to her mouth, jerked, and a few drops of coffee spilled on the table. "What the hell? Where's this third degree coming from?"

I waited.

After scowling at me for a moment through narrowed eyes, she said in a voice so flat it was almost spooky, "This visit isn't about zinnias, is it?"

"Only partially."

Those dark eyes narrowed even more. "Didn't anyone ever tell you that sticking your nose in other people's business could get you shot?"

Like all Marines, former USMC Captain Ariel Gonzales had been trained to kill, and given the size of those rockets on her helicopter, she probably had. Yet somehow I doubted she would harm me. "I've been told that. On several occasions."

"By your boyfriend?"

"Fiancé, actually. And my mother."

She motioned to my taped shoulder. "They were right. Why put yourself in harm's way?"

"Because a friend of mine is in trouble. She won't even be able to find a job until the real killer is identified, which means she could lose her home. And since she's prone to depression at the best of times..."

"You're talking about Lila Conyers." At my look of surprise, she added, "I not only anchor the news, I even remember it."

"Then you also know she lost her part-time job at the day care center because they were afraid they'd lose business if they kept her on staff."

She scratched Chaco's ugly head. "Life's never been fair for women, so why should it be any different for your friend?" Not one flicker of compassion showed on her scarred, paint-spattered face.

"Was it fair you had to change schools and majors because of Stuart Booth?"

"Any woman who expects fairness in this life needs an eye transplant because she sure as hell can't see what's going down." She gave a joyless chuckle. "People here in the U.S. of A. act all shocked and bothered by burkas and the fact that in an Afghan court, a woman's testimony is given only half the weight of a man's. Good luck for a woman trying to get an assault con-viction, eh? Or a rape? Ain't-a-gonna happen. Afghan women are aware of the inequity at the outset, whereas here in our own country it mugs us from behind."

"Sounds to me like you may have reported Booth."

"Of course I did. I wasn't the only one, either. Two other female students reported him, and guess what? Suddenly our papers started to get poor grades. My grades became so bad I was on the verge of losing my scholarship. What's that line in the Bob Dylan song? 'You don't need a weatherman to know the way the wind blows.' When the wind became a gale, I moved to Cal Poly and never looked back."

She stood up abruptly, making me aware that she was several inches taller than me and around twenty pounds heavier, all of it muscle. "Want some more crappy coffee?"

"I'm full up."

"Good. Now, this has been a whole helluva lotta fun, but I have to finish the living room. Will I see you tomorrow?"

"Tomorrow?"

"*Anteaters to Zebras*, remember? Your Loose-Sphincter-of-the-Week segment?"

Despite the tension in the room, I laughed. "I'm not up to that yet."

"No prob. We'll air a rerun." With that, she put a large hand on my back, and with Chaco following, steered me to the door.

Outside, the wind had come up and low-scuttling clouds obscured the sun. I was tempted to drive down to the harbor to talk to Darleene Bauer about the status of the otter count. The fact that Booth had died before sending in his numbers continued to nag at me. Would his count have been similar to mine? But my shoulder was signaling that it wanted some rest, so I pointed the truck in the opposite direction and headed for my current home-away-from home.

When I arrived, I found Colleen having tea with my mother.

Chapter Eighteen

Caro had brought Feroz with her. The Chihuahua showed a new side of his nature by the way he played with Joe's children. Instead of his usual growls, he emitted happy yips. Instead of snapping, he licked. For the first time I could remember, he behaved more like a dog than the Aztec warrior whose name he carried.

My mother, however, appeared unchanged. Ever the fashion statement, she wore a dove-gray silk Armani pants suit, offset by scarlet Ferragamo flats. Her eyebrows had been professionally plucked, her hair newly streaked, and her inch-long nails painted coral. In contrast, Colleen had ditched her green apron to reveal no-name jeans and a chartreuse tee shirt that shouted in blocky red letters YOU CAN'T SCARE ME—I HAVE GRANDCHILDREN.

"What were you doing, driving around town like a maniac?" Caro grouched when she finished hugging me. "You should be in bed."

"I'm taking plenty of naps."

"Not while you're driving, you don't! Where were you?"

"Out. Getting air. The ER doc said it would be good for me." Actually, the doctor had said no such thing, but Caro had been crying so hard at the hospital the night I was shot she wouldn't have noticed if the doctor had been speaking in ancient Sumerian.

"Colleen said you've been gone over an hour, Theodora. That's a lot of air."

"I needed a lot of it."

"How about some tea, everyone?" Colleen said, interrupting my mother's cross-examination. "It's peppermint, wonderful for frazzled nerves."

The tea turned out to be just what I needed to chase away the taste of Ariel's bad coffee.

"You should move to Old Town with me," Caro muttered, between sips.

"Where I'm at is quite nice."

"But it's so small."

"It's cozy."

"And noisy!" This, an apparent reference to

the Chihuahua-and-child commotion in the other room. "How can you possibly sleep?"

"The kids will settle down when Feroz leaves."

Giving up, Caro changed the subject. "Speaking of dogs, how's Bonz?"

"Doing well. The vet says he can come home tomorrow."

"'Home' being?"

"Here, for now. Don't worry, I'm not foolish enough to move back to the *Merilee* while Booth's and Amberlyn's killer is still on the loose."

"Promise me."

I crossed my heart. "Promise."

She didn't look convinced. "I know you think I'm a fussbudget, but your stepfather is worried about you, too."

"Tell Al to stop worrying. I'm perfectly safe here. Remember, Joe's the county sheriff and he carries a big gun."

"But how often is he actually here?"

She had me there. The past few days had been hectic in San Sebastian County. Two murders, several serious car wrecks out on the PCH, a couple of armed robberies, and the usual domestic call-outs. My stay here had given a taste of what my life would be like once Joe and I married, but that was okay. Given my job at the zoo and my TV program, I was a busy person, too. Caro, that lily of the field who toiled not nor spun, would never understand, but I loved her anyway.

"More tea?" Colleen asked, noting that my mother was winding herself up for another onslaught.

As further proof that miracles do happen, the next hour passed without any more cross-examinations. Caro even unbent enough to let Colleen show her the construction on the backyard granny cottage. Live oaks and fruit trees surrounded the still-skeletal building, but when finished, the living room would have a wonderful view of the steep hillside. As it stood now, the roof and framework for the walls were up, but no doors or windows had yet been installed; gaping holes revealed where they would eventually go. Joe was right—the site was a dangerous mess, with pieces of this and that lying in wait to trip the unwary.

Caro, aware of the damage a loose nail or rough boards could do to dove-gray silk, remained on the periphery. "It seems rather small to me," she said to Colleen. "Are you certain you'll be comfortable?"

Colleen smiled, perhaps remembering her childhood in a Dublin slum. "Living room, en suite bedroom/bathroom/office with built-in shelves for my hobby, a galley kitchen, and plenty of storage space—what else could a woman want?"

"More room," said Caro, who always thought big. "Maybe Joe could expand it? You've got almost three-quarters of an acre here. Cut down a couple of those trees, clear the brush, and you'd have…"

"Much more room than I need."

"What hobby are you talking about?"

Not actually answering, Colleen said, "We girls have to keep busy, don't we? As for the greenery, the live oaks were here before we were, so they're staying. Joe's grandfather planted the fruit trees and even what you're calling the 'brush,' which is actually a combination of lady fern and wild grape. Their scent is lovely, especially in the morning when everything is dewy. When I finally move in, I'll leave my windows open most of the time."

"But it looks so…so *wild*." Caro pronounced the word like it was a nasty one.

"Another reason I like it. All kinds of wildlife back here. I have to admit, though, that one night it was rather sad. A coyote came down the hill and caught a rabbit in the yard. Ever hear a rabbit scream?"

"No, and I never want to."

"And there've been cats…"

Caro held up her hand. "Stop! Don't tell me!"

"Well, the cats always escape up the trees you'd have me cut down."

That shut Caro up, and Colleen then gave us a tour of her organic kitchen garden, which was sectioned off by heavy plantings of bright yellow marigolds.

"The flowers give off a scent that discourages pests," she explained, "and keeps the lettuce less toxic. Oops. I didn't get a chance to put those things away before I answered the door."

Colleen bent over and picked up a pair of gardening shears and returned them to a whitewashed shed. Before she closed the door, I peeked in. Smiled. Along with the usual gardening tools, I saw a plastic garbage bin hand-labeled KOALA POO.

Wanchu would be so proud.

The rest of Caro's visit was pleasant enough, and when she scooped up Feroz to return home, everyone kissed her good-bye.

I slept away the rest of the afternoon, waking only when Joe came home.

"What, no more murders?" I asked, shuffling into the living room, where the smell of something wonderful in the kitchen mingled with the musky man-smell of tired sheriff.

He gave me a careful hug. "Not today. The only action happening in the more-or-less peaceful hamlet of San Sebastian was a shoplifting case at the new Walmart. It's still being picketed, by the way. As is the new Starbucks. How's the shoulder?"

"Trying to convince me it doesn't hurt. And quid pro quo, how's the Booth-and-Amberlyn case coming along?"

"Slowly."

"Did your techs find the bullet?" I motioned to my bandaged shoulder.

"They're very capable."

"Was it fired from the same gun that shot Booth and Amberlyn?"

"Why do you think I'm so worried about you?"

"Maybe if I..."

"*Don't*, Teddy!"

"But..."

"Dinner's ready," Colleen announced, exiting the kitchen and waving a spatula toward the already-set dining room table. Her inter-ruption was too timely to be coincidental.

I was beginning to appreciate my future mother-in-law more and more every day.

The next morning KGNN-TV aired a rerun of one of my least favorite segments, the screech-fest when the honey badger got loose in the studio. I wasn't pleased, but Colleen and the children found the mayhem highly amusing.

"You lead such an exciting life, Teddy," Colleen said, after switching the TV to *Sesame Street.*

"Sometimes too exciting," I muttered under my breath as she went into the kitchen to bake brownies or something. Cooking, cleaning, child-rearing…all commendable activities, but where was the fun?

I rotated my sore shoulder as far as it would go, which wasn't very far. Before turning in last night I had called Zorah at home to tell her I would be back at the zoo Wednesday, but not to expect any heavy lifting on my part. Understanding my situation, Zorah said she would enlist Janet Hewitt to help me out, which suited me fine. The trainee's relationship with Stuart Booth remained a puzzle, and having her by my side would give me a chance to question her. Come to think of it, I also needed to talk to river otter keeper Frank Owens. Since he and Ariel were supposedly together when I'd been shot, why hadn't he come to my aid along with her?

I was sitting in the living room writing down a list of questions that needed answering when the doorbell rang.

Colleen, who was typing away in the kitchen's office nook, yelled at me to get it. "I've got to get this last measurement down right!"

When I opened the door, I saw the deliveryman from Boutique de Fleur holding an outrageously expensive bouquet of orchids from Harper Betancourt-Booth. The bouquet included a note.

> *Teddy,*
> *I was out of town when I heard about your mishap. Please accept these flowers in lieu of my presence at your bedside. If you're recovered enough to join us in the main house for tea today, we'd love to have you.*

4 p.m.? And don't worry, I'll understand if you can't make it.
  Your dearest friend,
  Harper

Mishap?

Dearest friend?

One of us was delusional, and it wasn't me. However, the invitation played right into my hands. I texted her my RSVP, then headed out to pick up Bonz.

My three-legged terrier appeared pitifully happy to see me, and his joy only increased when I carried him to the truck. Dogs love car rides, and despite his bandaged ribs, he hung his head out the passenger's side window and slobbered all the way to Joe's.

The children were delighted to see him. They couldn't stop telling him what a brave doggie he was, and obeyed every time he made himself available for an ear-scratch. My only concern for his welfare remained the construction area in the yard. Loose boards, nails, packages of insulation…Accidents happen to nosy dogs, so after a discussion, we agreed to keep him in the house, and allow him outside only when leashed. This decision caused a brief argument about which human would be on the other end of the leash. Even little Bridie wanted to take him for walkies. Her older brother quickly overruled her, and he in turn was overruled by Colleen.

"It's not that I don't trust you, Tonio, because I do, but dogs can be devious when they spot a squirrel, so Bonz's only chaperones will be Teddy, me, or your father."

After much grumbling, the two returned their attentions to a grateful Bonz.

At three, I changed into my all-purpose black dress and drove to Old Town to take tea with my "dearest friend" Harper Betancourt-Booth, stopping along the way to visit Miss Priss at Caro's house. The one-eyed Persian had probably missed me, but cats being cats, I couldn't be certain. At one point she ceased terrifying my mother's Chihuahua long enough to brush against my leg and look deeply into my eyes for a half-second, but that was it.

"Would you say her behavior is normal for a cat?" Caro asked, rescuing her dog from the corner Priss had backed him into. "She won't leave Feroz alone. He's been a nervous wreck ever since I brought her here."

"There's no such thing as 'normal' for cats."

"Maybe you should take her with you to Joe's." Before I could answer, she said, "Oh, not a good idea. Bonz is still recuperating, isn't he? Miss Priss would make mincemeat out of the poor thing." She leaned over and kissed Feroz on the top of his trembling head. "Is my sweetums scared of Big Bad Kitty? Is hims? Mama not let Big Bad Kitty hurt her little sweetums, will she?"

With Miss Priss officially reminded of who she belonged to—me, more or less—I brushed some cat hair off my black dress and drove the rest of the way uphill to the Betancourt estate.

Imagine my surprise when I turned out to be the only guest.

"Oh, you poor thing!" Harper cried, throwing her arms around me.

"Easy on the shoulder, Harper. And by the way, where's everyone else? Your invitation said 'we' and 'us.'"

She smiled her perfect smile. "Dear Teddy,

always so suspicious. It must be because of your engagement to a cop." As if to punctuate her social superiority, she sniffed, then seemed disappointed to discover I smelled of Colleen's Lilac Beauty Bath Soap, not Monkey House Offal.

As if on cue, a maid entered, rolling a cart piled high with tea, watercress sandwiches, and a selection of scones and cream cakes. We were in the Orangery, a plant-filled, mostly glass-surrounded room that afforded a one-eighty-degree view of the Pacific. Although a few fluffy clouds dotted the sky, the air remained crisp enough for me to see all the way to Pacific Pride, the Betancourts' oil platform. Call me old-fashioned, but I thought it rather ruined the view.

"One lump or two?" Harper asked. Solid silver tongs hovered over a silver sugar bowl.

She had chosen a red Chippendale settee to sit on. I took the green one.

"No sugar, please."

"Because you're already sweet enough?"

"Right." Spode china cup dutifully handed over, I took a sip. I couldn't quite place the tea. Flowery, yet with a bite.

Puzzlement must have shown on my face,

because Harper said, "It's Tienchi flower tea. My life coach tells me it's good for allergies and insomnia."

"Having trouble sleeping?" I tried to look sympathetic. The woman had, after all, just lost her husband.

"On the contrary, I'm sleeping like a baby these days."

"Babies sometimes cry at night." I took a bite of scone. Cranberries in there somewhere. And maybe apricots. I eyed the serving cart again.

"Just between us girls, Teddy, I'm glad Stuart's gone. Whoever took him off my hands saved me a bundle in attorney fees. And I like living in the main house again, too. That cottage Daddy stuck us in was simply too small."

A slosh of Tienchi filled my saucer. "Attorney fees? You, ah, you..."

Ignoring my stammers, she continued, "I was going to divorce him anyway. And before you ask, only partially because of that grotesque Sugar Baby business."

Shock rendered me speechless. No matter. Harper was on a roll.

"When I found out about that Amber creature—it was about eight months ago, I think—I was already tired of him, because you know what they say, that some men are good for the short term, others for the long run. Well, Stuart was a sprinter. And as it turned out, he'd Hemingwayed his so-called past. Those tales he told about backpacking the two-thousand-mile-long Appalachian Trail while fighting off bears and wolves? The time at Pismo Beach when he punched out a shark to rescue a lifeguard? The stories were interesting the first few times I heard them but they paled with the retelling.

"By the time I heard them for the umpteenth time, I hired a private detective. Turns out there never were any bears or wolves or sharks. He'd only completed the first thirty-seven miles of the trail before being lifted off by helicopter after breaking an ankle. As for the sharks, zippo on that. The truth was that Stuart swam out too far, got a cramp, and the lifeguard dragged *him* to shore."

Having long doubted Stuart Booth's tales of derring-do, I merely said, "Sounds like you'd lost trust in him long before the Sugar Baby thing."

"I can put up with a liar and a cheater, but never with a bore. Besides, the detective gave me a nice discount."

"Ah, well."

"You had your own troubles, too, didn't you? With Michael?"

Harper knew how much I hated to talk about my ex-husband, but I answered her anyway. "Michael wasn't boring. Just unfaithful."

"All men are."

"Are you sure of that?"

"Trust me, Teddy. I know these things."

Instead of commenting further, I looked around at the Orangery, at the lush potted plants, the thick glass separating them from the manicured lawn. Everywhere Nature had been lopped and snipped to a fare-the-well. Brought under control.

Like she was hoping to do with me, maybe?

Harper was gazing at the offshore oil platform. She had a satisfied smile on her face, and why not? The ugly thing wasn't just pumping oil, it was pumping money. Betancourt money.

I couldn't help myself. "How's the cleanup going in the Gulf after that blowout last month?" The Prime Pacific Eagle, as the Gulf platform had been named, spewed thousands of gallons of oil on beaches across Louisiana, Mississippi, and Alabama.

Harper shrugged. "I haven't the slightest idea."

"Lots of dead wildlife, I hear."

"That's their problem, not mine. Or yours. That platform out there? Pacific Pride? It hasn't had so much as even one leak, let alone a blow-out."

"Yet."

"Don't be an alarmist."

"Harper, you know perfectly well that what happened to the Gulf shoreline could happen here. But even if it doesn't, just the day-to-day operation of every single Prime Pacific platform dumps tons of waste materials into the ocean. Brine wastes, toxic metals like lead chromium and mercury, oh, and let's not forget carcinogens like benzene. And now your father wants to build another platform just a few miles down the coast. Good-bye wildlife, good-bye dolphins, good-bye pelicans, good-bye otters. How can you not care?"

The satisfied smile disappeared. "If you want to keep getting gas for your nasty old truck, those are the risks. But they're minimal. Don't you realize the legal and environmental hoops Daddy has to jump through to get a platform up? The studies he has to present to the EPA? You and your tree-hugging friends should thank him for all the pains he's been taking.

Now, I suggest you stop insulting my father. Especially since your own felon of a father is nothing to be proud of. How about another cranberry-apricot scone?"

I gritted my teeth. "I'd love one, thanks."

She took one, too.

Maybe the Betancourts' cook included Valium in the cranberry-apricot scones, because as we munched, our tempers cooled, and Harper discussed more neutral subjects, such as movie stars (Harper had once dated Leonardo DiCaprio) and rock stars (she'd also dated Mick Jagger).

After giggling about what Mick had once supposedly done with her, she suddenly asked, "Is that cat hair on your dress?"

I looked down. "Can't imagine where it came from."

"Probably a cat." Finished with her I-Slept-With-A-Star tales, she returned to discussing her marriage, confiding that even before her husband took up with Amberlyn, he had visited other beds. The first affair began less than a month after their marriage. A student. Blond, of course. With big boobs.

"Stuart thought I didn't know, but I did. I'm not stupid. Daddy had a talk with him, said if the screwing around continued, he'd stop Stuart's allowance. That made Stuart straighten up, so he went out and got himself a mistress."

F. Scott Fitzgerald was right. The rich are different than us.

"You know, Harper, maybe you shouldn't be telling me all this."

She laughed. "Because then you might suspect me of murdering my husband? But Teddy, that's why I've invited you here today, because I know you already do! So for the sake of our long, close friendship, I'm going to save you time and assure you that no, I didn't kill Stuart, and I can prove it." She pulled some papers out of the Coach handbag at her feet and shoved them at me. Photocopies of airplane tickets and hotel receipts. "See, Miss Suspicious? I wasn't even in the country when Stuart died."

"Why bother proving it to me? Why not just...?"

"Because you and your boyfriend work together. He sends you out to act oh-so-bumbling-and-innocent, while you entice people to tell you their secrets. Then you..."

"Fiancé. And you're one hundred percent wrong. Joe hates it when I get involved in homicide cases."

"As if I believe that."

I looked down at the photocopies in my lap. "So how was Banff?"

"Canadian."

"Canada usually is."

"You can see I have an iron-clad alibi."

My cranberry-apricot scone now happy history, I helped myself to another, leaving only one. Munching delicately, I said, "With your money, you could have hired some rent-a-thug to do the deed."

Harper snapped, "Well, I didn't!"

"Hmm. The more you talk about Stuart, the less I understand why you married him in the first place. Please don't try to convince me it was because of his tall tales of derring-do."

She pressed her lips into a prim line. "The marriage was Daddy's idea."

"C'mon, Harper. As you pointed out, we've been 'dearest friends' for a long time—since we were children, as a matter of fact—and if there's one thing I know about you, it's that you have never at any time in your life, listened to anything your father said. Except when it would get your allowance raised."

I took advantage of the subsequent silence by grabbing the remaining scone. After I had wrapped it in a napkin and slipped it into my handbag, Harper finally answered.

"Remember when you got married and moved to San Francisco?"

Who could forget? Even living in one of the world's most beautiful cities hadn't been able to numb the pain I had felt when Michael left me for another woman. "What's San Francisco got to do with anything?"

"You weren't here, that's what. While you were up there, I was, uh, I was having some bad times." Her face flushed so deeply that it almost matched the red settee she was sitting on.

"Bad times meaning…?"

After clearing her throat, she said, "The usual. Booze. Drugs. I was living on my own, had started running around with a crowd that… Well, the less said about them, the better. My boyfriend at the time? He was actually my dealer. Daddy was so furious when I got my third DUI that rather than bailing me out, he let me go to jail for the full ninety days. The experience, it…it was grotesque. The women they threw me in with knew who I was because my arrest had made the local papers. Two of them beat me so badly that I lost a tooth." Still flushing, she tapped a canine. "Implant."

Not knowing what to say, I said nothing.

"The week before my release, Daddy came to see me. He said that since I'd been, ah, abusing my allowance, he was cutting me off. Can you imagine? Here I'd dropped out of school, had no skills, and unlike you, had no means of support. The only way Daddy agreed to give my allowance back was if I moved into the family compound and settled down. It was clear that 'settle down' included getting married. Daddy actually made a list of people I was allowed to date—you wouldn't believe how short it was—but Stuart was on it. For some reason, Daddy liked him."

I didn't know whether to laugh or get furious on her behalf. "What did your mother think about that?"

She shrugged. "Mother always agrees with everything Daddy says."

"But just because Stuart Booth was on the approved list doesn't mean you had to marry him. This isn't the Middle Ages."

"It is if you're a Betancourt."

She had a point there. Curiosity getting the better of me, I wanted to know who else in San Sebastian County came Betancourt-approved. "Could you tell me who else your father deemed appropriate?"

She reeled off several names, most of them mid-level county movers and shakers. A widowed congressman, two corporate attorneys, the owner of a famous winery—all either unmarried or wending their way through the divorce courts. The only name that surprised me was Frasier Morgan's.

"But Frasier was married then!" I said.

Here Harper managed a smile. "Daddy said his marriage would never last, but somehow Evelyn stuck it out with him until just recently. These days, nine years is practically a lifetime. Speaking of, how long were you married? Five years, wasn't it?"

"Four and a half."

"Why didn't you just let Michael have his affair? Eventually, the bloom would have been off the wild rose and you'd still be in the catbird's seat."

The former teacher in me cringed at the mixed metaphors, but eager to get her off the subject of my failed marriage, I said, "The choice wasn't mine. But back to Frasier. How'd he wind up on your dad's list? Financially speaking, at the time he was hardly in the same category as the others. He still isn't."

"True, but he'd just started at Prime Pacific and Daddy said he had an excellent future."

"Really?" The Frasier I knew wasn't "excellent" at anything.

"Really."

"So what are you going to do now? Have your father draw up another list?" The minute the words were out of my mouth I regretted them, but Harper didn't seem to mind. In fact, she laughed.

"He already has. He's even trying to interest me in Frasier again, but I've got my own plans. I'm Stuart's sole heir and the beneficiary of his insurance policy. When the funds are released, I'll be moving to New York, maybe work in fashion design. Or on a magazine. That's more my speed than playing dutiful daughter."

"New York's a pretty expensive place."

Her laugh sounded as airy as wind chimes. "I'll be getting just short of two million."

"I didn't know college professors made that much."

"They don't. Daddy paid him a bundle to marry me."

My shock must have been visible because she laughed again. "Oh, Teddy, you are such a prude! Payoffs like that have been going on for centuries. Besides, in the beginning, before I found out what a bore Stuart was, he wasn't all that bad. He could even be fun on occasion, especially once he got involved with that Amber person. She loosened him up in some fun ways, if you get my meaning." She winked.

It was doubtful that Booth's harassment victims would agree that he "wasn't all that bad," especially Lila Conyers, but I refrained from saying so. Something else had been puzzling me ever since I'd become interested in this case, and this might be my only chance to clear it up.

"Okay, I plead guilty to being a prude, but how did Stuart find out about SeekingSugarDaddy. com in the first place?"

The question didn't put a dent in her laughter. "Because Daddy told him about it. He's been a regular customer for years."

By five-thirty, I was back at Joe's with the napkin-wrapped scone in my hand. The days I'd spent in Casa Rejas had taught me how much Colleen loved to bake. No matter the time of day, she could usually be found in the kitchen. But instead of standing sentinel in front of the stove when I walked into the kitchen, she was typing furiously away on her laptop in the tiny office nook. Upon seeing me, she closed down whatever she'd been working on and asked, "What's that you've got?"

I unwrapped the scone. "I was wondering if you could match this."

With a bemused expression, she took it from me. After taking a bite of the delicious thing, she said, "Cranberries, apricots, a dusting of pistachio, sweetened with sugar *and* honey. Easy peasy."

She searched through the kitchen cabinets, laying out a collection of ingredients on the countertop. Taking inventory, she mourned, "Oh, fiddlesticks. I have everything but apricots and pistachios. It would have been nice to have scones for breakfast tomorrow. If only…"

Never let it be said I can't take a hint. "Whole Foods is only five minutes away. I'll pop over there and get some. You want dried apricots or fresh?"

"Dried will be fine. I'm a little low on baking soda, too. Used the last of it on the cake yesterday."

Bonz, trailed by Bridie and Tonio, followed me to the door. They would all have piled into my truck if I'd let them, but I made them stay home.

A good thing, too, because once at Whole Foods, I ran across Frank Owens in the baking goods aisle. He was putting a bag of chocolate chips into an already loaded shopping cart. Nearby, two female shoppers were goggling at him. I couldn't blame them. Hunky man. Buying chocolate. What's not to goggle?

"You bake?" I asked the otter keeper, pulling my mostly empty cart alongside his.

Those devastating blue eyes looked into mine. "On occasion."

"It's pretty hard to bake on a boat."

"That's not where I bake."

"Ah. At Ariel Gonzales' house, right?"

He pulled a face. "I guess the cat's out of the bag. Not that it was ever in there to begin with."

"How long have you known her?"

"Several years." He started rolling his cart down the aisle toward check-out, probably hoping I wouldn't follow. But I did. Baking soda, dried apricots, and pistachios already in the cart, my own shopping was done.

"I thought you worked on Tuesdays," I told him.

"Usually, yeah, but due to your being laid up, Zorah's shifted everyone's schedule around. Tomorrow was supposed to be my day off, but I'm working instead, so I have to do my shopping now." He gave me a near-scowl. "Look, it's always nice chatting with you, Teddy, and I'm glad to see you're feeling better, but I'm in a rush here."

With that, he wheeled off to a longer check-out line before I could say anything else. I let him go, even though I had wanted to ask him why only Ariel had shown up to help me the night I'd been shot.

Dinner could have gone better.

Bridie, that adorable little blabbermouth, had fallen in love with my Nissan pickup, and began pestering her daddy to buy one just like it. "Teddy drives all over in her truck!"

Joe frowned. "Drives? You've seen her drive, like today?"

"And yesterday! Back and forth! Back and forth! I want a truck just like it! We can put puppies in it! Daddy, can we get a puppy?"

At hearing the word "puppy," Bonz looked up from where he'd been lurking under the dinner table in hopes someone would drop something.

"You'll have a dog when your daddy and I get

married," I assured Bridie, hoping to steer the conversation away from me driving back and forth, and back and forth, in my truck. "And a cat, too."

My ruse didn't work.

"I thought you were going to take it easy," Joe said.

"Oh, but I'm feeling so much better! I'm even starting work again tomorrow. For a half day, anyway. Zorah's loaning me the new trainee to do the heavy lifting, so I'll be fine."

"Listen, Teddy…"

"For breakfast tomorrow we're having cranberry-apricot scones," Colleen interjected.

"What's a scone?" Tonio piped up.

God bless the boy. "Sort of a Scots biscuit, only bigger and more crumbly," I told him. "And sometimes with fruit in it."

"Chocolate chips are common, too," Colleen said, furthering my rescue.

Before I stopped to think, I said, "Maybe that's what Frank Owens was going to bake. Chocolate chip scones."

"Are you talking about the river otter keeper?" Joe didn't sound happy.

"Um, yes."

"When were you talking to Mr. Owens?"

"Today, in the baked goods aisle at Whole Foods. It was only a conversation in passing."

Joe was so unhappy with this turn of events that he delivered another lecture about the dangers of amateur sleuths mixing themselves up in murder investigations.

When he finally ran out of breath, I said, "Point taken."

Colleen, quick to take advantage of my apparent surrender, steered the conversation to a less incendiary topic.

Politics.

After we'd all peacefully agreed to disagree, I excused myself from the table, explaining that my shoulder was aching and I wanted to turn in early. Instead, I dragged my laptop out from under the bed and opened the BAC file—*Booth/Amberlyn Case*—and transcribed my conversations with Ariel Gonzales and Harper Betancourt as best I could. Once finished, I updated several other interviews, most notably those with Kenny Norgaard, Ariel Gonzales, and Darleene Bauer, president of the Otter Conservancy. While I was typing, it became clear that I needed to talk to Darleene again.

That otter count thing kept bothering me.

Something else was bothering me, too.

The behavior of Janet Hewitt, the zoo's trainee zookeeper, made no sense unless something had been going on between her and Booth. And, if so...I typed in my reservations about her, then moved on to someone else.

To keep my suspect list honest, even when it hurt, I added my conversations with Lila Conyers to the list. Just because she had saved Bonz from being euthanized didn't mean she was incapable of killing a human or two.

Then, hating myself, I shut down my laptop and tried to sleep.

Chapter Nineteen

An uneasy conscience prevents a good night's sleep, so the next morning I showered and dressed with the self-awareness of a robot. I didn't truly come alive until I arrived at the zoo, where I found more flowers waiting for me in the staff lounge. While I admired the American Beauty roses, several zookeepers squabbled over the right to fetch me coffee.

"Hey, I'm not all that sore," I told Robin Chase, big cats. "I can get my own."

"You'd say that if you were hobbling around on a broken leg," scoffed Manny Salinas, birds. Winning the coffee urn battle, he filled me an extra-large cup and brought it to the table. "Now tell us what happened. Unless you'd rather not."

The other zookeepers had such expectant

looks on their faces that I relented and told them everything, from my foggy walk, to the rustling in the bushes. "And that's basically all I remember," I finished, "until I came to and found Ariel Gonzales leaning over me."

"Did you get a look at the shooter?" said Myra Sebrowski, her beautiful face not looking cranky for once.

I didn't get the chance to answer because Robin gave her a how-dumb-can-you-get glance. "Of course she didn't, Myra. Otherwise there'd have been an arrest. And it'd be all over the papers."

The coffee was terrible. It usually was. Since we zookeepers had to furnish our own beans, we almost always wound up with the cheap stuff. But today I was feeling generous, so I made a mental note to stop by Dark 'N' Deadly Roasters for something tastier to contribute. As a further treat, I would bring in whatever cranberry-apricot scones were left over from Colleen's baking frenzy. Hers had matched the Betancourts', maybe even surpassed them.

Later, while driving my zebra cart toward Tropics Trail to meet up with trainee Janet Hewitt, I remembered that although Frank Owens hadn't been in the staff lounge, he was scheduled to work today. So instead of continuing south, I detoured up the path leading to the river otter enclosure. My luck was in. Frank was on the other side of the pond, scooping otter poop into a plastic baggie while four otters—three females and one male— looked on.

"Hi, Frank!" I called over the clear acrylic fence.

He jerked his head up. So did the otters.

"Oh. Hi." Frank didn't sound thrilled to see me, although one of the otters—Mr. Wiggles, I think—humped over to the fence to check me out.

"I need to ask you a question."

A scowl. "Can't you see I'm busy here? Mr. Wiggles has been acting mopey, so I need to take his droppings down to the Animal Care Center to be checked under a microscope."

Mr. Wiggles looked fine to me, but as any zookeeper knows, appearances can be deceiving. "Hope it's nothing. Um, there's something I've been meaning to ask you. The other night when I was shot, Ariel showed up to help me. Where were you? You don't come across as a man who'd ignore someone in distress."

With a sound of disgust, Frank stood up.

"Since when are my whereabouts any of your business?"

I pointed to my shoulder and the bandages peeking out from under my shirt's short sleeve.

"Aw, hell, Teddy." Clutching the bag of otter poop, he walked around the pond and approached the fence. Lowering his voice, he said, "For your information, I didn't know you'd been shot because I wasn't there when it happened. I was someplace else. Ariel stayed behind on the boat. When she heard the gunshot she did her Marine thing and rushed to the rescue."

"If you weren't on your boat, where were you?"

"You really want to know?"

"Would I be here if I didn't?"

A sigh. "I was at the north end of the harbor, attending an Alcoholics Anonymous meeting. By the time I returned, you'd already been hauled off to the hospital."

"Oh."

"Yeah, oh. Now, is there anything else?"

"Nope." Embarrassed, I started up the cart.

"Don't take off yet, Teddy. I have a question of my own."

"What?"

"In all this poking around into other people's business, did you ever find out what was going on with the otter count?"

"Why do you ask?"

"Those final numbers. They don't seem off to you?"

Shrugging, although it made my shoulder hurt, I said, "I've had other things to worry about."

"Hmph." Without further explanation, he went back to work.

Frowning, because he was right, I headed down to Tropics Trail to join Janet, my helper for the day. Her being assigned to me was good in more ways than one. I needed clarification on her relationship with Stuart Booth, given her tearful outburst while returning from the TV station last week. Maybe she was just the overly emotional type, but then again, those tears could have stemmed from something else.

True to Zorah's word, Janet was waiting for me next to the giant anteater enclosure. Lucy and her pup hadn't been let out of their night quarters yet, so Lucy was restless.

"I appreciate this." I told Janet as I climbed down from the cart.

No smile. "Yeah, well. So what do you want me to do?"

"Help me sweep up."

After I'd released Lucy and Little Ricky into the holding pen, Janet and I worked silently for the next half hour. Whenever I attempted conversation, she swept her way toward the other end of the enclosure, pointedly ignoring me. Once she came within the anteaters' grabbing distance at the pen's gate. Alarmed, I called out a warning.

"Get away from there! That anteater has four-inch talons!"

Janet moved, but not by much.

I spent the rest of our time in Tropics Trail making certain she didn't get herself killed. After the last animal was taken care of, I sent her over to Friendly Farm, where nothing would try to disembowel or eat her. As soon as she disappeared down the trail, I called Zorah on my cell, eschewing the more public radio frequency.

"Janet needs retraining. And she certainly doesn't need to work with big cats."

"Funny you should say that," Zorah replied. "Robin Chase told me pretty much the same thing yesterday."

"The girl's not careful enough."

"Robin said she actually tried to pet Maharaja."

I gasped. As beautiful as the big cat was, like all five-hundred-pound Bengal tigers, Maharaja was a perfect killing machine. You don't get cuddly with killing machines.

"Zorah, did you check Janet's references?"

"No references to check, since this is her first job at a zoo."

"She didn't do any volunteer work at one before getting her degree?"

"Not that I could find."

"Then why'd you hire her?"

Zorah's answer wasn't comforting. "Janet Hewitt is Aster Edwina Gunn's grand-niece, or something like that. She insisted I hire her."

Nepotism, thy name is idiocy. "I'm calling Aster Edwina right now."

"Better you than me." Zorah hung up.

Aster Edwina wasn't pleased to hear my complaint. "I asked you to keep me apprised of what's happening in the Booth case, not meddle in Gunn Zoo's hiring practices."

"You don't care if your niece gets her hand bitten off? Or something worse?"

"I'll speak to her about it. But the girl needs a job."

"Not one she's temperamentally unsuited for."

There was a long pause before the old harridan said, "Janet's had a rough time lately."

"Such as?"

"None of your business."

Even stone eventually wears away if water drips on it long enough, so I continued. "She could also wind up getting someone else hurt when they have to rush in to rescue her. Think of the lawsuits. Look, I know Janet has a bachelor's in Marine Science, so why not stick her in a lab somewhere like the one run by the Monterey Bay Aquarium? She'd help rehab injured otters, and they're not lethal." I was careful not to mention the open slot at Blue Seas because I was still hoping Lila would snag that job.

"I don't want the girl to be so far away."

"Monterey is less than thirty miles from here."

A note of disquiet crept into Aster Edwina's voice. "There are…ah, family complications. But you say she actually tried to pet Maharaja?"

"That's what Zorah told me. And just a few minutes ago I saw her leaning against the holding pen while the giant anteater was still in it."

"That anteater's a menace."

"The anteater is simply being an anteater. Janet is the menace."

Another long pause. Then, "I'll give the situation some thought." Promising nothing, she ended the call.

I wasn't happy. After dinner last night, Joe had hinted that time alone with just the two of us would be nice, so we'd driven down to the harbor. Before we boarded the *Merilee*, I had seen Lila Conyers sitting on the deck of her houseboat looking bereft. When I'd called out a hello, her return greeting was so feeble I could barely hear it. She'd been crying again. The realization had cast a pall over Joe's and my romantic tryst, and we returned to his house earlier than planned.

Now, as I checked on Janet's welfare at Friendly Farm—even chickens can peck until you bleed—I remembered the haunted expression on Lila's face. Since Joe was still refusing to share any information about the Booth/Amberlyn case, I could only assume the official investigation was at a standstill. Poor Lila.

Friendly Farm was a good place for hard thinking. Now that I didn't have to worry about Janet wandering too close to something lethal, I could concentrate. While the trainee raked out the communal paddock, I compiled a mental list of people who might have disliked Stuart Booth enough to murder him.

At the top was my "dearest friend" Harper Betancourt-Booth. Not being an idiot, I didn't buy her story about not minding her husband having a mistress; she might have murdered Amberlyn out of jealousy. And then there was the money Harper was about to inherit from her husband's death. She wouldn't have been the first woman to kill someone to gain financial independence. Regardless of the paperwork she had given me, I decided to do a little more checking on her story about being in Banff.

To be fair, my suspect list also needed to include Lila herself, because she had the strongest motive for killing Booth. But try as I might, I couldn't see her killing Amberlyn.

Which was the central problem, wasn't it? Why would Booth's killer also murder Amberlyn? At times it seemed that half of San Sebastian County—the female half, anyway—bore a grudge against the man, but the same could not be said for his Sugar Baby. Aside from the method she had chosen to get through college, Amberlyn had been no threat to anyone...

I stopped myself right there.

How did I know Amberlyn was no threat? Perhaps she had seen something, heard or seen something, or...

"Okay, I'm done. What do you want me to do now?" A sulky Janet stood in front of me, holding a rake.

I looked at my Timex. Eleven-thirty. "Why don't we get an early lunch?"

She didn't answer, just dropped the rake where she stood and walked off.

Jack Spence, bears, had made a pizza run into San Sebastian, and although the vegetarian pizza was only lukewarm by the time I bit into it, it was still delicious. The pizza made the staff lounge more crowded than usual, and gossip was rife. Over the weekend, Robin Chase, big cats, had broken up with Jack in order to reconnect with Buster Daltry, rhinos. Myra Sebrowski, apes, had been spotted at the San Sebastian Cinema's showing of the French classic, *A Man and a Woman*, with Manny Salinas, birds. Oleg Checkov, marsupials, had been involved in a fistfight at Ye Old Alehouse with Danny Wong, herbivores, over the charms of Betty Howell, reptiles.

My ears pricked up when I heard that Frank Owens, otters, had given Ariel Gonzales, anchorwoman, a big fat diamond ring. Since when did zookeepers have money for a big fat diamond anything?

Intrigued, I gobbled down the rest of my pizza and headed for California Trail, leaving Janet Hewitt still sulking in the lounge.

All five North American river otters were in their pool, rolling and tumbling in what appeared to be a group game of You Can't Beat This. Only half the size of sea otters, they were also more limber, and as a result, more playful. When they spotted me, Mr. Wiggles left the pond and weaseled up to the fence, hoping I would ignore the DO NOT FEED OTTERS sign. I didn't. Instead, I walked around to the keepers' entrance, where I found Frank tidying up their night quarters.

"You again."

Trying to sound non-threatening, I replied, "Just wanted to congratulate you on your engagement."

"Can't keep anything secret in this place, can I? But I doubt you came all the way up here for that. What do you want this time?"

"I hear the diamond was quite large."

To my surprise, he laughed. "Jesus, Teddy, do you ever listen to yourself?"

"Anatomically speaking, it's impossible not to."

"Always ready with the repartee, aren't you? Must be the Old Town blood in your veins. But okay. Get your questions off your chest so I can answer them and get back to my low-paying job."

I granted him the Old Town snipe since it was well-known that only the two-percenters could afford to live there, which we Bentleys had done for generations. "Okay, since you brought it up yourself, I was wondering how a zookeeper could afford what's being described as a real whopper."

"Seen my boat yet?"

"Huh?"

"As nosy as you are I'm shocked you haven't checked her out already, so let me describe *Ring of Bright Water* for you. She's a completely refitted 1965 Classic Feadship Motor Yacht, sixty-five feet long, fifteen-and-a-half in the beam, cruises at eleven knots, and has three double en-suite cabins. Cost me almost two mill."

I swallowed. "That's a lot of boat."

"Especially for a zookeeper, right?"

"Right."

"You've got guts, I'll give you that. So as a reward, Ms. Nosy, I'll tell you a secret."

After wiping his hands on his pants, he walked toward me. I hadn't realized until then how big he was, six-four at least. But I stood my ground as he leaned over and whispered in my ear.

"Lithium batteries."

I jerked my head away. "Huh?"

"Some lithium batteries have been exploding. But not the ones manufactured by Light, LTD."

"So?"

"Light, LTD, was started by a friend of mine. I'd come into a small inheritance, so when he needed funding for a project he was working on, I bought in. Just as a favor, old school tie, etc. Imagine my surprise when shares in Light, LTD, skyrocketed and I wound up rich." White teeth flashed.

I was familiar with the saga of Light, LTD, as was anyone who read the *Wall Street Journal* on occasion. "Then why are you shoveling shit in a zoo?"

His smile faded. "Because as it turned out,

being a member of the idle rich wasn't good for me. It gave me too much time to party, which I did. Big time. But you know what they say. All parties have to end, and mine ended with me having a near-death experience in the ER. After detoxing—booze wasn't my only vice—I quit living on my too-easily-gotten gains, and started working again."

"In a zoo."

"Did I happen to mention that I've always liked animals?" A wry smile.

"How'd you meet Ariel?"

"At Cal Poly. We were tight until I messed it up. She dumped me—hard, I might add—and joined the Marines right after graduation. Ariel isn't the kind of woman you forget, though, so once I cleaned up my act, I went looking for her. I didn't have any luck until one day in Seattle, while I was sitting on deck and watching *Good Morning, America*, they reran one of the interviews she did with you. You know, where the honey badger got loose in the studio. I was laughing my sober socks off when all of a sudden, there Ariel was, the love of my life. The second the program went to commercial, I set sail for Gunn Landing. So you see, my dear Teddy, you and that wild-ass honey badger inadvertently played Cupid for me, which is the only reason I'm telling you all this."

"You just showed up and proposed?"

"Don't I wish. It took almost three months of demonstrably sober behavior before that woman would even go out with me again. But once she did, the flame rekindled. Thus the 'real whopper' of an engagement ring, which I can certainly well afford."

"As well as the big boat."

"Yes, my beautiful *Ring of Bright Water.* She's large enough, by the way, to accommodate the engagement party Ariel and I are throwing next weekend. You're invited, of course. Just don't bring that honey badger."

Like most women, I love a good romance novel even when its plot seems implausible. Real life can be implausible, too. As I steered my zebra cart toward the koala enclosure, I thought about the number of coincidences necessary for Ariel's and Frank's love story to have a happy ending. Boy gets girl, boy dissipates, boy loses girl, boy goes to rehab, boy gets girl again, and somewhere in the middle of all that, boy amasses a fortune. Life being life, it could all have happened the way Frank claimed.

As soon as I had parked near the rear of the

monkey enclosure to visit Kabuki, my phone vibrated. While hurrying toward the night house, I hauled the phone out of my cargo pants, expecting a call from Joe, who had promised to call around noon.

But the voice on the other end of the phone wasn't Joe's.

In fact, the connection was so distorted I couldn't tell if the caller was male or female. His/her message was clear, though.

"Back off, or the next shot will be to your head."

Chapter Twenty

Reporting the threat to Joe was out of the question. He was already so apprehensive about my welfare that he had only half-jokingly threatened to lock me up in the San Sebastian Jail for my own protection.

If he knew about the call...

"Shoulder hurting?"

I glanced up to see Lex Yarnell sliding his cell phone into his pocket. Still grieving over Amberlyn's death, the park ranger's eyes were bloodshot, but he had pulled himself together long enough to send me a bouquet of orange-speckled tiger lilies, which his note said reminded him of me. Of all the flowers I'd received, they were my favorites.

"A twinge, that's all." I hoped he would interpret the quaver in my voice to physical weakness, not fear.

"Geez, Teddy. Should you be working so soon after being shot?"

"I'm fine. Who were you talking to just now?" I motioned toward his pocket.

"My sister. Why?"

"Merely wondering how your family is doing."

"They're doing fine, getting a lot of work in the fields. Thanks for asking." He didn't look grateful. If anything, he looked suspicious.

The fact that Lex and I were the only people behind the ape enclosure made me feel edgy, so I said, "Well, I guess I'd better go now."

"You be careful, okay?"

Were his words simple politeness, or a warning? Uncertain, I scratched my visit to Kabuki and climbed into my cart. When I drove away, Lex was watching me with an unreadable expression on his face.

As I disappeared over the hill, I considered two other doomed lovers. Would Juliet have loved Romeo if he'd been rag-picking poor? It seemed nice to think so, but…I was regretting my own cynicism when I saw another unlikely couple strolling hand-in-hand down the trail.

Harper Betancourt-Booth and Frasier Morgan.

I braked so hard I almost went through the cart's nonexistent windshield.

Harper looked smug, but Frasier appeared mortified. He couldn't snatch his hand away from hers fast enough.

"Goodness gracious, Teddy!" Harper said, a sly glint in her eye. "Shouldn't you be home recovering?"

"How odd you should ask since I've been out and about, even taking tea with my 'dearest friends.'"

"Taking tea is different than working like a field hand. Isn't that true, Frasier?"

Frasier duly agreed. At least he looked guilty about it.

What was going on? Harper had told me only yesterday that she was eager to escape from her father's Machiavellian matchmaking, yet here she was, strolling around the Gunn Zoo with Frasier. Had she already re-thought her bid for freedom? Maybe she was one of those people who dreamed of leading a different life but when the opportunity arose, decided the unknown was too scary. At least while living in the family compound she didn't have to worry about food on the table. Or rent.

While a red-faced Frasier pretended to be

interested in a pair of band-tailed pigeons hoo-hooing at each other from a nearby live oak, Harper continued, "Silly me. I forgot you're staying with that handsome fiancé of yours in San Sebastian instead of on your odd little boat. How gauche of me. Did you hear that, Frasier? Teddy's shacking up with the sheriff!"

Frasier's face grew even redder. "Um."

"What was that, Frasier dear?"

"Um."

If Harper was trying to make me jealous over the poor man, she was failing. I wasn't, and never would be, interested in Frasier. And anyway, he appeared to be firmly under her thumb.

His problem, not mine.

After bidding the unlikely couple a cheery farewell—at least they had Prime Pacific Oil in common—I delivered my zebra cart to the shed and clocked out for the day.

My conscious mind had planned a return to Casa Rejas, but my unconscious mind refused to cooperate, and I found myself driving toward

Gunn Landing Harbor. Something Frank Owens had said was bothering me.

Once at the harbor—oh precious ocean, oh precious moored boats, oh even precious thieving seagulls—I found Darleene Bauer enjoying a noontime margarita on the deck of her *Fleet Foot*. The president of the Otter Conservancy raised her gray eyebrows when she saw me. "Well, as I live and breathe, if it isn't the harbor's latest gunshot victim. Get your ass on up here, Teddy, and join me in a margarita. I made enough for two, although I'll confess I meant them both for myself."

I turned down the margarita but boarded the *Fleet Foot* anyway. Not wanting to waste any time, I started right in. "Was there anything weird going on with the otter count? I mean, other than Stuart Booth getting murdered while writing down the numbers."

Darleene snorted, blowing away a dusting of salt on the rim of her drink. "Funny you should ask. I was going to discuss it with you, but for obvious reasons you haven't been around much lately." She gestured at my shoulder. "But that can hold off until the next Conservancy meeting when we can all talk about it."

"Maybe you could let me know while I'm

here. I need to get back to Joe's or he'll send the Coast Guard out to hunt me down."

The crusty old thing actually smiled. "He is a bit overprotective, isn't he? Though not without cause."

"Darleene. The otter count."

"Oh, all right." She took another sip of her margarita and then cleared her throat. "This year we had four people tracking the otters. Me, you, Stuart Booth, and Frank Owens, who replaced Inger when she moved to San Diego. Granted, otters being what they are, mobile and such, we can only come up with estimates. We might miss a few and count others twice, but by and large, the individual counts pretty much agree. A hundred and five otters—give or take a couple—live in or near Gunn Harbor Slough. You following me?"

I nodded. After nearly being hunted to extinction by fur traders during the last four centuries, the Slough's otter population was recovering nicely.

"So four indiv—" Darleene was cut off when a fish-stuffed pelican flew by, one of its great wings almost touching her. Recovering from the near miss, she said, "Darn pests. Getting bold, aren't they? Anyway, as to the otter count.

Four individual counts by four individual people, with a combined variance of no more than four. That's not bad."

"Especially, as you say, with otters being otters."

Another pelican landed on *Fleet Foot*'s gunwale, cocked his great head at us, then flew off only to be replaced by an evil-looking seagull. He stared at Darleene's margarita.

She held her glass closer to her scrawny chest. "There is one glaring difference. I didn't think much of it at first, because as you know, Booth died before he could send in his numbers. But your handsome fiancé, after considerable nagging on my part for the last week, finally sent me a copy of Booth's count, took it right off that cell phone you found. Here's the weird thing. Booth's count was exactly the same as last year's, and I mean, *exactly*."

"What's weird about that? I think mine was, too. I counted a total of twenty-four in my sector two years running."

"You're talking live otters. You, me, Frank—and Inga before him—also counted sick and dead otters."

"Well, sure. We always take the sick ones over to the Monterey Bay Aquarium for treatment, and bundle up the expired ones for autopsy so the techs can get a handle on the toxoplasma gondii situation."

"Teddy, this year you rescued two sick otters. Frank, three. Me, one. Booth didn't rescue any."

"Pretty much the same as last year. I'm not sure if Booth…"

Darleene raised a cautionary finger. "Something else was off."

"Which is?"

"The number of deceased otters. This year you found two in your sector, Frank found three in his, and I found three. Last year you found one, I found two, and Inga found one."

"You're talking about the increase in deaths, then? That's what's weird?" I shook my head. "Numbers can fluctuate from year, especially since the toxo…"

"Teddy! Didn't you notice who I left out?"

"Booth's count of ill and deceased otters. What were they?"

After taking another sip of her margarita, she blew a raspberry at the seagull, who only ruffled his feathers to make himself look bigger and meaner. "For two years running Booth never counted so much as one sick otter, much less a dead one."

I frowned. "That sounds…"

"Fishy. Sure you don't want a margarita? Otherwise, I'm going to throw the rest out. I don't know what I was thinking, drinking this early in the day." She glared daggers at the sea gull, which finally flew off. "And I'm certainly not going to let the damned avian wildlife have it."

"It's too early for me, too, so no thanks. Ah, the Stuart Booth thing. Sounds like you suspect he was fudging the numbers."

"Sure looks that way. Otherwise, any otter who ever died in Booth's sector sank immediately to Davy Jones Locker, was eaten by a great white who could swim in two feet of water, or was carried away by pterodactyls. Seen any of them flying around lately?"

Given the rhetorical nature of the question, I didn't answer, just explored the reasons why Booth's count didn't jibe with the others'. During the silence, a small white object entered my field of vision. It crept slowly toward Darleene, ready to pounce.

"You're about to get another visitor," I warned.

She looked around. "Oh. Him. He's been hanging around all day. Come to Mama, sweetness."

It was Toby, the orphaned cat who considered all the live-aboarders his family. Needing no more encouragement, he leapt into her lap, turned around several times, then tucked his tail around his nose and went to sleep.

"Precious, isn't he?" Darleene asked, idly stroking the cat.

"But fickle. Bonz used to think he belonged to us."

"How is Bonz, by the way? I heard he got pretty beat up."

"One splintered rib and a couple of cracked ones, but he's home with us now. Got his spirits back, too. Loves the kids."

"'Home' meaning Sheriff Joe's house?"

"Until all this is over."

"Have you given any thought to what's going to happen to the *Merilee* once you two get married?"

"We've talked about it." I didn't mention that our "talks" always ended in an argument.

Feeling suddenly bereft, I looked down the pier and over to the slip where the *Merilee* rocked gently in the incoming tide.

What *would* happen to her? During the entire length of our engagement Joe and I had been at odds over her fate. In the beginning I hadn't taken his suggestion to sell her seriously, but as he continued his demand, I'd dug in. It was time to tell him the truth.

Selling the *Merilee* would be like selling my soul.

On my way to my pickup, I passed Lila Conyers' rickety houseboat. She wasn't on deck, but Pearl Jam's "Jeremy" floated out the open door. The song, about a teenager committing suicide, seemed an unwise musical choice for a woman who suffered from depression. I stood there for a moment, wondering if I should pay her a visit, then thought better of it. Instead, I called Preston Morrell and reminded him of Lila's interest in Blue Seas' job opening.

As before, he was noncommittal.

Overwhelmed by worry, I made the trip back to San Sebastian. Not a safe way to drive, but at least I could congratulate myself on having turned down a daylight margarita.

My gloom lifted when Tonio, Bridie, and Bonz met me at the door.

"Where'd you go?" Bridie.

"Did you solve the murders?" Tonio.

"*Arf! Arf!*" Bonz.

"I drove down to the harbor to see how the *Merilee*'s doing, Bridie, and no, Tonio, I didn't solve the murders because that's not my job." Lying to children. I'll probably go to Hell for that. "Hey, where's your grandma?"

"In the bathroom." Bridie. "She's…"

"Too much information."

Colleen, the wife of one sheriff and the mother of another, always kept a pot of coffee brewing. Desperate for a cup, I left the welcoming committee and headed to the kitchen. Passing the office nook on the way to the stove, I noticed that Colleen's laptop was still running. Curious as to what recipe she might be working on now, I bent over to take a look.

And was immediately sorry I had.

On the screen were detailed instructions for cleaning gunshot residue off your hands.

Chapter Twenty-one

Three years earlier Joe's first wife, Sonia, a San Sebastian assistant prosecuting attorney, had been found slumped over the steering wheel of her car in the emergency lane of the I-5, shot in the head.

Just like my attacker had threatened to shoot me.

Her killer had never been caught.

After a few moments of panic I forced myself to think things through. From everything I had heard, Sonia and Colleen had gotten along well. At first, the two had shopped together, attended church together, and occasionally even attended spiritual retreats together. But when the children came along, their relationship had changed. With two children and a full-time law career, Sonia had been squeezed for time, and Colleen had been elected Babysitter-In-Chief. Not the best situation in a small house. There were times when Colleen must have felt desperate to have a few hours to herself, yet from what Joe had told me, the subject of a separate granny cottage never came up.

So why did Joe suddenly think that a separation between a new wife and his mother was necessary? Had there been a rising tension between Sonia and Colleen he had never told me about and wanted to avoid this time around?

I knew that Joe locked his service Glock in the master bedroom's wall safe, but I had no idea where Colleen kept the firearm she so obviously owned. Come to think of it, wouldn't her gun—if it had originally belonged to Joe's deceased father—be registered, and its ballistics a matter of record? The fact that Joe had either not noticed or...

Suddenly feeling wobbly, I grabbed the nearest coffee mug and stuck it under the coffee-maker's spout.

"Watch yourself." Colleen said behind me.

Mug half-filled, I turned too quickly and sloshed coffee all over the kitchen floor.

"I didn't realize you were still so shook up, Teddy. Why, look at you! Your hands are trembling." Colleen's face radiated concern. Or maybe she was a good actress.

I glanced past her toward the laptop. It now showed a babbling brook running through a green glade. She had hit the Escape key.

"I, uh, I, uh…I'd better clean that up." I reached out for the dishrag hanging over the faucet.

My future mother-in-law grabbed my wrist. Her grip was surprisingly strong. "Don't be silly, I'll do it. Why don't you go lie down for a while? I've been suspecting you were doing too much for someone who's been through what you have, and now it looks like I was right."

I thought getting away from her might be a good idea, too, so I fled into the bedroom and breathed deeply until the shaking stopped.

Dinner was a strained affair.

The children kept quarreling over something called a FuzzBot, Joe seemed to be a million miles away, and every time I looked up from my plate, I found Colleen staring at me. Even Bonz, who usually hid under the table hoping for scraps, stayed slumped against the sofa in the living room.

I halfway expected Joe to invite me down to the *Merilee* again for some romance, but it didn't happen, so out of disappointment I turned in early.

Colleen was right about one thing.

I had definitely been doing too much.

The next morning Colleen insisted I take the leftover cranberry-apricot scones to the zoo, where my arrival was greeted with celebration.

"Man, these are killer!" enthused Robin Chase, while crumbs fell onto her khaki uniform.

Wishing the big cat keeper had chosen a different metaphor, I gave her a weak smile, then hurried off to accomplish whatever I could on another half-shift. There would be no helper today, the careless Janet Hewitt having been temporarily reassigned to office work. The buzz in the staff lounge was that Aster Edwina took our safety concerns seriously, and that Janet's brief tenure at the Gunn was nearing the end.

On my way to Down Under to care for the marsupials, I detoured past Quarantine to visit Clarabelle, the female Japanese macaque who had just arrived from the National Zoo. As soon as she proved free of health problems she would be introduced to Kabuki, whom we all hoped would replace her former lost love.

Clarabelle was a petite monkey, as attractive as Kabuki in her way, with brown-gray fur and a red face. Intelligent eyes gazed deeply into mine when I cooed, "Is Clarabelle excited about meeting her new boyfriend?"

She cooed back. "*Oooo!*"

"So glad you feel that way. I'm certain Myra Sebrowski, your new keeper, has told you how handsome Kabuki is."

"*Oooo.*"

"I'm sure she's also told you how naughty he's been behaving, too, what with all that nasty poop-flinging."

Clarabelle pursed her lips. "*Oooo.*"

"Right. I don't approve of it, either, but we here at the Gunn Zoo believe you'll have a calming effect on him and demonstrate the proper way to behave in public. In fact, I hear from your keeper at the National that your own conduct has always been above reproach."

"*Oooo!*"

We conversed for several more minutes until Myra came in and ran me off. As I drove my cart down the hill, my concerns about Colleen's gun cropped up again. Something was wrong there.

Dangerously wrong.

That night, I got little more than two hours' sleep—no good when you're trying to recuperate from an injury. Every time I drifted off, dreams of gunshots and crying dogs jolted me back into consciousness.

At three a.m., awake and staring up at the ceiling again, I realized that my situation was untenable. *I had to get out of this house.*

But how could I do that without offending both Colleen *and* Joe?

At Down Under the next morning, the koalas were awake for once, and their constant scrabbling for affection kept my mind off the Colleen situation. Cleaning their enclosure was a joy, even though Wanchu kept wrapping herself around my leg, forcing me to hobble while I pushed the rake around.

The day was a beautiful one, with a cloudless sky and a freshening breeze blowing in from the Pacific. The fact that the breeze also carried the scent of animal offal made no difference to my lightened mood. I had come to enjoy the differing odors. For instance, koala poop had a faint medicinal scent, whereas tiger poop was gamey.

"You're a sweet-smelling girl, aren't you, Wanchu?" I asked the still-clinging koala.

"*Arrr.*"

"You're welcome."

I hated to remove her from my leg, but I was needed elsewhere, so I lifted her into her tree. Instead of being upset about that, she fell asleep.

All was peace and light with the wallabies, wombats, and echidnas, too, which helped me relax further. In truth, my zoo world seemed so rosy it made me question my paranoia about Colleen.

My future mother-in-law had always behaved warmly toward me, and from all accounts, had behaved the same way with Sonia. If I had seen a questionable website on her laptop, it didn't mean she was a serial killer. Hadn't I ever mistakenly found myself on an offensive website simply because I'd inverted two letters in a search engine?

Besides, Colleen didn't even know Stuart Booth. Or Amberlyn Lofland.

Joe was right. I needed to start minding my own business.

That determination lasted only as long as my half day at the zoo. Upon leaving, by unconscious habit I turned southwest on Old Bentley Road toward the harbor, instead of northeast to San Sebastian. By the time I caught myself, I was already nearing the parking lot at Gunn Landing Harbor. My mistake turned out to be fortunate, because when I started to make a U-turn, I saw Lila Conyers' 2012 Ford Focus being hauled away by a tow truck. Shrieking, she ran after it while a small group of liveaboarders looked on unhappily.

"What happened?" I asked, braking next to her.

Tears streamed down her face. "I was three months behind on the payments. Now even if I get a job, I won't be able to commute 'cause there aren't any buses around here. It's no use, no use. I don't know why I even try."

She turned to go back to her houseboat, but concerned about her distressed state, I exited the truck and caught her by the arm. "Here's what we're going to do, and don't you dare argue about it."

It took several hours and myriad phone calls before the towing company released Lila's car. The irony in all this came when I called her finance company to make the past-due payments, along with several other fees accumulated by the repossession. There had been only four payments left before the car would have been paid off. Furious at such financial heartlessness, I made those payments, too, so that when Lila finally drove the Focus out of the Castroville impound lot, she owned it free and clear.

"I'll repay you as soon as I get a job," she insisted, giving me such a strong hug that it made my shoulder throb. I had followed her to the harbor to make sure she arrived safely.

"No hurry, Lila. Take your time."

After waving her off to her houseboat, I walked down the dock to check on the *Merilee*.

My boat looked fine. No dry rot, no graffiti, not even any barnacles I could spot through the murky harbor water.

"You don't look like you missed me," I said, caressing her gunwale.

She didn't answer, just bobbed in the wake of the twenty-seven-foot SeaRay Sundancer purring by.

Someone else spoke to me, though.

Maureen.

Upon spotting me, the otter swam up to the *Merilee's* stern, chattering for a handout. Not wanting to incur her wrath, I went into the cabin and found a tin of sardines packed in oil. I washed off the oil as best as I could, then took the tin on deck and dropped one fish to her.

She caught it, but after a couple of sniffs, gave me a less than friendly look. *You can't do any better than this?*

"Sorry, Maureen, I've been busy trying to stay alive."

"Did you ever find out who shot you?"

Not believing in talking otters—besides, Maureen was female and the voice was male—I turned around to see Kenny Norgaard, half-sloshed as usual, holding a martini glass. His clothes smelled none-too-clean and there was a faint tremor in his hand.

"Nope," I answered. "Whoever shot me is still on the loose."

"Permission to come aboard, dear heart?"

I waved him aboard and unfolded a deck chair. As for me, the gunwale made a fine perch. Below, Maureen—still irked—swam away, leaving the rejected sardine to float down to its watery grave.

"Re you getting shot the other night," Kenny said. "Surely someone must have seen something."

"What makes you say that?"

He took a sip of his martini and smacked his lips. "Because you know how gossipy this place is. Can't get by with anything without someone getting all googly-eyed over it."

"Unfortunately, no one seems to have gotten all googly-eyed that night. I was the only person in the park. Besides the shooter, that is. At least until my rescuers showed up."

Another sip. "Untrue. The park was crawling with people."

"Are you talking about the Montinis and Ariel Gonzales?"

"Them, too."

"Too?" I frowned. "Are you saying you saw someone else out there around the time I was shot?"

"Ruth Donohue and Dee Dee, for starters."

"For *starters*?!"

"Calm down, dear heart. I'm sure it was all innocent fun."

I didn't know whether to strangle Kenny or hit him over the head with the sardine tin. Because of the state of my shoulder, I did neither. "Perhaps you'd be good enough to explain. In detail, and not one sentence at a time."

He downed the rest of his martini. "You remember how foggy it was that night? And cold?"

"Skip the weather report."

"But it's pertinent, because that's why Ruth and Dee Dee were out there." Maybe it was my imagination but I thought I detected a note of malice in his voice.

"Explain."

"Dee Dee got the idea when everyone was playing that ridiculous *Pokémon Go* game, you know, rushing around trying to find some silly pocket monster and get points or some such. They were both into it, but Dee Dee decided to create a game of her own." He looked at me as if waiting to be praised.

"Kenny…"

"You can be so impatient, dear heart. Ah,

you wouldn't happen to have any gin below deck, would you?"

"No. Are you going to tell me what you said you would tell me or are you just going to babble?" I stood up, too irritated to remain sitting.

Perhaps Kenny thought I was getting ready to throw him overboard, because he delivered the rest of his tell-all in a rush.

"Okay, okay. Dee Dee designed this new game called *Find Susie Seagull*, and it takes place in a marina that's something like ours. According to the game, Susie could be anywhere, on the pier, on a boat, in one of the restaurants, on shore, in a park, in a car, out in the hills, wherever. She and Ruth had been waiting for a foggy night to give it a dry run, so to speak. Dee Dee didn't want it to be easy, because *Find Susie Seagull* was designed for mid-level gamers, not beginners, a combination of *Pokémon Go* and geocaching, that thing where you hide a box full of stuff and the gamer who finds it takes one thing and puts another thing in the…"

"I know what geocaching is. So what you're telling me is that Ruth and Dee Dee were both in the park when I was shot? But if they were out there, why didn't they say so when the police questioned them? Or did they?"

He shrugged. "Haven't the faintest, dear heart. Um, I wouldn't mind vodka. Or tequila. Or even wine, if that's all you have."

"Sorry, all out." I waved my hands in a shooing motion. "Now, thanks for the information, but I've got business to attend to."

"You mean you want me to…?"

"Leave. And maybe make yourself some coffee."

"Mmph."

Aggrieved, he clambered out of the deck chair and none-to-steadily stepped onto the dock. After regaining his balance, he tottered toward his *High Life*.

The second he was out of sight, I made a beeline toward *Clear Light*, where I found Ruth and Dee Dee enjoying a late lunch on deck.

"Come aboard," Ruth said, waving a hunk of cheese. "There's enough here for you, too." Her smile looked strained. So did Dee Dee's.

Rather than abuse their hospitality, I turned down the offer of food even though I was starving. "Kenny says you two were in the park the night I was shot. Is that true?"

They exchanged guilty looks.

"More or less," Dee Dee confessed, her usually cheerful face folded into unhappy winkles.

"Mostly less." Ruth.

My puzzlement must have been obvious, because Dee Dee continued, "I'd designed a new game and we were trying it out when we heard a noise, but I swear to you we didn't realize it was a gunshot or we would have…"

"…would have done something about it," Ruth finished, her soccer-strengthened body taut with tension. "Instead, we kept moving on to the next spot, then the next, working our way inland toward Goat Hill, where the game was supposed to end. We didn't know something awful had happened until the next morning when a certain someone told us all about it. Talk about feeling like crap! Anyway, a few minutes later the cops came knocking, asking us if we'd seen or heard anything."

"Did you tell them about hearing the gunshot?"

"Of course we did." Dee Dee.

"That 'certain someone' who told you there'd been a shooting, would it have been Kenny Norgaard?"

Unison nods.

Remembering the malice in his voice, I asked, "Have either of you had a disagreement with Kenny about something?"

Double head-shakes.

"We've always been careful not to say any-thing that would upset him," Ruth said, her big hands clenched tight. "Because of, well, you know."

I stared at her. "On second thought, I'll have some of that cheese. And a pear."

Ruth loaded up a paper plate for me while Dee Dee fetched another chair. In no time my stomach was pacified into silence by Brie, crusty sourdough, and slices of Bosc.

"Those were lovely flowers you sent," I told them, after licking remnants of Brie off my fingers. "Pink and lavender carnations, such a comforting color scheme. They smelled lovely, too."

"Dee Dee picked them out. She has a bet-ter color sense than I do. Comes from all that game designing."

"Oh, don't be silly," her partner said. "You're the one who talked me out of buying that chartreuse and purple rug."

Ruth smiled. "True. It would have clashed with our red slipcovers."

After thoroughly discussing sea-going home décor we moved on to the weather. When we had said everything about the weather that could be said, I dropped my empty paper plate into their recyclables bin. "Well, gotta be going," I announced.

"To the sheriff's house?" Dee Dee.

"Yep."

"Definitely safest, considering," Ruth said. "And again, we're so sorry about the other night."

"Don't worry about it. You couldn't have known." Relieved to have allayed my suspicions of the two, I got up to leave. But before stepping off the *Clear Light*, I remembered Ruth's odd comment. "Wait a minute. You said something about always being careful around Kenny. May I ask why?"

The long silence that followed had me thinking neither was going to answer, but then Dee Dee blurted out, "Kenny's last name isn't Norgaard. It's Norton. He…"

Ruth held up a restraining hand, silencing her. "On second thought, we've said too much already. Just watch yourself around him, okay?"

As if to punctuate her words, they grabbed the remains of their lunch and scurried inside, firmly closing the hatch behind them.

I was halfway down the dock when the hatch popped open and Dee Dee stuck her head out.

"One more thing!" she yelled. "That night you were shot? We thought we saw Preston Morrell headed into the park, too."

The hatch closed again.

I stewed about that conversation all the way to San Sebastian. Upon arriving at Joe's, I wasted no time in firing up my laptop. It was a relief in a way, because I was able to hold my worries about Colleen in abeyance while I Googled every combination of Kenneth Norton, Kenneth Norten, Kenneth Norrton, and Kenneth Nortten. The various spellings of this simple name being both numerous and creative, I got hits on hundreds of men, including a trapeze artist, the owner of a dry-cleaning chain, several accountants, and multiple handymen. Weeding through all those Kenneth Whatevers took a couple of hours, but I considered the time well-spent after finding a Kenneth Nortten mentioned in an article from the *Tampa Herald*, dated twenty years back.

LOCAL MAN FOUND NOT GUILTY OF KILLING PARENTS

GRAYTON BEACH, FLORIDA—In a verdict that stunned many onlookers, the jury acquitted Kenneth Nortten, 33, in a controversial murder trial lasting more than two and a half months.

Nortten, a Grayton Beach resident, took the stand in his own defense. He testified that while he and his parents were sailing on the *Logos*, the family's racing catamaran, a sudden storm swamped the boat, washing his parents overboard. According to Nortten, he was the only one of the trio wearing a life jacket. Nortten's emotional account of the storm and his subsequent efforts to save his parents—Edna Stokes Nortten and Karl Nortten—made several jurors weep.

In a fiery summation, prosecuting attorney William Masden claimed that Nortten knocked his parents out before the storm hit, removed their life jackets, and threw them into the Gulf.

Nortten's motive, Masden said, was

financial. Karl Nortten, a respected naval architect, founded West Winds, a privately held ship-building company. Lowell Price, a family friend, testified that two months before their deaths, the elder Nortten said he was thinking of changing his will so that his nephew, Samuel Barrington, could inherit the family business.

Price testified that Karl Nortten frequently referred to his son as "a wastrel."

At the time of the deaths, Samuel Barrington had been attending a Miami seminar on double keel design. In his own testimony, Barrington said that under no condition would Karl or Edna Nortten have set sail into the Gulf without wearing life jackets.

"They were safety first people," Barrington testified. But the jury believed Kenneth Nortten's tearful testimony and found him innocent on all counts.

While leaving the courthouse, Avis Stokes, a distant cousin of Edna Nortten's, who had attended the trial every day, commented, "The Scots allow jurors to render a third verdict—Not Proven—and that's what should have been available to the jury here. To let that spoiled little snot walk away free and clear is a travesty. At least my cousin and her husband had the foresight to rewrite their wills in favor of Sam and to tie up Kenny's remaining portion in a trust. Now he'll have make do with a small monthly check instead of the fortune he erroneously thought he'd inherit."

Neither Karl's nor Edna Nortten's bodies were ever recovered. Their catamaran washed ashore near Tampa a week after the incident. It had sustained major damage.

Several photographs illustrated the article, including one of the battered catamaran. Although the man in one of the photographs was twenty years younger and approximately forty pounds lighter, he was definitely the Gunn Landing Harbor resident I knew as Kenny Norgaard.

"What's wrong, Teddy?" Colleen asked, when I came into the kitchen. She was in her usual place, hovering over the stove.

Although anxiety had made my shoulder ache, I managed a weak smile. "Oh, nothing."

Nothing, other than the fact I'd just found out that a friend might have murdered his parents, that my trusted almost-stepfather had been in the park the night I was shot, and that my future mother-in-law had been researching how to rid herself of gunshot residue.

"Did you have lunch? If not..."

"I already ate." *Not only that, I ate lunch with two more supposed friends, who upon hearing a gunshot, didn't do squat about it.*

"Dinner won't be ready for another hour, so why don't you go lie down for awhile?"

"Good idea." *It'll give you a chance to slip rat poison into my food.*

Ultimately deciding that paranoia was not helpful to the healing process, I trudged into the bedroom, whereupon I promptly fell asleep.

Chapter Twenty-two

I survived the night.

My shoulder, not so much.

When I rolled over to turn off the alarm clock, a wave of pain surged through my left shoulder. The wound had begun to bleed again. Badly. The sheets and one of the pillowcases were soaked.

Bonz, who had been sleeping at my feet, looked at me with a worried expression.

Arf!

Keeping my shoulder as stable as possible, I swung my legs around to the floor and discovered to my relief that they would hold me up. Unfortunately, my attempt to put on clothes made the bleeding intensify, so I threw a housecoat over my Otter Conservancy nightshirt and staggered into the living room with Bonz tagging behind me. Joe had already left for work so I had no choice other than to throw myself on Colleen's mercy.

"Um, can I get a lift to the doctor's office? I'd drive myself, but, I, uh…"

They say you see stars when you pass out.

Naw.

You see nada.

I woke up in the ER with Colleen on one side of me and Joe the other.

"Didn't I tell you to take it easy? Now you've gone and pulled out your stitches!" Joe.

"Oh, you poor, poor thing." Colleen.

"Sorry about the bed linens." Me.

"Move, the both of you. Can't you see I'm stitching here?" Cross-looking doctor.

"Uh, could you all..?"

No stars again, just a big black nothing.

When I next awoke, I was tucked into bed at Joe's, where Colleen had changed the sheets and pillows. The only thing that remained the same was the three-legged terrier snoozing at my feet.

A big man was sitting on a chair in the corner. His eyes were red. If I hadn't known him as well as I did, I would have sworn he'd been crying.

"Finally awake?" Joe grumped.

"Either that or I'm dreaming about a hot cop."

"Sheriff, not cop."

"Same thing."

"The San Sebastian County electorate beg to differ. How many fingers am I holding up?"

"Two."

"Now?"

"Six, if I count the thumb."

"What's your mother's name?"

"Caroline Piper Bentley Mallory Huffgraf Petersen Grissom."

"What day is it?"

"Friday."

"Try again."

"Saturday?"

"Again."

"Sunday?"

"Bingo."

"What the hell?"

"Teddy, you lost so much blood they had to give you a transfusion. Then they kept you in the hospital for two days. This isn't the first time you've woken up, by the way. You were conscious, more or less, when we brought you home, but this is the first time you've made any sense."

"Your eyes are red."

"I have a cold."

"Help me get up."

"Like hell I will. You're going to stay right there."

"But you said I was making sense!"

"Oops, I was wrong."

The door opened and my mother stormed in. Her eyes were red, too. Those summer colds are so contagious. "She's awake! My baby's awake!" She flung herself at me, kissed me all over my face, then leaned away and threw Joe a dirty look. "You said you'd call me the minute she woke up."

He glanced at his watch. "There were eight seconds left in that minute."

"Smartass."

"Is that any way to talk to your sheriff?"

"It is when he's fam…" She caught herself and resumed her usual haughty manner.

"You're a bad influence on my daughter, that's what you are." To me, she said, "How are you feeling, Theodora?"

"Like I've just had a transfusion of blood donated by a marathon runner."

Colleen peeked around the door. "Hey, you're awake!"

"That seems to be the consensus." I gave the gunpowder residue expert a big smile, just to stay on her good side.

It must have worked because she smiled back. "I bet you're hungry."

I was probably still on pain meds, because at this point I didn't care if she poisoned me or not. My stomach was growling. "Any scones left? And Joe, I don't care what you say, I'm getting out of this bed."

Once in the kitchen, I scarfed down a ham sandwich, a cranberry-apricot scone, and a glass of milk. Feeling almost human again, I returned to the bedroom long enough to change out of Colleen's loaned green nightgown into jeans and my favorite HONEY BADGER DON'T CARE tee shirt. Joe scowled while I tottered around the house in a wimpy form of exercise while Bridie, Tonio, and Bonz followed me from room to room.

Bridie offered encouragement while the adults sat and watched. "Left foot, right foot, left foot, right foot…"

After two complete tours—while passing through the kitchen I'd snuck a look at Colleen's laptop, which was showing that harmless mountain glade again—I felt winded, so I sat down on the sofa next to the scowling Joe.

"See, everyone? I'm fit as a fiddle."

"Fiddles are always going out of tune," Tonio offered. "That's what our music teacher says."

"Then I'm healthy as a horse."

"The school librarian has a horse and it's always sick."

"You should let me take you to my place," Caro said, interrupting the flow of clichés. "You'd be safer there."

I was tempted, but then reality set in. Leaving with Caro could easily be interpreted as a lack of trust in the Rejas household, and I couldn't allow that to happen. Not if even it killed me.

"That's sweet of you to offer, Mother, but I'll stay here where I've got a sheriff on duty twenty-four/seven."

She humphed. "He's always at work."

"His office is ten minutes away."

"A lot can happen in ten minutes, as you

should very well know." She gestured at my shoulder.

My shoulder was throbbing again. In the movies, the hero is always getting shot, then he gets up and chases down the shooter as if nothing's happened. It's sure as hell not like that in real life.

I kissed my mother on the cheek. "I'm fine where I am."

"Hmph."

Those twinges as I walked around had taught me something, though. I wouldn't get better keeping to my usual schedule, so I called Zorah at the zoo and told her I needed to take a couple of weeks off. Since I hadn't had a vacation in three years—that's how much I love my job— she didn't quibble. Neither did Aster Edwina, who during our brief phone call, growled that if I didn't take care of myself she'd fire me.

Emboldened by the old woman's concern, I asked the question that had been bugging me for days. "Did you have an affair with Stuart Booth?"

A long silence. Oh, I was in for it now.

"Aster Edwina, did you hear me?"

"*Ack*! I... I... I heard you all right. *Ack! Ack!*"

Choking sounds. Dear God, the woman was having a heart attack!

"Are you okay, Aster Edwina? Should I call 9-1-1? Please, I didn't mean to..."

Ack! Ack!

No heart attack. Aster Edwina was snort-laughing.

Between guffaws, she told me her sex life was none of my business, then repeated her threat: if I didn't take care of myself, she would fire me.

"Now get some rest, you silly girl."

Ack!

Dial tone.

That afternoon I felt good enough to sit in the kitchen and watch Colleen bake. From time to time I was even able to help her, if you count handing someone a measuring spoon "help." Every Friday evening she supplied cookies for the San Sebastian Library's Open Mic Night for Teens, a community service that encouraged teens to perform self-written poetry instead of shooting each other. Every now and then I snuck a look at her laptop, but never saw anything more interesting than mountain glades or, at one point, a blank screen.

She had learned to be more careful.

Monday was Joe's day off, and he had decided to spend it working on the granny cottage. Bundled up against the cool morning air, I sat on the sunroom steps and watched. There was something oddly reassuring about seeing the man I loved create something from nothing, and as the interior walls began to take shape, everything I had been through in the past few days ceased to worry me.

I was here now, and safe.

As long as Joe was around, I would always be safe.

Colleen, though…

After two days of semi-bed rest, I felt strong enough to walk around the block, and by the end of the week, I could make it all the way down to the campus of Betancourt College.

Serendipitously, as I approached the drinking fountain in the quad, I ran across Harper Betancourt-Booth as she emerged from the Marine Sciences building with Frasier in tow. He was pulling a cart loaded down with books and papers.

"Cleaning out Booth's office?" I asked Harper.

"It had to be done. Nice to see you up and around, Teddy. We heard you were in the hospital again. Did you get our flowers?"

We. Our. The ensnarement of Frasier was pretty much a done deal. I glanced at her ring finger. No ring yet. Frasier could still escape.

"I thought you'd be in New York by now, Harper."

"Plans change. I'm starting a fashion magazine."

"Where?

"Here. Daddy's fronting it, but I'll be editor-in-chief. Maybe I'll ask your mother to write an article or two. She knows a lot about fashion."

The thought of Caro actually working at something made me giggle.

"What's so funny?"

"Don't give Mother the check until you get the article."

"But isn't that the way it's done, pay the writer first?"

"You might want to bring a professional editor on board to take care of the day-to-day stuff, Harper."

She sniffed. "I'm more of a hands-on person."

That pesky giggle threatened to erupt again. After I'd successfully squelched it, we chatted about fashion magazines while Frasier remained as quietly obedient as a well-trained dog. Finally, in an attempt to draw him into the conversation, I asked, "So how are you doing, Frasier? Busy as a bee at Prime Pacific?"

"Things are going well. Looks like we might get the go-ahead on that new drilling platform." I could almost see his tail wag.

The news made me less happy. Another oil platform to despoil the Coast.

"Well, although it's been nice seeing you folks, I need to continue my walk, regain my strength."

I gave what I hoped was a polite wave and made a beeline for the drinking fountain. When I looked back, Harper, her face a mask of fury, was giving Frasier a piece of her mind.

Probably for speaking without permission.

Chapter Twenty-three

The two weeks off helped. My shoulder stopped hurting around the same time Bonz stopped limping. Miss Priss had moved in to keep him company, and for once the dog and cat appeared to have reached a détente.

Or at least my cat had stopped trying to kill my dog.

When I returned to work on a Friday—the zoo was expecting several busloads of summer campers—the other zookeepers greeted me with enthusiasm. Hopefully, it wasn't just because I arrived with a box of cranberry-apricot scones.

While nibbling on a scone and sipping at my dark roast Kopi Luwak—I'd also brought in better coffee—I thumbed through the *San Sebastian Journal*. The Booth/Amberlyn murders, still unsolved, had moved to page two, due to a more recent crime. Yesterday afternoon, three men wearing blue jumpsuits and Abraham Lincoln masks had held up the San Sebastian Bank, escaping after a fierce shoot-out with the bank guard. Following surgery for a bullet in the lung, the guard was now recovering in the ICU. Meanwhile, a statewide manhunt was ongoing for the robbers, who had fled in a black Cadillac Escalade.

But I hadn't needed to read the article to know that.

Yesterday Joe had been working on the granny cottage with Bonz and me as his faithful audience, when he'd received a call from Deputy Gutierrez. After listening for a few seconds, he'd dropped his tools and raced out of the backyard without bothering to change. As far as I knew, he was still out there somewhere in his dirty civvies, chasing down the bank robbers. In the meantime, the police scanner on the kitchen island kept Colleen and me apprised of the manhunt. This morning we'd breathed a sigh of relief to learn that no officers or innocent bystanders—other than the unlucky bank guard—had been hurt.

Yet.

In the zoo's staff lounge, the newspaper

article occasioned yet another argument on California's lax gun laws. Gun-owning Myra Sebrowski and no-guns-for-anyone-except-the-cops Buster Daltry were all but spitting at each other. Not wanting to hear any more about bank robbers on the loose with guns, I headed out on my rounds.

While raking the wallabies' enclosure I noticed how strong my right arm had grown during my layoff. I had been babying my left side, and as a result, the right arm actually gained muscle. Good news, since zookeeping, with all its heavy lifting, wasn't for wimps. Even better, my left arm was gaining back some muscle tone.

Humming a happy tune I moved on to the koalas, where I found Dr. Preston Morrell, my almost-stepfather waiting for me. His expression was that of an old sea captain ordered to shore, and none too happy about it.

"Morning, Teddy. I was under the impression you started your day with the koalas."

"The koalas are usually asleep when I arrive, as you can see, so it doesn't hurt to mix it up a bit. But, hey, this is a rare honor. What's going on?"

He pawed at his salt-and-pepper beard for a moment, then said, "I didn't want to bother you while you were recuperating, but..." He sighed. "It's just that I'm afraid someone may have given you the wrong impression about something."

"Someone? Something?" Such vagueness wasn't customary for Preston; scientists specialize in specifics. "Perhaps you could clarify."

"Dee Dee Pascal told you she saw me going into the park the night you were shot, and I'm here to tell you it never happened. I can prove I was nowhere near that park."

"How'd you know what Dee Dee said, not that I'm...ah, confirming anything."

"Oh, please. The harbor has always been a breeding ground for gossip, and for the past few weeks it's continued nonstop. Since that strange rumor about me being in the park started going around, people already have me tried and convicted for not only shooting you, but murdering Booth and that poor girl, too. I never thought I'd be in this situation, having to defend myself, but...but I don't want this to spoil my relationship with you. Or your mother."

For a man who wanted to defend himself, he was being murky about it. "I'm afraid I don't understand."

"He cleared his throat. "Okay. I...ah, I wasn't anywhere near the park or the harbor that night. I was with...with..." A flush colored his face.

"Spit it out, Preston."

"I was, er, I was... in bed with, ah, Harper Betancourt. There! I've said it."

It took me a moment to find my voice. "Harper? You were in bed with *Harper*? You've got to be kidding."

The pained expression on his face told me he wasn't.

"How could you, Preston? You, of all people, know what her family wants to do to the shoreline. And already has!" I gestured in the direction of Prime Pacific's offshore drilling platform, which at least couldn't be seen from the zoo.

"Even a marine scientist can get lonely. After your mother wouldn't marry..."

"Old water under old bridges."

His hangdog manner intensified. "Yeah. Anyway, there's no way Dee Dee could have seen me at the park the night you were shot, because that's when I was busy being an idiot with Harper, whose family's beliefs and actions, yes, I've always found abhorrent. In my defense I swear to you it was nothing more than what the kids today call a 'hookup.'"

"Oh, Preston, I thought you were above that."

"So did I."

Conscience cleansed and alibi delivered, he was about to leave, but I wasn't ready to end the conversation. "How did that ridiculous hookup happen?"

A sheepish smile. "Blame it on Phil's monthly Two-Fer Night. I was in the restaurant having the clam chowder and the two-for-one drinks when I spotted Harper. Just to be neighborly, I asked her how she was doing after her husband had, er, become deceased, and she told me she wasn't taking it well, that she felt...um, *bereft*, was the word she used. Honestly, I was just trying to be comforting, that's all, but we wound up ordering a bottle of wine, which turned into two, then three, and…"

"No, Preston. I meant who approached whom first?"

"Eh?"

"Before the conversation started, did you go over to her table or did she come over to yours?"

Preston didn't answer my question right away. He couldn't. During our conversation, the koalas had woken up. Wanchu and Nyee trundled over to the fence, looking up at us with expectant faces. Wanchu, that sly girl, reared up on her hind legs and waved her forepaws at me.

Hugs, please.

Overcome by such cuteness, Preston responded, "Awww."

I leaned down and hefted up the koala. "Is Wanchu hungry?"

She chirped a yes, then snuggled against me. Her joey stuck his nose out of her pouch, gave me a look, then disappeared back in. He wasn't human-friendly yet.

"Stay here, Preston," I ordered.

After carrying Wanchu over to her favorite feeding area, a wooden manger, I set her down and stocked it with the fresh eucalyptus leaves I'd brought in my cart. Nyee, who had followed close behind, tried to edge his mate away. She slapped him.

"Be nice," I told the two.

They tried, but a hungry koala can be a rude koala, and the slaps continued. At least no blood was drawn.

Once the two settled down, I returned to the hangdog marine scientist. "As I was saying, did Harper come up to you, or did you go over to her?"

He gave the koalas a final awww, then replied,

"I was sitting by the window with my chowder and the next thing I knew, Harper was standing at my table. Just to be polite—a lady alone, you understand—I asked if she would like to join me. She did, and we started talking..."

"And drinking three or more bottles of wine. Okay, I get it."

Harper had targeted Preston.

The question was, why?

Chapter Twenty-four

When I joined Colleen in the kitchen after my first full zoo shift in almost three weeks, she informed me that Joe had briefly returned home, showered, changed clothes, scarfed down a sandwich, then left again. The bank robbers were still out there.

"Life's not easy for county sheriffs," she said, wiping flour off her hands.

"Or their wives. Or mothers."

An unconvincing smile. "We get used to it."

Two dozen cookies were already cooling on the kitchen island as she slid two dozen more into the oven. Tonight was Open Mic Night again at the San Sebastian Library, and I knew the entire batch would disappear within the first half-hour. For mouths, teenagers had open maws.

"Did you worry about Joe's father, too?"

"Not as much as I should have." Unhappy with the subject, she changed it. "Think four dozen cookies will be enough?"

"It was, last week. And the week before that."

We talked baking for a while, then changed the topic to the weather. It might rain. Then again, it might not. Fog was possible, but this far inland, not probable. Our inane conversation kept being interrupted by updates from the police scanner. Although trying to keep the conversation light, Colleen kept glancing at the noisy thing.

So did I.

Unable to stand the scanner's scary updates anymore, I went into the living room and watched television with the children. Since it was too late in the day for *Sesame Street*, they were making do with *SpongeBob Square Pants*.

"Looking forward to Open Mic Night?" I asked Tonio.

He nodded so energetically that red curls flopped over his eyes. "Delilah might be there!"

In a previous Open Mic Night outing, nine-year-old Tonio had fallen hard for the fifteen-year-old Delilah, a budding poet. Ah, young love.

Bridie, a simpler soul, said, "Gramma says I can have all the cookies I want!"

For a while I thought about accompanying them to the library but in the end decided not to. It was past seven now, giving me almost two hours of alone time before Colleen and the children returned. Enough time for me to figure out if what I had begun to suspect could possibly be true. The two weeks I'd taken off from work had given me plenty of time to think, and I was almost to the point where I felt comfortable sharing my suspicions with Joe.

But not yet. There were still a few things I needed to clear up.

As soon as Colleen and the children left, I led Bonz into the now-darkened yard to do his business. To make certain he wouldn't hurt himself further, I kept him away from the construction site. Although the granny cottage was coming along nicely, there were still too many loose boards lying around, and too many nails, not to mention several heaped bags of insulation material. Terriers are curious animals, and it would be just like Bonz to tear open a bag and insert his face into the intriguing pink stuff.

"Sorry, no can do," I said, legging him away from a half-open bag.

He gave me a searching look. The poor thing was desperate to go into the cottage and explore all those lovely new smells, but after several attempts, he gave up and attended to his business. That included watering every plant in the vicinity.

As he made the rounds, I smiled. Thank goodness Colleen had had the foresight to enclose the kitchen garden in a sturdy slatted fence.

Colleen.

I looked at my watch. Seven-thirty. Time to do what I'd been putting off.

"Hurry up, Bonz," I called. "I need to check something."

There's no hurrying a pissing terrier. When he finally finished, I picked up his more solid contributions to the ecosystem, enclosed them in a plastic bag, and dropped it into the outdoor waste bin.

Bonz looked gratified that his offerings were being saved, but as we returned to the house he gave a final longing look at the cottage and all the imagined treasures waiting inside for him.

"Not until it's finished. Then you can snoop and sniff all you want."

He sneezed.

Before starting up the stairs, I noticed that an errant two-by-four with a nail protruding from the end was lying uncomfortably close to the stairs, where Joe must have dropped it when informed about the bank robbers. Rather than take it back to the cottage where it belonged, thus giving Bonz another chance to get into trouble, I turned it over and edged it flush against the side of the bottom step. Tomorrow morning, as soon as it was light, I would return it to the lumber pile near the cottage.

Once in the kitchen, Bonz lapped at his water bowl as I turned on Colleen's laptop to do some snooping of my own. At first Microsoft greeted me with friendly chimes, then refused to show me anything else. Password protected.

Putting aside my disappointment, I went into the bedroom, hauled my own laptop out from under the bed and made myself comfortable by using pillows as a backrest. Bonz joined me. After turning around several times, he laid his head across my left shin and fell fast asleep.

Happiness is a warm terrier.

Comforted by the snoring Bonz, I opened a Word file to "BAC." *Booth/Amberlyn Case*. Not subtle, but when it comes to computers, I'm not as slick as my future mother-in-law.

I scrolled down to the list of suspects. Colleen's had been the last to be added, and the notes were sketchy.

```
METHOD: Booth, Amberlyn,
me, shot wi same firearm?
Colleen's?
```

```
MOTIVE: ???
```

```
OPPORTUNITY: How Colleen
get from San Sebastian to
harbor, kill Booth, go home
& no one noticed??? Where
were Tonio & Bridie? Same
childcare prob for Amberlyn's
murder. And shooting me.
```

The more I stared at my notes, the more I realized how much the child care situation impacted my suspicions about Colleen. Sure, any woman could commit murder, especially any woman who owned a gun, but there was no way a grandmother as devoted as Colleen would leave those two children unattended while she drove around murdering people. She also wouldn't have taken wise Tonio or blabbermouth Bridie with her. Smiling at my own former paranoia, I typed...

LIKELIHOOD TO BE KILLER: ZERO

Satisfied, I scrolled down to the other names on my list, stopping at Dr. Preston Morrell, my almost-stepfather and head of the internationally respected Blue Seas Marine Laboratory. The last time I had worked on this list, something odd happened: I'd heard the voice of my old French teacher intoning, *"Le nuit, tout les chats son gris."*

At night, all cats are gray.

Time to double-check that, too. I punched in Dee Dee's number on my cell. When she answered, I asked, "What made you think you saw Preston Morrell going into the park the night I was shot?"

"The guy looked like him." She was hard to understand since I'd obviously interrupted her in the midst of dinner and her mouth was full.

"Looked like him how?"

A gulp, then her voice cleared. "Beard."

"The guy had a beard? What color?"

"Gray." More chomping, then another swallow. "And he was wearing that sweatshirt with the marine lab logo on the back. I have one just like it, only mine's burgundy."

"Okay, the gray-bearded guy you saw, what color was his sweatshirt?"

"Gray."

I had a Blue Seas sweatshirt, too. It was blue. The sweatshirts carried in the lab's gift shop were available in Blue Seas Blue, Blue Seas Burgundy, Blue Seas Green, Blue Seas White, and Blue Seas Black. They didn't come in gray.

But *le nuit, tout les chats son gris.*

Maybe beards, too.

After thanking Dee Dee for her help, I hung up, and with a feeling of relief typed...

LIKELIHOOD TO BE KILLER: ZERO

Wading through some of the other names was fairly easy, especially once I placed another call, this time to Preston himself. No wonder telemarketers pick dinnertime to call: everyone's stationary while chowing down.

"Sorry to bother you while you're eating, Preston, but when you met up with Harper at the restaurant the night I was shot, did you notice who else was there?"

"Can't you call in, say, a half hour?" Munch, munch.

"It's important, Preston."

A gurgle. Water? Wine? "Okay, let's see. Hmm. Well, as I said, it was their big Two-Fer night, two drinks for the price of one and two entrees for the price of one, so the place was

packed with locals. I saw Kenny Norgaard, but
he was just drinking, not eating, no surprise
there. And, hmm, that park ranger guy whose
girlfriend was killed? Lex-something? He
was with that pretty little ape keeper, Myra-
something. Oh, and I saw that *Good Morning,
San Sebastian* gal who's always interviewing you,
and hmm, let's see… " He took another bite of
whatever it was, and garbled on. "The TV gal
was sitting with Frank Owens, the river otter
guy—you know they're a couple, right?—and
he was telling her all about otters, you know,
the differences between sea otters and..."

Once Preston got onto marine animals he
never shut up, so I hurried him along. "Who
else?"

Another chomp, another gulp. "Ruth and
Dee Dee, of course, they never miss Two-Fer
Night. Oh, and Zorah, the zoo director, she
was there, but I can't remember who with. The
bear guy at the zoo? I remember being surprised
that you and the sheriff weren't there, like you
usually are…but, whatever. 'The course of true
love never does run smooth,' right? I'm sure
you two will kiss and make up over the problems you're having, especially now that he's got
you stashed away at his place. Very romantic."

Not with a mother-in-law and two kids hanging around, it wasn't. "Skip the editorial commentary. Anybody else?"

"Touchy, touchy. A few tourists came in, and a gaggle of liveaboarders, but by then Harper and I were well into our third bottle. Listen, I've got some Rocky Road ice cream here, and it's going to melt if…"

"You didn't say you saw Darleene Bauer there."

"The president of the Otter Conservancy? Because she wasn't. Not that I could see, anyway. Now, please, my Rocky Road is doing a Wicked Witch of the West and…"

"Melting. *Bon appetite*, Preston, and thanks."

I ended the call, wondering what the heck Zorah was doing dining out with Roger Daltry. One thing was for certain. If Robin Chase heard about it, she'd throw a jealous fit. Big cat keepers were funny that way.

Speaking of zoo employees, why was Lex Yarnell eating dinner with Myra Sebrowski only a couple of weeks after the supposed love of his life had been murdered?

Curious, I called him to find out, only to wind up on voice mail. Then I called Myra.

Voice mail.

A coincidence? Or…

I punched in another number. Darleene Bauer wasn't picking up, either.

Where was the rest of the world tonight, if not at home, eating? At the library, listening to teenagers recite poetry?

Unable to contact Darleene, I reread, for approximately the tenth time, the notes I'd made about our last conversation. Then I looked at the info on Preston again. Something was off, so I began at the top of the file and reread everything I'd written about the case. It took almost an hour. Finally, eyes blurring and head hurting, I gently nudged Bonz's head off my leg and went into the kitchen for a cup of coffee. The police scanner was in full yip, calling out codes I didn't recognize. It sure was a hot time in the old town tonight.

But here, with everyone gone, it was…

Boring.

Which was odd, because as slow as things sometimes were at the harbor, I had never felt bored on the *Merilee*. Perhaps because boats, unlike houses, existed on a near-human level, and humans can be quite entertaining.

I smiled, visualizing the *Merilee* rocking peacefully at her berth, an island of hush in a loud world. When all this was over, Joe and I needed to have a serious talk, because there was no way I could give up my *Merilee*. Hopefully that wouldn't end our wedding plans, but if it did, so be it. If he couldn't understand my love for my boat, he didn't understand me.

Regardless of our disagreement on the issue of the *Merilee*, it was now time to confide my suspicions about the Booth/Amberlyn case to Joe, so I picked up my cell and punched in the direct line to his office.

Voice mail.

Considering all the traffic on the police scanner, I wasn't surprised. I left a brief message for him to call me as soon as he had a chance, that I had figured out something he should know, then hung up. Yes, Joe would be angry when he found out I'd ignored his orders to cease messing around in police business, but it couldn't be helped. Booth and Amberlyn's killer had to be stopped before another victim was added to the list.

Me, for instance.

As added insurance, I called my old friend Deputy Emilio Gutierrez, but wound up on his voice mail, too. I left the same message and told him to pass it on to Joe as soon as possible.

All this yakking to faceless recordings woke Bonz up. Ears pricked, he stared at me with alert brown eyes. Then he made a sound that could have been a growl. Or a moan.

I looked at him with concern. "Is Bonz hurting?"

He jumped off the bed and landed with a yelp.

"Is it bad?"

You can never tell with an animal. One minute they seem fine, the next minute they're dead. Bonz had seemed to be healing well from his splintered rib, but a couple of weeks ago I'd seemed to be healing well from my gunshot wound, too, and look what had happened to me.

That growl/groan again.

On stiffened legs, Bonz moved slowly toward the kitchen. Phone in hand, I followed. Maybe he was simply thirsty and wanted to visit his water bowl, but if I saw one more sign of discomfort, I was calling the emergency vet.

When we made it to the kitchen, I heard the same thing he'd heard.

A cat.

Wailing in agony.

I remembered what Colleen had told me:

A coyote came down from the hills back there, and caught a rabbit in the yard… There've been cats, too…

Nature, raw in tooth and claw.

If I stayed in the kitchen, Nature would take its savage course.

But any animal lover, upon hearing those heartbreaking cries, wouldn't let it.

I started to grab a broom from the hall closet, but then remembered the sawed-off two-by-four lying just outside. Intent on using it as a scare tactic only, I barged through the sun porch and out the back door, closing it against Bonz, who howled in protest.

"Hey, coyote!" I yelled into the darkness, picking up the two-by-four. "Leave that cat alone!"

Sometimes the mere sound of a human voice will chase away a coyote, but this time it didn't work. The cat just kept screaming as if it were being torn…

There!

Movement inside the cottage. The coyote had ducked into it and was hiding in the shadows with its screaming prey. I might still be able to rescue the cat in time. If not, the coyote would leave the yard with a full belly.

"Coyote! I'm coming for ya!"

Making as much noise as possible, I held the two-by-four at an angle in front of me to enlarge my silhouette, and then ran, yelling, toward the cottage. The new moon was hiding behind a cloud, lending the yard little light, but from my earlier trip outside with Bonz I knew the location of every board and bag. Coyote would not eat tonight.

But there was no coyote.

Only a less honorable killer.

Chapter Twenty-five

When I charged through the unfinished doorway, my upraised two-by-four took the brunt of the killer's downward blow, knocking his knife to the ground.

Frasier Morgan stood there, a stricken look on his black-bearded face while his cell phone yowled on.

I didn't give him a chance to pick up the knife. Instead, I smashed him across the face with the nailed end of the two-by-four and sent the fake beard flying.

The result was ugly.

"That's for Bonz!" I spat.

For no reason other than the memory of my little terrier's splintered rib, I hit him again, splattering blood all over his Blue Seas Green sweatshirt.

He stopped moaning.

On my way out the door to rescue the nonexistent cat, I hadn't stopped to look for a flashlight, but since my eyes had become accustomed to the dark, finding Frasier's knife wasn't too hard. Touching it with only my fingertips, I tossed it out into the yard so that when—or if—he regained consciousness, he couldn't use it again. Finding his phone was even easier since it was the source of the wailing cat recording. I picked it up, muted the recording, and punched in 9-1-1.

"Attempted murder at 49784 La Paloma Lane," I said. "Attacker down. Send officers and ambulance."

"Wait! Isn't that Sheriff Rejas' address?"

"Yes, and hurry, before my attacker wakes up."

"How about his mother? And his kids?"

"Safe at the library. Now, hurry!"

"Already on it," the dispatcher on the end of the line said. "But you need to know that all the cars, including the sheriff's, are at the Grampions' farm on the other side of the valley. They, ah, they're…" She halted for a moment, then asked, "This is Teddy, isn't it?"

"Yep, and I don't care what they're doing,

you need to send someone here right now. The guy I clocked, his name's Frasier Morgan, and he killed Stuart Booth and Amberlyn Lofland. And he's tried to kill me, too. Twice!"

The moan on the other end of the line almost matched the renewed moaning of my assailant. Then the dispatcher—I think it was Carol Langley, who kept a small sailboat moored near my *Merilee*—said, "Oh, Teddy, I'm so sorry, but those bank robbers? They're barricaded in that farmhouse with Pete and Ellie Grampion and their four kids, and…" Her voice trailed off. "It's a mess."

"Are you telling me I'm on my own?"

A quick gulp of air, then "Get out of there now, Teddy! Get in your truck and drive to someplace where there are lots of people!"

"And take a chance Frasier could get away? I don't think so." I ended the call and punched in another number: Colleen's cell.

"Don't come home," I told her when she answered. "Booth's killer is in your yard. I've got him down on the ground. He's only semiconscious right now, but he's coming around again, so neither you nor the kids should be here. As for Joe, he and everyone else in the department are at the Grampions' farmhouse where those bank robbers are holding hostages. I'm on my own, but don't worry, I can handle it."

I didn't wait for her reply, just slid the phone into my jeans pocket and gave Frasier another whap with the two-by-four. As soon as he stopped moving, I tucked the two-by-four under my arm and ran to the garden shed.

Like most smartphones, Frasier's had a flashlight app, and once I clicked it on, finding what I needed was easy. I gathered up a pair of gardening shears, some wire cutters, and what was left of the two-gauge wire Colleen used to attach green beans to their trellises. After picking up one more item, I hurried back to the cottage, where Frasier had regained consciousness and was attempting to stand.

He went down again when I dropped the gardening supplies and gave him another whack with the two-by-four. Geez, the man had a skull like a rock.

Tying someone up with gardening wire isn't as easy as it sounds. You can't actually tie the ends together in a nautical knot, just twist them around each other. Doing my best, I bound Frasier's hands and feet. As an added precaution, I wrapped a longer piece of wire around his ankles, took out the slack, then looped the wire twice around his neck. If he moved, he'd strangle himself.

Satisfied, I stepped away and admired my handiwork. Frasier now lay in a tightly rolled ball, looking like a spooked armadillo.

The next time he regained consciousness I was sitting five feet away from him on a bag of insulation, a pitchfork in my hands, the tines pointing toward his eyes.

"Move and you're blind."

"You…you wouldn't…wouldn't do…that."

"You broke my dog's ribs, you piece of shit."

"He bit me!"

"Hope it hurt."

"You…you don't understand."

Actually, I did, but it would be nice to have him explain it all to me now that I'd hit the Record app on his phone. Gotta love those things. "What's to understand, Frasier? Enlighten me."

"We need…Prime Pacific…" He gulped, then tried again. "America needs oil."

"In other words, you killed two people out of patriotism? Same reason you tried to kill me? That's rich. You sure know how to spread the pain around, patriot that you are."

"Pain? No! If you'd just…stood still when… when I shot…You wouldn't… wouldn't have felt…a thing. *They* sure didn't!"

I motioned outside, to where I'd tossed the knife. "I hear getting stabbed hurts like hell."

"Not… not if…you do it right."

"Okay, you great humanitarian, you. But why not use the gun again when it worked so well the first two times?" I sneaked a covert glance at his smartphone. Still recording merrily away. Maybe it would even pick up the coyote yips drifting over the hill behind us. Drawn by the nonexistent cat's cries, the animals were ranging close to the house. Maybe they believed I would feed Frasier to them. Which wasn't a bad idea.

Oblivious to my thinking, Frasier babbled on. "After I…after I shot you…I threw the rifle…into the…the Slough. Had to get rid of it before…"

Into the Slough? That meant the murder weapon was lying in the water, waiting for some curious otter to latch onto it. Joe's minions would have to fish it out before some innocent otter got shot.

I leaned forward. "Where exactly in the Slough, Frasier?"

"Near where I...I shot Booth. I figured the cops had already searched there, and wouldn't search again. Please, please loosen this wire. I can't breathe."

"You're breathing fine, you phony." I shook the pitchfork at him. "Now explain your reasoning behind killing two people. This all started with the otter count, didn't it? Somehow you talked Stuart Booth into fudging his numbers to make it appear Prime Pacific's offshore platform wasn't harming the area's wildlife. I get that. What went wrong? Judging from this year's fake numbers, Booth was still doing his job, so why'd you kill him?"

I had already figured out why, of course, but I wanted the entire rotten scheme recorded on Frasier's cell.

"Blm."

"Stop mumbling." I poked the pitchfork toward his eyes, stopping less than an inch away.

"Booth was blackmailing me!" he shrieked.

"That's more like it. Now tell me everything, from the beginning."

It went like this.

As a prerequisite to rising in the ranks at Prime Pacific Oil, CEO Miles Stephenson Betancourt IV had made it clear to Frasier that he expected him do everything necessary to "soften" the state's resistance toward any new offshore drilling. It had been an uphill battle for years, since California's State Lands Commission had already begun decommissioning oil and gas platforms in state waters, making the licensure of new platforms highly unlikely. Part of the reasoning for CSLC's position was that in the immediate area of the already-existing platforms, more and more dead otters and other marine life had begun washing ashore. Autopsies had proven that toxoplasma gondii had accounted for only some of those deaths; pollution linked to drilling accounted for the others. Thus the importance of accurate otter counts.

Frasier, an ambitious man with access to Prime Pacific's slush fund, had approached Booth with a proposition: find no sick or dead otters and earn tens of thousands of dollars. The greedy Booth had immediately accepted.

But then the unforeseen happened: Booth fell in love with his Sugar Baby.

"The idiot wanted to divorce Harper and marry that slut," Frasier moaned.

Infuriated by the slur toward a young woman I had rather liked, I stabbed Frasier's ass with the pitchfork. Once he got through screaming, he continued.

"Okay, okay! Booth started hitting us up for more and more money until it got to the point where Miles said it had to stop."

Us? The word made me set up straight. "Miles Betancourt knew what you were doing?" I looked over at the cell phone again: red Record light still on.

"Of course he did." Frasier nodded his head as much as he was able, given the fact that it was encased in loops of gardening wire. "He began making noises about me finding other work. At the time, Evelyn was bleeding me dry in divorce court, so I…So I did what I had to do."

"You set up a meet at the Slough, then shot Booth."

"Mph."

"Diction!" I shook the pitchfork again."

"Yes! Yes, I set up the meeting! Yes, I shot Booth!"

"But why kill Amberlyn?"

He took so long to answer I had to poke him again. Once he was through squealing, he said, "She was going to blackmail me, that's why! After I…After Booth died, she remembered some of their pillow talk, like the time he told her about the otter count, and she figured it out. So the little slu—" He eyed the pitchfork. "Uh, she called me at my office and told me she needed help with her tuition and maybe I could help her out and that she thought I was sexy so maybe we could have the same sort of arrangement she'd had with him and…"

"And?"

"Me? Sexy? Oh, please. I'm not stupid. I could tell what she was leading up to, the hold she'd always have on me, and you know what I did about it."

"Say it. Please." A little politeness never hurt anyone.

"I shot her."

"But how did you know where she'd be that morning? I doubt she sent out an e-mail blast telling everyone where she was going to be and at what time."

"Aw, c'mon, Teddy. That blabbermouth Booth wouldn't shut up about her, always yakking about how pretty she was, how great her body was, how…how flexible. It got to the point where it was downright disgusting. He even told me what gym she belonged to, when she worked out, every piddling detail of her exercise routine, and where and when she jogged. Five miles a day at the same park. PhD or not, the man didn't have any common sense at all. He'd have flunked out of business school in the first semester."

Too bad Frasier hadn't. "Tell me, after all this manipulation, all this killing, what did the officials at the State Lands Commission tell you?"

A bitter laugh. "They wouldn't give me the courtesy of a meeting, not even when I e-mailed them about the great otter counts. I knew what that meant, that I was dead meat as far as Prime Pacific was concerned."

"So you started wooing Harper."

"It was the only thing left to do. Marry my way up the ladder."

"Did Harper know about any of this?"

He shook his head. "She wouldn't have cared. But she didn't know, so you can forget about her. The minute she found out her father was going to help her set up a magazine here in town she dropped her plans about going to New York. As if anybody in New York would put up with the cranky bitch."

Poor old Harper. She had been nothing more than a rung on a ladder for two different men.

I motioned toward the corner, where Frasier's fake black beard had landed. "Why the beard?"

"I thought that if anybody saw me messing around at the park, they'd think I was that uppity Preston Morrell."

This infuriated me all over again, so I gave him another hard poke in the ass. "Don't talk like that about my almost-stepfather!"

Frasier began to cry.

All that bloodshed, just so a hollow man could climb the corporate ladder. Besides killing two people, Frasier had purposely implicated a good man, and made a good woman unemployable. Talk about scum.

Disgusted, I poked his ass with the pitchfork again. "Stop being such a baby. You're lucky I don't have…"

I had meant to say "…a gun," but the sound of several cars roaring down the street toward us silenced me. No sirens?

Brakes screeched. Car doors slammed. Women called out to one another.

Within seconds, the back porch light clicked on.

"Teddy! Are you all right?" Colleen.

"Don't let the kids come out here!"

"Gotcha!"

A thunder of feet down the steps as the porch light revealed the forms of several women I recognized as librarians from the San Sebastian County Library.

Their hands were outstretched, clasping dangly keyrings.

No.

Those dangly things weren't keyrings.

They were pepper spray canisters.

The heavy artillery arrived when Colleen fetched her Glock 19 from the house.

"How long have you had that thing?" I asked.

"It belonged to Joe's father. I kept it because… Well, because you never know, do you?"

Colleen and the librarians and I sat in a circle around Frasier, each of us aiming our weapon of choice at him. The reference librarian was uncertain if her pepper spray canister worked because she'd owned it for almost two years and hadn't yet tested it.

So she tested it on Frasier.

It worked.

Frasier was still crying when we heard sirens approaching.

"Guess the bank robber situation has been resolved," Colleen said.

"About time," the child's librarian grumped. "I've already missed *South Park*."

Chapter Twenty-six

All was well that ended well with the hostage situation, too. The bank robbers had indeed surrendered, leaving the Grampion family unharmed. Swarmed by the press, the Grampions left the farm to the various factions of law enforcement and skedaddled to the San Sebastian Holiday Inn Express. There was a rumor going around town that a producer from *Sixty Minutes* had called, and that a New York literary agent had already inveigled the rights to a hostage tell-all with the working title, *Hot Hostage Hearts*. According to town gossip, Peggy Sue Grampion, a cheerleader at San Sebastian High, had fallen for one of the hostage-takers— the cute one—and promised her undying love as he was led away in handcuffs.

Saturday morning's edition of the *San*

Sebastian Journal screamed in eighty-four-point Gothic,

LIBRARIANS CAPTURE MURDERER WHILE BANK ROBBERS SURRENDER

The newspaper sold so many copies the presses had to roll for a second edition, and why not? Their subscribers received two big stories for the price of one. With pictures.

The Rejas residence was declared a crime scene, with the yard off-limits for the next few days. No one was happy about that, especially not Tonio and Bridie. Although the adults had agreed to withhold the grisly details from them, the children had figured out enough that they wanted to see Frasier's bloodstains for themselves. Every cop who trudged through the house was subjected to so many pleas for information that I eventually called Bucky Snow and requested another favor. Happy to oblige, Bucky duly escorted the kids to the San Sebastian Cineplex where they were treated to a double feature of *Wonder Woman* and *The Muppets in Outer Space*.

But the best part of the day arrived when I received a call from Lila Conyers to inform me that on Monday, she would be starting work at Blue Seas Marine Laboratory as Preston Morrell's personal assistant.

"And the Lab's paying my tuition so I can finally get my masters!" she enthused. "Oh, Teddy, I can't thank you enough. Um, by the way, did you know Toby's moved in with me? He's so precious."

"Don't get too attached," I warned. "That cat's middle name is Unfaithful."

Thinking about Toby called up a vision of my *Merilee*. Unlike Toby, my boat was always there for me, a comfort when I was upset, a joy when we were out on the water together. If these past few days had taught me anything, it was to remain true to my values—and I valued the hell out of her.

The struggle over my boat's fate had to end now.

But how to tell Joe?

By Sunday evening, things had calmed down enough at Casa Rejas that Colleen was able to bake another batch of cranberry-apricot scones. These were greatly appreciated by Bridie and Tonio, the deputies, the crime scene techs— and my mother.

Caro had stormed the house less than fifteen minutes after the police had arrived, demanding I return with her to the safety of Old Town. Upon my refusal, she had bunked down overnight with Colleen, and the two had chattered into the wee hours like a couple of teenaged girls at a pajama party.

"May I have another of those scones, Colleen?" Caro asked, the next morning. "They truly are delicious."

Colleen beamed at her new BFF. "Not only can you have another scone, Caro, but I've made an extra dozen for you to take home."

My mother looked down at her miniscule waistline. She had always fiercely protected her size 0. Nevertheless, she said, "A dozen sounds perfect."

The two air-kissed, and Caro headed off to Old Town, clutching a box of scones to her surgically enhanced breasts.

Relieved, Joe pulled me into the hallway and kissed me so passionately I had trouble catching my breath.

"Promise me you'll never get mixed up in a murder case again," Joe said, as I came up for air.

"I promise."

"You almost got killed. Again."

"I said I promise."

Joe wasn't finished. "Let's elope."

"You don't want to wait until the granny cottage is finished?"

"Nope. I want you right here where I can keep an eye on you."

Another long kiss.

Resurfacing, I said, "Um, about that. You need to know I'm not giving up the *Merilee*."

He looked at me in shock. "But I thought you'd come to your senses, that…"

I held up my hand, stopping him. "The *Merilee* is my sanctuary. We're a package deal, Joe. Love me, love my boat."

When he frowned, I thought we were about to have another argument, but that didn't happen. Instead, he said, "Besides the needless expense, I thought she was added work for you."

"Work that I love. Like my job at the zoo."

He frowned. "You're saying I've been blind, is that it?"

"No blinder than me. I didn't realize how much I loved that boat until…Well, until it looked like I might have to give her up."

"That's an emotion I can understand."

A few minutes of heavy-petting later, Joe climbed into his cruiser and took off for his office to begin work on a mountain of paperwork. After straightening my clothes, I went into the kitchen to help Colleen put away the breakfast dishes.

I was too late. The kitchen was already spotless and Colleen was sitting in the office nook, hunched over her green laptop. The minute I walked in, she threw me a startled look and hit the Escape key.

"I thought you and Joe were…"

"He's off to supervise again."

She smiled. "He loves to supervise. Don't let him go too far with it. Not with you, anyway. He's always loved your independent streak."

"No worries there."

I looked at the laptop. It was time to clear the air. "Colleen, I have a confession to make. One day when I came through here, I saw that you'd been looking a rather odd website. Something about how to clean gunpowder off your hands."

She flushed so deeply that her freckles almost disappeared. "Oh, no! You saw that?"

"I'm afraid so. And I thought…I thought…"

"You thought I might be the killer?"

"Well, kinda." Never had I felt so uncomfortable.

Colleen began to laugh, great howls separated by guttural snorts. Her reaction was so unexpected that I just stood there and watched. After she'd howled herself out, she wiped her eyes and said, "I guess I'll have to divulge my awful secret. But if you tell Joe, I *will* kill you!" At the expression on my face, she added, "Joke!"

Still laughing, she walked over to the laptop and brought up the file she'd been working on when I entered the kitchen.

"Take a look, Teddy."

I leaned over and began to read…

> The brave zookeeper faced down the killer with only a rake for a weapon. Behind her, the macaque monkeys cringed in fear of the menacing man.
>
> "And that's why you shot Emaline DeBussey!" Lettie Hently spat, brandishing her rake at the leering David Randolph Wilkerson IV. She wasn't about to let that monster hurt her beloved

animals. "You thought merely wiping your hands with a HandiWipe would make the gunshot residue go away, but…"

Epilogue
Three Months Later

The gossip going around town was that Frasier Morgan wanted to plead Not Guilty. His argument was that he'd been in the Rejas' yard, innocently looking for his lost dog—he didn't have a dog—when he was assaulted by a group of radical feminists who had just returned from watching a re-screening of *Wonder Woman* at the San Sebastian Cineplex.

But he changed his mind when his attorney, a high-roller from San Francisco, played him the recording of that evening's events. The attorney duly warned him that even if the recording, made under duress, was eventually thrown out of court, there was still the matter of the rifle dredged out of the Slough. The authorities had traced the Remington Gamemaster 141 to Frasier's father, who had used it on hunting trips with his then-friend Miles Stephenson Betancourt IV, CEO of Prime Pacific. So upon his attorney's advice, Frasier accepted a plea deal wherein his sentence would be reduced from life without parole to a mere sixty years.

At least Frasier came from a long-lived family.

The county attorney's attempt to link Miles Stephenson Betancourt IV to bribery was proceeding slowly. After much thought, Frasier had retracted what he had said on the recording about Miles' knowledge of the otter count problem, and so far, no evidence of tampering had surfaced.

I had my suspicions about who was paying Frasier's legal bills.

Which brings me to Harper Betancourt-Booth. After second-guessing her plan to start a fashion magazine—too much work—she whirlwind-romanced Lex Yarnell, the Gunn Zoo's park ranger, which terminated in a suspiciously hurry-up wedding. Zoo gossip had it that as part of the prenup, Lex's extended family would be moving out of the trailer park and into a new five-bedroom, five-bath home in one of San Sebastian's tonier suburbs. The

Yarnells would never need to work in the fields again. As for Lex's part of the bargain, he had signed an agreement that "any children arising from the union of Harper Genevieve Betancourt and Lex Michard Yarnell would henceforth and hereafter carry the surname name 'Betancourt.'"

The news from the zoo was even more satisfying. Clarabelle, our new macaque monkey, had finally been introduced to Kabuki. It was love at first sight, and Clarabelle, like Harper Genevieve Betancourt Booth Yarnell, was already pregnant.

In another satisfying piece of zoo news, Janet Hewitt, whose carelessness around dangerous animals had worried us all, accepted a job at the Monterey Bay Aquarium, where the worst thing that could happen to her there was to be stung by a jellyfish. Since she was so close to Aster Edwina, we'd given her a farewell party at Phil's Fish Market, where she'd gotten plastered enough to confess to a brief affair with the despicable Stuart Booth. The affair had ended in tears when he left her for a younger woman— Amberlyn Lofland.

Closer to home, Colleen's cranberry-apricot scones became such a hit in San Sebastian that she was thinking about opening a small bakery named Scones 'R Us. It would operate out of the recently completed granny cottage.

"She's doing too much," Joe grumbled, stroking my frizzy hair.

I snuggled closer to him under the cool sheets. "Oh, stop worrying about your women, Joe. We're fine."

It was just past sundown, and we were lying together in the *Merilee*'s aft bunk, while Miss Priss, wayward little Toby, and a completely healed Bonz snoozed in the bow bunk. The tide was coming in, and the *Merilee* rocked sleepily with it. With the next ebb tide, we would leave for San Diego, making stops at friendly ports along the way.

"I still can't believe I wanted you to give her up," Joe said, holding me tight.

"Well, you did. But I should have been more open with you and not allowed everything to build up."

"Let's promise to always be open with each other from now on."

"Pinky swear?"

"Pinky swear!"

We pinky-swore.

He was quiet for a while. Just as I thought

he'd drifted off to sleep, he said, "Baking for hundreds of people will take up too much of my mother's time, Teddy. We have to do something to stop her. She's almost in her sixties, for Pete's sake! And then there's that damned book. So how could she…?"

Ah, yes, that damned book.

Colleen, that sly Irish businesswoman, had contacted the same New York literary agent who had wrangled the book/film contract for *Hot Hostage Hearts*, and wound up with a contract of her own. As a result, *Murder At the Zoo* was slated to be released next spring, with a TV series to follow. She was already halfway through the sequel.

"Colleen's doing fine, Joe."

"But she's working too hard! She…"

"Cm'ere, handsome."

For the next few hours my new husband was too busy to worry about overworked women.

Colleen's Cranberry-Apricot Scones

INGREDIENTS:

12 ounces self-rising flour
5 ounces whole milk
3 ounces chilled cubed butter
3 large eggs (1 for egg wash)
1 tablespoon baking powder
½ tablespoon baking soda
1 tablespoon sugar
1 tablespoon honey
1 1/2 ounces dried and diced apricots
1 ounce dried cranberries
1/2 ounce chopped pistachios
1/2 ounce crushed pistachios for topping
1 ounce brown sugar for topping
Pinch of salt

INSTRUCTIONS:

Preheat oven to 400 F.

Mix dry ingredients (except for crushed pistachios and brown sugar) together in large mixing bowl. Blend well. In a separate bowl, whisk two eggs into the milk. Add the liquid to the dry ingredients. Mix. Add butter to mixture, cutting butter into pea-sized lumps. Add honey to cranberries, chopped apricots, and chopped pistachios. Fold in to dough mixture.

Put dough/fruit mixture onto a floured surface and roll out to a 1-inch thickness. Use a cookie cutter or glass rim to shape dough into circles; there should be approximately ten. Place on well-buttered cookie pan. Wash top of scones with beaten egg mixture, then sprinkle with brown sugar and crushed pistachios.

Bake scones 12 minutes or until golden.

Serve with butter, fruit jam, and/or clotted Devonshire cream—if you can find any.

To see more Poisoned Pen Press titles:

Visit our website:
poisonedpenpress.com
Request a digital catalog:
info@poisonedpenpress.com